LAKE REDSTONE

J.D. HOLLYFIELD

Lake Redstone
Copyright © 2019 J.D. Hollyfield

Cover Design: All By Design
Photo: Adobe Stock
Editor: Word Nerd Editing
Formatting: Champagne Book Design

ALL RIGHTS RESERVED. This book contains material protected under International and Federal Copyright Laws and Treaties. Any unauthorized reprint or use of this material is prohibited. No part of this book may be reproduced or transmitted in any form or by any means, electronic or mechanical, including photocopying, recording, or by an information and retrieval system without express written permission from the Author/Publisher.

This is a work of fiction. Names, characters, places, and incidents either are the product of the author's imagination or are used fictitiously, and any resemblance to actual persons, living or dead, business establishments, events, or locales is entirely coincidental.

MORE FROM J.D. HOLLYFIELD

Love Not Included Series

Life in a Rut, Love not Included

Life Next Door

My So Called Life

Life as We Know It

Standalones

Faking It

Love Broken

Sundays are for Hangovers

Paranormal/Fantasy

Sinful Instincts

Unlocking Adeline

#HotCom Series

Passing Peter Parker

Creed's Expectations

Exquisite Taste

2 Lovers Series

Text 2 Lovers

Hate 2 Lovers

Thieves 2 Lovers

Four Father Series

Blackstone

Four Sons Series

Hayden

Elite Seven Series

Pride

Casey doesn't have much luck in the dating department, so when her girlfriends ditch their girls only weekend for a couple's retreat, she's forced to take desperate measures.

Refusing to be the only single one, she does what any quick-thinking girl would do:

She lies.

It was almost too easy hiring a stranger to pretend to be her hot, rich, successful boyfriend. What she didn't plan on was him being hot, successful, and *way* too much trouble for her liking.

Jim was in a slump in his everyday life. He was bored and needed something to spice up his life. Accepting a gig to play the perfect boy toy was not what he had in mind, but it was too good to turn down.

What he didn't plan for was the smokin' little spitfire who hired him. It's a con, a job, a fraud. But the more she's in his presence, the more he realizes she may be more than just a ruse.

Three days at a lake house.

Two strangers who cause a lot of mayhem.

One little lie.

What could go wrong?

When you're at the lake, it's all puppies and daisies.
   —*Gary Rodgers*

pick·le·ball
/ˈpik(ə)lˌbôl/

noun
noun: **pickleball**; noun: **pickle ball**

Google
A game resembling tennis in which players use paddles to hit a perforated plastic ball over a net.

Wikipedia
Pickleball is a paddle sport (similar to a racquet sport) that combines elements of badminton, tennis, and table tennis. Two or four players use solid paddles made of wood or composite materials to hit a perforated polymer ball, similar to a whiffle ball, over a net. The sport shares features of other racquet sports, the dimensions and layout of a badminton court, and a net and rules somewhat similar to tennis, with several modifications. Pickleball was invented in the mid-1960s as a children's backyard game.

Urban Dictionary
Combination of tennis and ping pong, legit Olympic sport, way to determine friend status or sponge-worthiness.

The greatest game of all time. Played typically in gym class. Oversized table tennis or miniature tennis, played with a wooden paddle and whiffle balls. Those who are skilled in pickleball are considered the shit.

Right Service Court	Left Service Court

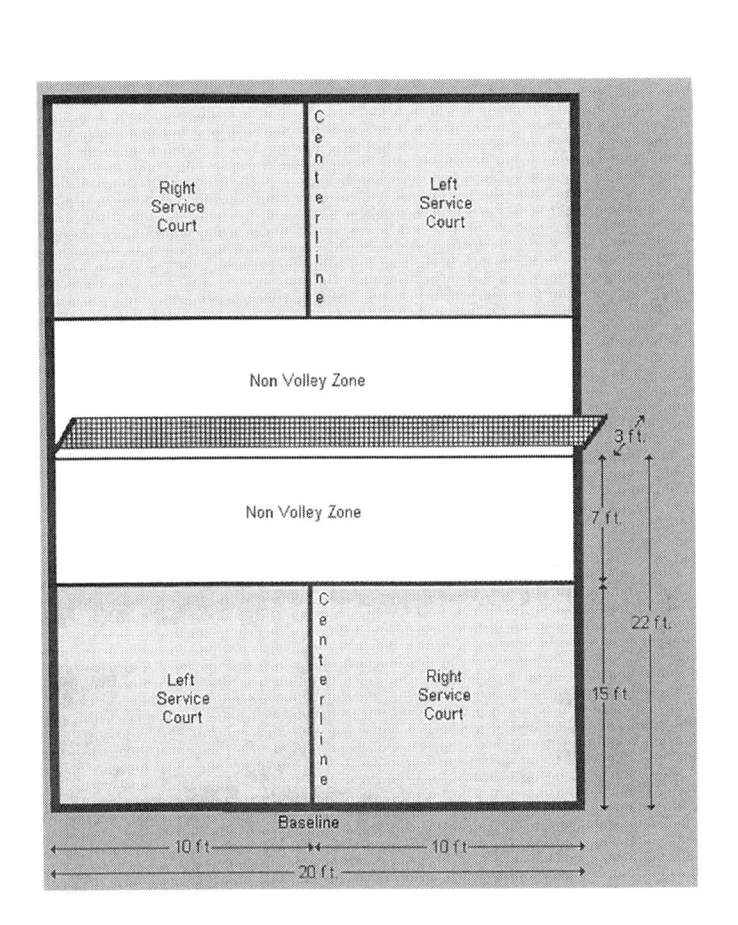

Centerline

Non Volley Zone

Non Volley Zone

3 ft.
7 ft.
22 ft.
15 ft.

Left Service Court	Right Service Court

Centerline

Baseline

← 10 ft → ← 10 ft →
← 20 ft →

To the Lake Redstone crew:
Beware…
What happens at the lake, ends up in a book.

LAKE
REDSTONE

CHAPTER
ONE

Dreams are awesome.

Especially the one I'm having right now—dirty sex with 1980's version of Axl Rose, the lead singer of Guns N' Roses. "Paradise City" is playing in the background while I ride the hell out of him...in my parents' bedroom, my childhood dog, Muffy, staring at me while a pair of wings unfurl on my back.

What the heck?

Okay, I take that back. Dreams are plain ol' weird.

The song gets louder, and I begin to lose my focus on the good part. I yell, "Ride 'em, cowboy!" and move faster, because...well, dreams can end at any time. If the only time I get action is while I'm unconscious, I gotta get movin' with this.

Sadly, the song continues to get louder while the dreamy schlong gets softer.

No, no, no...

I need this! Don't go away, wet dream! Come back!

The lyrics from *Paradise City* blares from my phone as

my eyes begin to blink awake. My phone continues to ring, and Axl fades out of existence.

Go figure.

Even in my dreams, I can't keep a guy. I roll over to my phone and see a Facetime call coming through from Poppy. *Shoot. What time is it?* My bloodshot eyes search out my clock. It's way past ten in the morning.

With the most dramatic sigh, I reach for my phone and accept the call. I see her smiling face, along with three other of my best girlfriends.

I was supposed to meet them for breakfast to discuss our annual girls' trip.

Shoot!

"Jesus, you look like hell." That's Poppy, my best friend since grade school. The one I had my first tea party with, sleepover, and first real cry over a boy where we spent all night eating ice cream like they do in the movies, only to spend the rest of it vomiting from stomach aches. Typical Poppy, she doesn't bother to coddle me or my sensitive emotions. Normally I would tell her to buzz off, but I bet *looking like hell* is putting it nicely.

"Casey, girl, you get yourself into a little bit of some trouble last night?" That's Katie, third in charge. Katie and I met at a Girl Scout retreat when we were thirteen. Neither of us wanted to be girl scouts, but our moms thought it was our legacy to follow in their footsteps. We ended up ditching our tribe, and a few hops and a skip later, found the pot of gold: the boys' cabin. The rest is history. "Come on, girl, don't hold out!" Katie says, popping her bubble gum.

A little bit of trouble would probably be an understatement of what I accidently got myself into last night. And I say *accidently*, because no one actually *plans* to go out and get so drunk they end up at a strip club with a random guy, getting a massage from a stripper *and* the random guy. The déjà vu where I promised myself I'd never drink again is hitting real strong right now. "Let's just say I let Jesus take the wheel and he definitely crashed and burned."

Poppy rolls her eyes, while Katie laughs hysterically. We're exactly the same. Or should I say *used to be*—until Katie got married and knocked up. Now, she's all strapped down by kids, being a second-grade teacher to even more kids, and expects me to be disaster enough for us both. Tough shoes to fill.

"Oh, girl, start talking. I want every single detail." Last, but not least, that's June. The innocent—the friend who married right out of college and started changing diapers and planning dinner menus fresh off the alter.

"No can do, my little June-Bug," I say, scraping some dry drool off my cheek. "I'd have to remember the night to tell." Not that I don't remember taking body shots off the stripper, or offering my random date a lap dance, but I'm still trying to forget the whole barfing and slipping off the stage part.

Poppy straightens in her chair and leans forward, taking up most of the screen. "Well, hangover or not, it's time for us to plan our annual trip."

Yeah it is! I love these trips. Every year, we pick one weekend out of our busy lives and get together for three whole days of fun and destruction. When I say busy, though, I'm clearly not referring to my own. Out of the four of us, I pulled the short straw. You know, the girlfriend who isn't married with kids and can't hold down a man or a job to save her life. That's me. Casey Kasem—not the reincarnated radio jockey, to be clear. My parents didn't think about the lifelong jokes they were opening up for people before they wrote on my birth certificate. Thanks, Mom and Dad.

While all my friends were finding love, happiness, spitting out kids, and being successful, I was refusing to be attached to a man, settle down, or grow up. And, at thirty, I'm *never* growing up, holding down a job, or spitting out kids. Because *I'm* the short straw.

"So, I found this lake house," Poppy starts, and I sit up, ready to hear her wild plans. She may be a cop by day, but when it comes to planning these wild, inappropriate weekends, she's always on point. "And I think it would be a great place for the seven of us to relax and get some sun."

Okay.

Hold the phone.

I might be lacking a really good job or maturity, but I passed math in college. Well…what I attended of it, and I'm pretty sure four girls does not add up to seven. "Yeah, you mean four." There's a bit of silence. Unfortunate thing about Facetime is you can't hide expressions. And why are my friends sporting pity faces?

I'm not *that* bad at math…

Am I?

Three girls, plus myself, equals—

"So…we were thinking the guys could join us…"

No.

No!

I drop my phone, then scramble to pick it up. "Sorry, I could have sworn I heard you say the G word. Okay, so what is this lake you speak of?" Man, is my headache kicking in.

"Case, I did say the G word. I know! It's always us girls, but we were thinking maybe we could invite the guys this *one* time."

I'm still drunk. There's no way they would—

"Case…"

"Guys…as in strippers?" What do they not understand about girls' weekend? Why would they want their husbands on *girls'* weekend!

"I know, it's not our norm, but Mick's agent found this location and—"

"Then have *Mick* go to this lake house. Let's go to Vegas. Oh! Wait! How about Tahoe again?"

June grumbles. Maybe she didn't enjoy Tahoe as much as I did. But how was I supposed to know you can get poison ivy in the desert? "Okay, fine, no Tahoe, what about New York again? Or Mexico! I hear they're having major deals due to all the crime out there."

That earns me a snort from Katie. I know she's on my side. She lives and breathes these girls' trips as much as I do. She has two wild boys. And by wild, I'm talking about the amount of time she spends in the ER because her children attempt jumping off the roof into baby pools, bonfires in the living room, and competitions of who can eat more dirt and not throw up.

"I know this isn't our usual, but it's a great deal. Mick's agent wants to book a modeling shoot up there, so he's gonna hook us up on this beautiful summer house on the lake. Every amenity you can think of—and it's all free!"

Free schmree.

No husbands.

Girls weekend dammit! What do they not understand about *girls* weekend!

"Casey, it's kinda a good deal. We can still do all the girl stuff. The guys can go off on their own. We'll lay out, drink, and talk crap about everyone who's turned into a total loser since high school—"

"*Heyyy!*" I let out a loud whine. *I've* totally turned into a complete loser since high school.

"You're a cool loser, though," Katie pipes up, trying to save Poppy from my tongue lashing.

I don't like where this is going. It's like, all of a sudden, my friends don't know the meaning of just girls. And also forgot I'm as single as single gets. Party of one. Numeral Uno. A-L-O-N-E.

"I know this isn't ideal, but it could be a great time! What ever happened to that guy you were seeing? Invite him along!" Pfft. What guy? "You two seemed really into each other the last time we all hung out."

My brain is trying to search for who in God's name she's referring to. When you have all married friends, no one really pays attention to the single one. Which is a good and bad thing. Good because they spend less time judging your actions, but bad because they always think you need saving. *Let me hook you up with my boss's brother. I know a guy from the grocery store. I met a bum on the street and he's willing to date you...*

It never ends.

"Who was that cute guy you brought to June's anniversary dinner?" Katie asks.

I have no idea. Because that's the problem. There are so many ifs, possiblys, and failed one-nighters coming in and out of my life, I have no idea who I took to that dinner. I also don't want to admit I have no idea, but I have to act like I have *some* class. And maturity. And respect...

"Oh, yeah…you mean Bob?"

Stupid Bob…

"Sure, he was nice. Why don't you ask if he wants to come with us for the weekend? He seemed like a keeper!"

He did? Good to know.

"Case," Poppy starts in again, "I know. This is not ideal. But it's free. And it's in a great location."

So is Vegas, Tahoe, the Bermuda Triangle…when you don't have your *husbands* trailing along…

"Call Bob. Never know. Maybe some nice lake time will help you realize he may be the one!"

Yeah.

Not today, Satan.

CHAPTER TWO

Two weeks later...

I'm sitting at the local coffee shop, having a long go-around of sending out my resume. Once upon a time, I used to have a pretty solid job...until I got laid off. Nothing I did, just bad timing, but what's even worse is the economy and trying to get back on that horse. I've worked odd and end jobs since—coffee barista, daycare, receptionist—but nothing has really sparked my interest. I obviously need to get back out in the real world, but since I've been a victim of corporate America, I struggle with trust. Who really deserves my time? My dedication? I can't simply work for anyone, ya know?

Okay, so maybe I struggle with working in general. It's not that I don't have the drive to move up the corporate ladder, it's just that my drive tends to lean more toward "live free and semi-buzzed."

It's been two weeks since our disastrous girls weekend call, and nothing I said was going to get me to convince them bringing their husbands was a major red flag—horrible idea—total girls weekend game changer!

They also wouldn't let go of who I was going to bring. Being single sucked sometimes. I guess when you're married and trapped in a relationship you willingly signed off on and can't get out of, you spend way too much time focusing on other's relationships—especially your single friends. *Who is Bob? What does he look like again? What does he do?* After all the questions, I found myself lying through my teeth about *Bob*, this amazing guy I wasn't sure was even worthy of coming on this trip because he was just so worthy!

The question still remained: who the heck is Bob?

I hung up the phone wondering what the hell I'd just gotten myself into. Why didn't I speak up and say I made Bob up? I'm so single, my plant won't even stay alive long enough to hang out with me.

One thing's for certain: I lost at having a girls' weekend.

The second thing: I have to find a Bob.

It's only noon and even though I'm bathing in the mist of free air conditioning, the sun outside looks hotter than the devil's sweaty balls. Living in Chicago sounded like a good idea, until I realized it's expensive and I'm poor—and trying to land a job is impossible. Personally, I think my skillset in problem solving, multi-tasking, and communications is on point. But apparently when they ask, *"Define what makes you the right candidate,"* a reply of, *"I'm always the life of the party and can speak to a group of people while dominating a game of twister"* is not the right answer.

I finish applying for a CEO of a makeup company position, since I practically own stock in Sephora and would make a super cute CEO, and call it quits for today. Right when I start to shut down my computer, I get a text from Poppy.

Poppalicious: Have you heard back from Bob? Trying to get a final count for the pontoon boat party.

If I took a shot for every time one of them sent me a text about good ol' Bob and whether he's gonna make it…

I'd be dead.

Me: Oh yeah, took me to the fanciest steak house last night. Wined and dined me. Can't say much more. Not a kiss and tell kinda girl…

I laugh at myself. The only steak I ate last night was inside a burrito from a local taco truck at one in the morning.

Poppalicious: Glad he's feeding you. But is he coming? Have you even asked him? The trip is in three weeks!

Technically, neither of us is *coming*. Mainly because he doesn't exist. And me because…well, he doesn't exist. But man could I use a good bang around the bedroom. My phone dings again.

Katie: Heard you got it good last night. How big is he? Is he coming?

Jesus, my fake love life is becoming the topic of the year.

Me: Sore Sally down below. All I can confess.

I leave out "I wish." It's not really lying, more like being too lazy to type out the full sentence. I mean, who even does that anymore? Full-length words are so yesterday.

JuneBuggy: Please tell me you asked him. I'm dying to meet him.

Well, June…me too, girl. When pigs fly and perfect made-up Bob falls into my lap, you'll be the first to be introduced.

Me: Not sure he can make it. Super busy with work.

I can't even keep up with all the lies I've told about Bob—what he does for a living, his favorite food, his dick size, does he snore, the car he drives, cologne he wears…

Jesus, I can't even hire a guy to fit all these fake attributes…

Or can I?

I flip my laptop back open and type in a few words that land me on a site for wanted ads. With a few short requirements, and compensation, I hit submit.

BOYFRIEND FOR A WEEKEND and FAST

Looking for boyfriend material. Be one for three days on a weekend trip. All expenses paid.

Rental Time: Friday-Monday.

Requirements: Hot (cute will do), able to lie on a dime (rich, successful, possibly athletic), no priors or police record. Good teeth. (I hate guys with bad breath).

PRICE: $50
(Possibly made through a payment plan if you're cool with that).

Okay, Bob, come to momma…

CHAPTER
THREE

Two weeks, six days, and twelve hours later...

"Screw you, Bob!"

I throw my back against my tiny sofa, in my tiny apartment, and sigh. Yet again, I check my ad—and nothing—not a single potential hit.

Well...I got *hits*—from serial killers, because that's what their profile pictures looked like. I asked for hot. And like most, my version of hot had teeth. The people who applied to my "Boyfriend for a Weekend" ad were clearly not reading the requirements. I need him to be attractive, fake wealthy, fake kind, fake good in bed, large and in charge—that, he can't fake—and he needs to pretend to be Bob for three whole days. What's so hard about that!

Taking another huge sip of my homemade margarita, I start to come to one conclusion.

I'm done for.

The trip is tomorrow, and I'm going to have to show up with no Bob. Even after I made the biggest mistake of telling them he agreed to go! This, of course, was *after* I submitted my ad thinking it would be a piece of cake to get a guy to be my fake boyfriend, but *before* I realized no one in the entire state of Illinois wants to be my fake boyfriend!

Down goes more margarita.

I should back out.

Pretend I'm sick.

I have the flu. The shpoops. I'm projectile vomiting resembling the girl from *The Exorcist*! If I drink anymore of this mix, it won't be far from the truth. I'm pretty sure these margarita jugs are meant to be shared with more than just one person.

I'm not sure what else to do, and I'm out of time. Re-reading the ad, I don't understand why I'm not having any luck. All my expectations are easy to meet—hell, most of them have to be lied about!

Maybe I should expand my geographic search…

I change the span out to a hundred-mile radius instead of twenty-five, then sit back and take a few more swigs. Nothing. Every so often, I press my nose against the screen because my eyesight is about as gone as my margarita.

"Eat a bag of buttholes, Scuba Bob! It's a paid weekend! Who says no to a *paid* weekend!"

All of Illinois, apparently.

Maybe that's it. No one wants to do it for fifty dollars.

So, I low-balled it, but hello! I'm poor!

I guess I can spare a few more bucks since it *is* my dignity on the line. I press edit again. With one eye open, I add another zero, having no idea how I'm going to pay Bob even if he does show up in the next twenty hours, and click "yes" to update.

I go empty out the last dredges of the bottle—just like Bob will be doing to my bank account if he ever shows up.

7:30 a.m.

The sound of my alarm wakes me from my perfect slumber. Just kidding. My slumber consisted of crawling to my room from the bathroom and passing out between my dresser and bed. I really need to invest in a floor mattress.

I lift my head, wiping the lime-flavored drool off my face, and reach up to shut my alarm clock off. Great. Today's the day. Where I lie and pretend I'm dead or confess I made Bob up and show up alone.

Dead it is.

I reach for my phone to send a text letting my friends know I've sadly passed and they'll have to go on this trip without me. When I flip it over, I notice a few missed calls from June, a text from Poppy demanding I be sober and showered because they're coming to get me soon, and a notification from—

What!

"Holy smokes! No way!" I pop up, using both hands to unlock my phone, scroll through my screen, and open the app.

One new application.

Someone replied to my ad! I swear, if he's at least half decent and has less than a five-year prison record, he's in. I open the application, but my phone freezes.

"Oh, Mother of pearl!"

I close the app and reopen, but a call coming through interrupts. Poppy. "Hey, girl, what's up?"

Okay, maybe less than a ten-year prison record. I can't afford to be picky at a time like this.

"Um…hey, girl, as in *hey*, where are you? I've been calling. Mick and I will be there in thirty minutes. Are you ready? Is Bob riding with or meeting us?"

Good question.

"Yeah, I'm not sure. He's finishing up some marathon." Lies! I lay in a bed of lies—correction, a floor of lies!

My phone dings, and I pull it away to check.

Jim_Strums35: You still need a boyfriend this weekend?

"Wow, running a marathon already this morning? I tell ya, you sure found a keeper. Can't wait to get to know him this weekend."

Ha! Me too!

Another ding.

Jim_Strums35: Gotta know soon.

"Anyway, we're making great time. Traffic wasn't as busy as we thought. So, hurry and be ready. Our GPS puts us there in twenty."

Twenty! I need more time than that to stalk this dude's social media networks and make sure he isn't going to chop me up and dump me in the middle of a lake.

I put Poppy on speaker and scramble to open the app and respond.

PrtyGrl_Casey: Show me a pic and prove ur not a psycho murderer.

"Did you hear me, Case?"

Jim_Strums35: *photo attachment*

"Oh, give me a break," I gripe as I stare at a photo of John Wayne Gasey, the biggest known serial killer.

"What? I didn't know how the roads were gonna be!"

Oops. "No, not you, ugh...Google alerts. News these days. How soon again?"

PrtyGrl_Casey: Very funny.

Jim_Strums35: There's more where that came from, but humor is extra. What's it gonna be? I have another opportunity waiting, but this pays better.

Geez! What a pushy jerk. No thanks, pal. I don't need anyone who's gonna boss me arou—

"...and if we make it in time, we can go to the couples late-night swim."

Being bossed around isn't the worst thing that can happen...

PrtyGrl_Casey: You're hired.

Oh, Casey, what did you just do?

Got out of couples' late-night swim alone?

Sure, sure. We'll go with that. Not that I signed on to hire a stranger to pretend he's dating me and we're insanely in love.

He asks me where he should meet me, and I shoot off my address, telling him he has seventeen minutes to get here or the deal's off.

Jim_Strums35: See you soon, schnookums.

For real, what did I just *do!* Oh my god, I just said yes without any background checking, photo referencing, preparation—

"Fudge nuggets!" We didn't even go over details. How is he going to know what my favorite color is or how I like my feet rubbed when those pack of wolves start grilling him? I open the app again and try to reach out to Jim... whoever he is. He needs to know all the stuff he has to go along with. I send him a message, but it bounces back.

I'm so screwed!

Drowning. Head falling below water. What in the fresh hell have I done? He's going to be a creepy old guy. The creepiest. With creepy eyes and untamed nose hair. And he's going to tell everyone how I love yoga and long baths and cuddling and...*ew, cuddling.* I shake my head, shuddering. I peek at the time. I have fifteen minutes to shower, pack, and hope fake Bob doesn't dupe me.

CHAPTER
FOUR

What do you mean you didn't know I was into short, bald guys?

It's what's on the inside that matters.

He's rich. Very rich.

While standing outside my apartment waiting on Poppy, I'm preparing all my reasons for why Bob is Bob.

He's funny.

He's got a great dog.

He's the last man on earth who was willing to pretend date me.

Another long, dramatic sigh falls from my lips as I squint down the street wondering where the hell everybody is. Poppy told me twenty, and I told Bob seventeen. It's been twenty-two minutes. Is anyone ever on time anymore?

Heck with this, I'm going back upstairs.

Plans canceled.

I spin around and catch my reflection in the front door. My hair, brown and blah, looks like I stuck it in a light socket. I throw my hands up and run my fingers through it to calm it down. Damn Illinois humidity.

My eyeliner is smudged. "Crap on a cracker." I lick my finger and try wiping under my eye to fix it, only to make it worse. I scrub a little harder when I suddenly see a stain on my tank top. "Seriously?" I grumble. I pull my shirt away to further inspect. Toothpaste.

"Yeah, party's off." I reach for the handle to ditch this disaster vacation when Poppy pulls up.

"Where you going? Get in. Where's Bob?"

Dammit.

I turn back, a wide smile on my face. "Heeey there!"

She jumps out of the car and gives me a hug. Man, I've missed her. Before real life got in the way, we were inseparable. But then she had to go to the academy and become a badass, while I stayed back and just became an ass. She and Mick met while Poppy was on a routine call. Mick had fallen from a trapeze rope during a modeling shoot and Poppy was there to save the day. It was love at first sight, and the rest is history.

"Missed you, girlfriend."

"Missed you too." We're so cute.

"Where's Bob?"

And then she had to ruin it.

I pull away and stare my best friend in the eye. I should be honest. Confess all my sins and be free with the truth. I go to open my mouth when a guy appears out of nowhere, heading straight toward us. Oh God, my worst nightmare is coming true.

Dirty overalls.

Stained white shirt.

He resembles your typical plumber. And *not* of the PornHub variety.

My mouth falls open. *He couldn't even put a clean shirt on for this?* Just kill me. There's no way I can go through with this.

"Poppy, I have to tell you something," I say, staring at Bob as he gets closer and closer.

"What is it? Is something wrong? You look freaked out."

'Cause I am! "I...I...I lie—"

"This fourteen-thirty-two Cresthaven?" Bob asks.

It's now or never. Go along with this or pull the plug...

With a deep breath, I take a step forward. "Yes. Actually, it—"

"Schnookums, sorry I'm late. Traffic was a bitch."

My head whips to my right and away from train wreck Bob as a set of warm lips cover mine. I become stone-still as a strong, muscular hand wraps around my neck and pulls me into a hard chest. I'm not sure what to do. Weirder things have happened to me, but—a. Man. Is. Kissing. Me. Like, *kissing* me. I would pull away—I *should* pull away—but he smells good, and his lips feel nice. *Real* nice. And man, he can kiss. I find myself relaxing into his hold, and when he uses his tongue to part my lips, I allow it. When in Rome, right? Just as our tongues touch, a zap shoots down to my toes, and I lose my balance.

And the moment is gone.

He pulls away.

Turning to Poppy, he sticks out his hand. "Hey, you must be the best friend. I'm Jim."

"Oh, you mean Bob?" Confusion spreads over Poppy's face.

"No. Jim."

"You mean Bob?" Still confused.

"Nope. Still Jim."

I'm too busy staring at him to step in. I should step in. He's singlehandedly blowing my cover.

Which is what again?

Lies. He's blowing my lie. "It's *Bob*." Holy hot guy, Batman. Is *this* Bob?

"No, my name is Ji—"

"Jim-Bob! It's Jim-Bob. I call him Bob for short. But he likes to go by Jim sometimes, right, *Jim-Bob*?" I give him my crazy eye, silently telling him to go along with it. Then, I stop, because who *is* this guy? He's insanely hot! Tall, dark, sexy hair, hazel eyes, tats sticking out of his black t-shirt, and muscles—lots of muscles. I take back my crazy eye and try relaxing into a sexy face. A single brow rises as he slightly tilts his head. Oh hell. Sexy face is…not so sexy. Why is someone as hot as him taking paid dates with on-line strangers? Back is my crazy eye. If he even thinks about sawing me up for my organs…

"Oh yeah, I forgot. My girl likes calling me Bob in the bedroom. Such a little role player, right, babe?" He glances at me with a fiery smile I bet melts panties off women daily. Then he smacks my ass. "So, we doin' this?" He aims his devilish smile on Poppy, who is equally as flustered.

"Earth to Poppy," I speak up, because it looks like she's in need of a reboot.

"Oh, uh…yeah! Yes. Husband. I have one. Hi, I'm Poppy. My husband, Mick, is in the car. We should get going before we hit traffic. Yes, traffic." She shakes off her moment of weakness and walks back to the car, leaving me alone with Jim—or *Bob*.

"A little much, don't ya think?" I say, annoyed my bestie now thinks I'm a perv in bed.

"Is that not what you're paying me for? To be your fake

boyfriend? Though, why is it you need to pay someone to fill the role again?"

Now I see why *he's* single. He's a jerk. "For your information—"

"You two lovebirds comin'?" Poppy yells from the car window.

Not willingly.

"Yeah," I grumble while Jim—*Bob*—laughs. Grabbing my bag off the ground, he starts walking, and I'm left with no choice but to follow. Before he makes it to the car, I shout after him.

"Yeah, sugar plum?" He stops, turning back to me. Long lashes and eyes bright with mischief steal my breath as he gazes at me like I'm the only one who matters—the only one he sees.

My mind blanks.

I have no idea what I was going to say.

I stand, like a goldfish gaping in water.

"Gonna spit it out, babe? Or you gonna stand there and stare at me like you want to eat me for lunch?"

A horny goldfish apparently. My cheeks blaze as humiliation courses through me. This guy has some nerve. "I am *not* staring at you like that," I snap.

"Yes you are. Like you're picturing me naked. If we weren't already madly in love, I'd almost feel violated." He takes two steps toward me to eliminate the space and speaks softly. "Wait, *are* we in love?"

My heart thumps at the sound of his deep voice. His expression tells me he already has me naked, and I'm pretty sure I'm okay with a "clothing optional" weekend.

"You two can make out in the backseat. We won't watch. Let's go!" Poppy yells, breaking the weird moment.

Jim's backpack slides off his shoulder, and my eyes shift to his inked bicep as he tosses it back over. I'm not sure why I'm acting like I don't know how to function. One foot in front of the other. I've been doing this since before I could talk. I'm thankful when he grabs my hand, sending a shockwave up my arm. "No worries. We'll work out the kinks on the ride," he says, then pulls me toward the car.

I'm thankful for the quietness—all thirty seconds of it before Poppy starts firing off question after question. I instantly panic, debating on causing an accident. Fake choking to shut her up. Screaming *"spider!"* since she's deathly scared of them.

Instead, I nudge Jim.

"Ouch."

Okay, maybe I punch him in the thigh. Either way, I get his attention and point to his phone. He drops his eyes to his lap, then back up. Leaning closer, he whispers, "Babe, I get they said we can make out, but asking for that is not cool. We'll be there soon, I'm sure, and you can have it all you want."

Good grief, this guy is infuriating!

Stupid attractive but infuriating. Great lips too. Geez, mine are still tingling from the way he swooped in like my knight in shining armor, rescuing me from Plumber-Bob with those chivalrous lips. My heart stopped when I saw the disaster of Plumber-Bob playing out in my head. But it jolted and skipped a beat when the real Bob came in, turning me into some punch-drunk swoony teenager. Kind of how I'm eyeing him now—a hazed over gaze. Stupid, *stupid* attractive.

Okay, pull it together!

I roll my eyes, and mouth, "No, not that. Our app." I wink a few times until he gets it. He finally obliges as Poppy asks another question.

"So, Jim-Bob, Casey's told us a lot about you."

Jim smirks at me and winks. "Has she now? That's sweet. What exactly has she told you?"

"Oh, the basics. You're successful, great taste in food. How was that new steak restaurant you two went to?"

Fiddlesticks! I start firing off a message.

PrtyGrl_Casey: We went to the Hildebrandt's. We both had steak. You fed me dessert.

"Hildebrandt's, yes. It was delightful. The service was impeccable, and dessert was my favorite part. Up until the last bite."

Jim_Strums35: Why did we order steak? And what was for dessert? Tell me we had mousse. I've never had mousse. Did I enjoy it?

I gawk at him with a *what the hell, who cares?* look.

"Sounds like I'm going to have to make Mick take me there. What exactly is it you do to be taking my girl to such a fancy dinner?"

PrtyGrl_Casey: You're an investor. Own your own company. Travel a lot.

"Oh, you know, I invest here and there. Mainly in my girl, though. Most important investment yet." He turns and winks at me.

Jim_Strums35: Where do I travel to? I've never been outside the U.S. I love Mexican food, though.

Jesus all mighty. I have my work cut out for me with

this guy. There's no way I'm going to get away with this. I'm estimating an hour max before I'm busted and pushing us both out of the car.

"Wow, that's exciting. Mick and I have always wanted to invest. Got any pointers for us?"

He certainly does not! I shut this ridiculousness down before it gets too out of hand. A subject change is in order. "Hey, Mick, Bob is *really* interested in your modeling career. Why don't you tell him how you got started?" I say, a winning grin trying to escape. No one will get a word in the rest of the ride.

CHAPTER FIVE

Casey

For the record, I wasn't always such a screw up. Believe it or not, when I was younger, I actually had dreams and set goals for myself. It's just…life happened. Reality versus fantasy. Everything is so shiny and beautiful when you're small, then you grow up and fantasies become just that. When I was nine, I wanted to join the circus, paint my face, dress up in a bunch of colorful outfits, ride on elephants, and balance on a trapeze pole—the whole shebang. And at that young, fragile age, William Kasem III told me no child of his would be running around with savage townies and carnies. I would go to college and follow in his footsteps of becoming a lawyer. I could barely pronounce the word, let alone muster up enough gumption to do it.

At age eleven, I wanted to be a veterinarian. After I did my research on circuses, I realized I wanted to *help* animals, not be part of their cruelty. Once again, my father stepped in and said playing with pets all day was a low man's job on the totem pole and no daughter of his would be working in such a mangey profession. He then went and used the whole l-a-w-y-e-r word again.

At thirteen, it was an actress. At fifteen, an interior designer. Dream after dream, my father said the same thing: my heart and goals were in the wrong place.

"And how exactly do you think you'll live on such a fickle income? Your entire life has been made up of these silly dreams, Casey. No one will accept you if you can't even take yourself seriously. Lawyers and surgeons thrive in this world, not filthy pet doctors or D-list movie stars. Get this nonsense out of your head and start thinking about a real life for yourself. You'll become no one if you continue on this puerile path of yours."

I spent my whole life being told who to be, how to act, to stop living my fantasy life and start living in reality—status, prestige, and how much you're worth is what people judge you for.

It just wasn't who I was. In my second year of barely passing my college classes, I decided to finally take Daddy Dearest's advice. I started thinking about living my real life. I quit school, took all the money I had in my bank account, and traveled, lived wild and free—until William Kasem got wind of my shenanigans and pulled the plug.

The university sold me out. My father's golf buddy had been my psychology professor, and when your best bud's daughter stops showing up to your class, I guess you become five and tattle. My dad lost it. Made so many threats, I couldn't even keep up. *Get back to school or I'm cutting you off. Grow up or get out.*

So, I got out. I used the rest of the money I had to settle into a small apartment and found a job waiting tables close to my place so I didn't need my car. Life was great. I had my friends. My freedom. I could do whatever the hell I wanted.

So, I did.

And did.

And did.

I was wild and free all right. Along with broke and jobless and basically the big ol' loser my dad said I would be. But I had my independence. That had to count for something, right? I made sure not to live by my father's rules, up to the very last one, claiming my only hope left was to marry a wealthy man and pray he tolerated my lunacy. But as for the rest of his silly rules, I refused to be tied down to money *or* a man. I didn't need either to define who I was. I forbade it.

Some might ask how it's all working out for me, and considering I just blew the last remaining money to my name on a fake boyfriend, not great.

Getting lost in my own thoughts, I must have dozed off. Voices filter through the car, and my ears pique at the conversation.

"...wow, I didn't realize you two were that serious. Do you live together?"

"No, but I stay at her place all the time. It reminds me of her. Cute and feisty."

Wait, what?

"Such a snuggler this one. Like a little spider monkey. Can't get her off me at night—*ouch!*" I pop my head up, my hand cranking back and flying into Jim's chest.

"Look who's awake! Finally, we couldn't hear each other over the snoring."

"I don't snore!"

Poppy sticks her head back. "You snore."

"Do not!" I argue.

"Like a gorilla. I was telling them how it's one of my favorite attributes. Cute little growling you do when you… okay then." He shuts up real fast. Thank God my crazy eye does the trick…this time.

"Case, I didn't know you two were living tog—"

"Oh, look! We're here!"

Major disaster averted. Everyone watches ahead as we pull down a steep gravel driveway, gigantic thick forest pines enclosing above us. I'm not sure where *here* is. The accidental cat nap has me unsure how long we've been driving, but the view tells me it was long enough to end up in a secluded patch of heaven deep in the country. I roll down my window and inhale the warm summer air. The breeze strokes my cheeks, a hint of earthiness rushing over me. We're close to the lake.

We're all still quiet, waiting for something to appear as the road becomes more vertical than I'm comfortable with. I'm about to tell Poppy I think we made a wrong turn and should go back when the trees open up to the most amazing view. My breath catches as a gigantic lake appears like magic as soon as we crest over the ridge. My eyes transfix on a stunning two-story summer home, covered by clear panes of glass. With the house facing the lake, the rays of the summer sun cascade off the windows, illuminating the glimmer of rays from the water, the lake a skyline silver. Calm and peaceful.

"Holy Heaven."

Sure seems like it. I stick my head further out my window, and the smell of nature sifts inside my nostrils. The dew pearled grass tells me they must have had some rain recently. I ache to snuggle my bare feet in the damp grass and feel the warmth of the sun on my face.

A black SUV is parked in front of the house, and I spot June and her husband Jason right away. It's kind of hard to miss him. He used to be a linebacker for the Oakland Raiders. And talk about super dreamy. Who would have thought our sweet little June-Bug would catch the eye of a famous football player and bring him to his knees? Literally! They met at a bar, and while she was trying to squeeze through a group of giants, she tripped, tossing two full hands worth of shots. Jason had taken the brunt of the booze, not only catching a lime to the face, but when he tried to steady June, he slipped, and his knees met the bar floor. June was completely mortified, but Jason, as he says, fell head over heels in love. It took two minutes of some cheesy pick-up lines for June to give in and offer up her number.

"Oh, great! Everyone's already here." Poppy unsnaps her seatbelt as Mick parks, and they both climb out. When Jim reaches for his door handle, I catch hold of his shoulder.

"Wait."

He pauses, setting those seductive eyes on me. His lips turn up in a sultry smile as his eyes drop to where my hand is touching his shoulder. I quickly retreat, pulling my hand away. "Listen, we need to get our stories straight. They'll catch on right away if we don't get our act together. Especially June. She's like a hawk."

"Hmmm, June, we don't want her to blow our cover. Okay. So, more making out, less cuddling. Do you prefer pet names or—?"

"Stop! I'm being serious. If my friends find out this is all a scam, they'll—"

"What? Disown you because you made up a boyfriend? He sounds super boring by the way."

"No, they'll think I'm pathetic for making you up, then feel all sorry for me because I'm still single, *then* they'll try to set me up with their dentists, dog walker, or God knows who else!"

Great, now *he's* looking at me like I'm sad and pathetic. "Stop looking at me like that. You're not here to judge me. You're here to play nice and get paid."

"Speaking of getting paid—"

"Get out, you two!" Poppy opens Jim's door and tries dragging him out of the car. I grab for him and play tug-of-war with Poppy but lose. We didn't go over anything, and I can already see curiosity piquing in June and Katie's eyes.

"Jim—I mean *Bob*, wait!" I yell to get his attention. The vultures are swarming, and that *up to no good* look on Katie's face as she makes her way to our car is confirmation enough to hurry up and spit out the basic needed facts. Jim finally turns to lean inside the car, his arms flexing above his head, making it hard to focus. "No nicknames, even less PDA, okay?" His smile is big and sexy, and I mentally want to take back the PDA comment. I think he catches on because his smile turns deviant, and delicious while mischief glints in his eyes. Jesus, what have I gotten myself into?

"Cool. Got it. Let's go make all your friends gush over your perfect boyfriend." He leans farther in to grab my hand and pulls me out of the car. I throw my hand over my eyes to block out the blazing sun when Katie pounces on me.

"Dude! What the hell! You guys took forever. Ew, you smell funny. Is that…the lingering scent of sex?" Katie and I are similar in appearance. Brown hair, hazel eyes, cute button noses. Kidding on the noses, but we have passed for sisters before when it came to snagging family discounts. She releases me and turns her attention on Jim. "Oh, and you must be the cause of said scent, you dirty little muncher."

Jim laughs while I slowly die of embarrassment. "Katie!" I snap, but she has no interest in me. She's set her eyes on my boyfriend—*fake* boyfriend.

"Hi, you must be Bob. Katie. Heard a lot about you."

He wastes no time unleashing that smile on my friend as he sticks his hand out. "It's actually Jim."

Utter confusion strikes as her eyebrows go up, up, and away.

"Wait, I thought your name was Bob?"

"It's Jim."

"But..." She turns to me for help. I taser Jim with my glare, wanting to punch him for not playing along.

"It's Jim-Bob. I like to call him Bob for short." Why is he making this so hard?

"Oh, okay then. Jim-Bob it is. Since you guys are the last ones here, you get the room next to us. Beware, Jim-Bob, the walls seem thin. No funny business if you don't want us hearing anything." She winks, and I debate throwing myself in the lake and never resurfacing. *Why* do all my friends have to be so *strange*?

And why hasn't Katie let go of his hand? Like a jealous girlfriend, I slap their hands apart, only realizing my action after the fact. "Oh, sorry. Uh, your husband was looking over here. I think he was getting jealous." That's right. Point blame elsewhere.

Katie swipes her hand in the air. "Oh, it's fine. Jerry's high as a kite. He probably can't even see this far." We all take sight of her husband, who, indeed, is trying to catch a butterfly, Mr. Miyagi style. "Anywho, let's go in. The house is dope. Some sort of famous couple owns it. Not to mention, there's a weird obsession with koozies going on in there."

My eyebrows shoot up. "Koozies?"

"You can look later. Just hurry up and change. The pontoon boat is sick," she says, then starts to walk off.

Still confused, I shake it off. No time for questions. Side leaning into Jim, I whisper, "Her husband's Jerry. He's a financial advisor. They have two kids, boys. She's a teacher, second—"

"What was that?" Katie turns around.

I open my mouth to tell her I wasn't talking to her, but Jim beats me to it. "Oh, she was just telling me she's not worried about the thin walls. She brought her favorite ball-gag."

Gosh *darn it*, Bob.

I wind my hand back and take a nice swing into Jim's chest.

"Ouch!" he gripes, bucking forward.

"Are you for real right now?" I yelp.

"You two are cute. Fighting like a married couple already," Katie awes, and she's off again. We're both still standing there, Jim rubbing his chest while I snarl at him.

"Seriously?"

"What? You're a freak in the sheets. Don't chicks envy other chicks like that?"

"What? *No*! It's *guys* who envy dudes who have chicks who are freaks in the sheets."

"Oh, so I should have used the line on the other guys here?"

Jiminy Cricket.

Turn around, Casey. Go home. Cut your losses.

I'm starting to think this might be the best course of

action, but when Jim turns and starts walking toward the house, I want to take my grabby hands and see just how tight his butt cheeks are. Man, he has a nice tush. Every time he sways from side to side, one cheek flexes, and damn…

Just damn.

"Hey, girl—"

"*Gah!*" I jump, startled by June, who pops out of nowhere. "Jesus, you're like a little ninja."

"I was calling your name, weirdo. Sure it wasn't due to something—or *someone*—catching your eye?" she jokes and leans in for a light hug.

I turn back as Jim disappears into the house. "I'm not sure," I say honestly. I've been in the presence of this odd stranger for approximately four hours and he's already managed to get deep under my skin. Not sure if that's a good or bad thing, but he's succeeded in hitting both emotions. Bad, because why doesn't he know how to listen? I tell him to say one thing, and he says another. Reminds me of an untrained dog. But then there's that smile. That kiss. What *was* that kiss? He didn't even introduce himself before he shoved his tongue down my throat and made my knees turn to Jell-O.

And then the nicknames. Small little gestures are so not my style, but he's making me kinda, sorta, possibly, maybe enjoy them. Hello! I'm single. I don't get called sweet things. Sweet little nicknames are not because someone is all fancy on me. It's because I'm about to make awful choices and won't even remember the pet names come morning.

And, ugh…even in the short four hours of having a fake boyfriend, it's making me think maybe it wouldn't be so bad to have a real one.

"You going to elaborate on that one?"

I forget June's standing there waiting for an answer. "I don't really know how. Let's just say my boyfriend is a mystery to me sometimes."

An understatement of the century.

I wish it were possible to stall. Click my heels and it be the end of the weekend. But time is ticking normally, each minute the required sixty seconds, each hour the required sixty minutes, and sadly, I don't have ruby red shoes. *Lucifer's sweaty balls.* A big huff and a puff and I wrap my arm around June and walk us up to the front porch.

"Wow, this place is beautiful," I gasp, stepping inside the lower entrance of the house. Katie's mention of koozies instantly makes sense as my eyes focus on an array of shelves holding row after row of colorful foam sleeves—or what I like to call beer huggers. "Holy Hoarders Anonymous, what is all this?" I don't know whether to be impressed or confused. "Who likes koozies this much?"

"You should see the back room. Locked glass case of 'em. I assume those are the ones off limits. Jason and I took a peek. Some big autographs on them. There's a blue one with a light beam guarding it. Super strange."

"Yeah, but why koozies?"

June shrugs. "Why *not* koozies?"

Oh, June, my little intellectual know it all. I shrug when Katie's voice booms as she comes out of the bathroom. "Case, you're upstairs to the right. Hurry up and change. Boat leaves in five." She stops to snag a koozie off the wall. "I mean…they obviously have enough to share." She jams her corona into an "alcohol you later" koozie, and walks past, offering us both her *toodles* wave as she skips down the hill leading to the water.

Great.

I turn to June to suggest we stay at the house and admire the koozie hall of fame when she gives in and pulls one off the wall. "Cute, huh? Matches my bathing suit. See ya down there." Then she's gone too.

I find myself staring at the endless wall of colorful drink holders, one from Siesta Key, Florida, another from Hooters. I give in and snag one that says, "You have some big pickleballs."

"Wish I had some big pickle*balls*." Ones that wouldn't have me running for the hills thinking about having to trek my sorry butt upstairs to face the attractive predicament I got myself into. Speaking of predicament, how could I have not thought about room situations? Did I not think I would have to share a room with this dude? You know, my *boyfriend*? I smack my head with the squishy foam. Maybe the room has two beds. Possibly a big enough closet for one of us to sleep in.

I grunt, keeping the koozie, because I do enjoy a nice cold drink, make my slow journey up the long set of stairs, and peek into the room.

"Jim?"

Maybe I got lucky and he's already changed and is on the boat. When I push the door open and walk in, I'm met with silence. No sign of fake boyfriend anywhere. My backpack is on the bed, and a pair of men's jeans are over the small rocking chair in the corner. He's already gone. Good. Hurrying to my bag, I rip down the zipper and reach for my bathing suit. I don't know what I was thinking when I decided buying a hot pink bikini with lollipops on it was smart. But I was day drunk and internet shopping to make myself and my high-interest credit card feel fulfilled.

My fingers latch onto my jeans, and I shove them

down, along with my underwear. I kick out of them, then off goes my top. Unhooking my bra, I toss it to the side—

"Hey, I forgot my...*holy fuckin' Jesus.*"

I whip around to the deep voice, and it takes a few seconds for my brain to catch up and remind me I'm naked. *"Jesus!"* I jump, throwing my hands over my boobs, then my crotch, then I try to mastermind a full body cover up with my arms, hands, and legs. "Dude!" I scream.

"Dude," Jim groans.

"Don't you knock?" I turn around and hurry into my bottoms.

"Knock knock?"

I whip my head back to give him my perfected eye snarl and throw my bikini top over my boobs. I fumble with the string, but I'm all out of sorts and can't seem to get it tied.

"Here, let me help you."

"Yeah, no need. I got it," I snap, but still can't get this damn strap to—

I shut up real fast the second his warm hands land on my back. He's slow and gentle as he adjusts the straps, securing them in place. "There. All good now."

I want to turn around and say thank you, but my face is hot, my ears burning, and there's a flutter in my belly I can't quite place. Embarrassed? Turned on? Both? He may have removed his hands from my back, but I can still feel the warmth of his fingers lingering on my skin. "Mmm... okay, great. Thanks."

"Yeah, great. So, I forgot my sunglasses. Just gonna grab those. Yep. Right there. Cool. See you out there."

He's gone, and I'm pretty sure I have a lady boner.

Ugh.

Seventy-two hours. You can do this, Casey.

CHAPTER SIX

Jim / Bob

What the hell have I gotten myself into?

I stand at the top of the stairs a few seconds longer because I need my fucking boner to go down. I adjust the big guy. I really don't want to be standing near the door when she comes out thinking I'm some creep. Not that I'm *not* a creep. Who agrees to be someone's fake boyfriend for money? *You do, asshole.* Not that I need the money. The traffic at the bar is doing okay and the band gigs are steadily coming in. I just figured, how bad could it be hanging out with a random chick for three days? And get paid to do so.

Making my way outside and down the grassy path leading to the dock, I try to dissect why this girl needs to pay someone to date her. She's hot as all get out. A little feisty, but that body? Damn. I'm forced to make another adjustment down below, replaying the images of her naked and perfect in all the right places. And fuck, that cute little ass.

She's gotta be crazy.

One of those bat shit crazy chicks who reels in guys, then goes all psycho when you eat the last bite of their taco or don't hold the door open for them. *Man, speaking of, tacos sound good right now. When was the last time I ate?*

"Hey, bro. You must be Bob."

This damn Bob bullshit. Who the fuck names their kid Bob? Who names their fake boyfriend Bob? She couldn't have given me a cooler name? Something more badass? Like the dude who drove us, Mick. He sounds badass. "It's Jim, actually." I stretch out to take his hand. He looks familiar. TV maybe?

"Oh, sorry, man. Thought the girls said your name was Bob."

"Yeah, it's confusing. It's Jim and Bob, and just Jim." I should just go with Bob. She's paying me enough money to call me whatever she wants. "You look familiar," I say as we release hands.

"You watch football?"

"No way! Jason Maniac from the Oakland Raiders? Holy shit."

"Yeah, retired now, but I'm assistant coaching for the Bears."

"You were a badass on the field. What'd you have, like, over eighty solo tackles last season?"

Jason laughs and opens a cooler. Tossing me a beer, he grabs one for himself and cracks it open. "Something like that. But I tore my ACL at the end of the year and that was that." I remember that now. A running back from the Broncos side charged him during a tackle causing him to land faulty, taking him out the rest of the season. "So, how's Casey treatin' you? Never thought I'd see her settle down."

"Why's that?" *Inquiring paid boyfriends need to know.*

"Well...you know her, wild party girl. Don't get me wrong, we love her, but it's definitely time for her to grow up and find a man to put her in her place. You get me?" He laughs and takes a swig of his beer. *My girl is not only crazy, but wild. Interesting.*

I open my mouth to grill him for more information, but chatter from up the hill has us both turning. Three girls and two husbands join us on the dock. I stare at Casey, trying to get her attention, but she seems to be avoiding eye contact.

"Let's get this party started!" Katie sings, walking past me and jumping on the pontoon boat. I'm quickly introduced to Katie's husband, Jerry, and when everyone is loaded and seated, Mick pulls away from the dock. I take a seat in the front of the boat next to Casey and inspect the crew. Everyone seems relaxed, hanging on their better halves. I also notice they're all staring back at us, as if we're a goddamn circus act and they're waiting for us to put on a show. I gaze over at Casey, who's stiff as a board. She's sure doing a bang-up job at convincing her friends we're a couple with the whole cold shoulder act.

Looks like I'm going to have to take the lead on this.

Definitely gonna have to work for my money.

She squeals when I capture her waist and pull her into my lap, cuddling her in my arms. My smile outshines the noon sun as I rest my hand on her bare thigh, her skin soft and smooth like silk. Damn, just the simple gesture has me giddy, feeling like I won the lottery with this gig. I stroke my thumb up and down the inside of her thigh, still sporting a happy-go-lucky smile on my face, when she whips her head around, a fire in her eyes making this even more enjoyable. If this is how it is to get paid for my company, I would have applied to these ads a long ass time ago. The only problem is when I lean in and kiss her shoulder, my sugar momma becomes rigid in my arms. There's no disguising the rumble of her anger as her body quivers within my hold. I lean in even closer, my lips still grazing the corner of her shoulder. My voice dips to a husky whisper. "Baby, you gotta learn to relax. Don't think about work—"

"You have a job!" Poppy blurts out.

Fuck.

"No. Yes, I mean, I—"

Shit. That didn't help. How was *I* supposed to know she didn't have a job? "She's...uh, actually doing work for me." *Which is what again?* My actual job is far from what the ad requested. How the hell do I fight the can of worms it seems I just axed open? *I'm rich, I invest, and I like fancy steak restaurants.* Go with that. "Investment stuff. Lots of it. Really great with her hands. All professional, though." Winking, I give her a big squeeze. Man, I almost blew it. It does strike me as a little concerning, though, considering she still has to pay me. I bring my mouth to the back of her ear, keeping my voice low. "How are you going to pay me if you don't have a job? And *why* don't you have a job?"

Her elbow goes into my gut, and I grunt.

Damn, she's feisty.

"That's great, Case! I thought you were still walking dogs. Glad to hear Jim-Bob's getting you on the straight and narrow career path finally," Poppy says, opening a spritzer.

"Yeah, ya know, really movin' up in the world." She wraps her arms around my neck and digs her nails into my skin. I fight through the pain and match her by sliding my hand farther up her thigh. Her nails dig deeper, and I'm forced to call uncle because I'm pretty sure I'm about to start bleeding.

"Cool. So, what exactly is it he has you doing?"

I brace for her nails to hit a vein at Poppy's next question.

"Um…just research. Lots of research. *Hey!* What's this amazing spot June was telling me about? Something about a rope swing?"

Subject change. Thatta girl.

Her nails ease up as Poppy drops the subject. She begins explaining all the activities they have set for the weekend. I play fair too, forcibly dropping my hand from her thigh, and I say forcibly because damn, her thigh under my palm feels fucking fantastic. My mind heads down a bad, bad place at what that thigh leads to, and I have to adjust her on my lap because I'm starting to poke her with my bad, bad hard-on.

The boat slows, and I stare straight at a steep rock ledge dangling over the lake and an old rope hanging from an even older looking tree branch. Yeah…fuck that shit. Casey jumps off my lap like it's on fire, and I adjust myself to hide my semi-boner. Mick parks the boat and drops an anchor.

"Oh boy! Who's going first on that?" June pops up next.

Not fucking me. I'm more of a keep my feet on the ground kind of guy. I get up to head to the back of the boat, pretending to need anything but a lunatic dive off that sketchy ass rope, when I hear my name.

"Jim-Bob! Dude, where you going? You're up first, man." It's fucking *Jim*. Deep breath. I turn around, facing my audience, including Casey, who's smiling.

"Yeah, *babe*. You first. You're always telling me how adventurous you are at *work*. Show us what you got." Her celestial smile is cute and sexy and also about to disappear when I take a hand to her perky ass.

"Nah, *babe*, I'm good. Tired from all my world traveling. You should go first, since you did tell me on our app site where you hired—"

"SHUT THE FU—front door. Babe, no business talk." I'm pretty sure she wants to throw me off the side of the boat, which wouldn't be the worst thing. The fire in her eyes keeps waking up my little buddy down below. Actually, big buddy. Fuck. He's big. Huge.

"Why don't you both go? It'll be romantic. Hold hands and jump together!" Poppy chimes in. We both snap our heads her way, our expressions matching. *No fucking way.* "Staying on the boat and making out is not allowed, kids." She laughs, and my horny mind creates this awesome visual of my tongue passing those adorable pursed lips and exploring her mouth, which I bet tastes sweet from her fruity spritzer.

Fuck…

"Let's go!" I blurt, then grab her hand and jump off the side. I force her in with me, because it was either that or introduce everyone to my dick. Casey squeals as we go under, and the moment we pop up, I prepare for a lashing. I wipe water off my face and catch her breaking the surface. Just in time for her to throw her hair over her face all *Baywatch* style. And why the fuck is this chick single again? Smokin' hot, kinda scary when mad, and yeah…crazy. She must be crazy.

"Why the hell did you just do that?" she hisses. Her eyes shoot such fiery flames, the lake water should fear evaporation. But I'm more focused on her cute little nose and running my tongue over her wet lips.

"'Cause I had a boner thinking about making out and had to hide it. I did you a favor."

Her cheeks begin to match the blaze in her eyes, forming a rosy tint across her face. "How's *that* doing me a favor?"

"Because I'm not an escort. I don't have sex for money. And if you saw him, you'd want him. He's not for sale." Her eyes go wide, and I laugh knowing he'd take her for a fair price. Which is free. He would take her right now in the water three times over if he was calling the shots.

She splashes me, followed by a loud huff. "This isn't what I signed up for. I've clearly made a mistake thinking this was a good idea." She pivots and starts swimming toward the rock.

I swim after her, trying to keep up. "Well...too late, sweetie pie. I blew off a good paying gig for this. So, unless you wanna pay me now and send me on my way, you're stuck with me." She doesn't stop swimming until she reaches the rock and begins climbing out. Her ass cheeks flex as she slips and almost falls back into the water. I mistakenly start to chuckle, and she whips her head around, giving me that stare.

"You're a jerk."

"And all yours for the next three days, babe." I make it to shore and start climbing up the slippery rock behind her. She's pretty quick to make it to the top. I'm hot on her tail as we hit the flat surface. "What's your problem? Why are you so angry all the time?"

Wrong thing to ask.

"I am *not* always angry. I'm annoyed. I hired you to be someone you're clearly not."

"Well, no shit, princess!"

She raises her hand to take a slap, possibly a punch, since she's nuts, to my actual nuts, when I seize her wrist, interjecting her assault. "Not nice, babe. They didn't do anything to you."

"Oh my god, why is everything sexual with you?" Is it? Maybe she should stop being so damn hot so my mind will get out of the gutter. "Hello? Staring at me like a creep doesn't help you."

"I'm normally not. Apparently, my dick has a fetish for feisty, crazy chicks. I can't help—"

Dammit!

I missed that one. She gets me good, kicking me in the shin. I buckle down, holding my ankle like a fucking pansy. What I also do wrong is look slightly up and realize simply how high we climbed. My nuts suck up into my stomach as fear hits me. During our little fake relationship scuffle, I forgot I was afraid of heights. Staring at her ass the entire way up kept me from realizing just how high we went.

I panic and step back, bumping into Casey. "Whoa, watch it! You almost threw me off! Who's the crazy one now?"

"You, for bringing us up here!" I snap. Shit, I can't breathe.

"You followed me!" she yells back.

My eyes scan the rope. It looks to be a billion years old and hanging on by a thread. Hell no. The branch...it's frayed and dead—just like we're gonna be if we attempt that. "We gotta go back down," I freak, turning around to find the path we took. Fuck, why is it so steep?

"Jim, we can't go back down, we have to jump."

"You jump. Enjoy! I'm going back down." Or I may just live the rest of my days on this ledge, 'cause goddamn it's too steep.

"Oh my god, are you scared to jump? Not only are you a pervert and a jerk, you're a scaredy cat?" Oh, that's it. No one insults my manhood. I turn back around to face the lake.

Okay, just this once, I'll let it slide.

"Chicken, *bawk-bawk-bawk.*"

Dammit! That one hurt.

Choices need to be made. Mainly on how I want to portray myself as a man. A big, bad, tough, testosterone-filled man.

"*Bawk-bawk-baw—*"

I grab her hand and say fuck the rope. Giving her no choice, I force her to jump off the cliff with me. The screaming on the way down is loud, though I'm not sure if the louder, girly one is me or her. The water smacks into us within seconds, and we're engulfed under. I lose Casey's grip in the process, and when I pop back up, she's nowhere around.

My head whips around in both directions. "Casey!" Shit. I shift toward the rocks. "Casey!" I shout again, suddenly feeling like that was a godawful move. Without using the rope, we could have landed too close to the rocks. My adrenaline spikes thinking the worst. Fuck. "Casey!" I yell, and finally, I hear her voice, laced with annoyance of course.

Whipping to the right, I see her on the other side of the water's edge and swim like a man on a mission until I clutch her and pull her into my arms. "Jesus. I thought...I thought...well...it doesn't matter...why are you all the way over here?" I ask, keeping my thoughts that I assumed I tugged her off a cliff to her death to myself. And then I realize something else. "*Jesus.* Why aren't you wearing a top?" The swell of her tits press against my bare chest. I squeeze her closer, because…well, I'm a man. They're full and real and wonderful.

"My top fell off when I hit the water." Her response is so soft and innocent, I almost forget the hellion girl in my arms. She's flushed with embarrassment. Gone is the fire in her eyes, and in its place, shyness. I can't help but crave more of this new person while being curious to see more of her. Learn more about her. I look down as she peers up at me. For the first time, we're seeing one another, not on a battlefield, but in a moment of possible surrender, where we both call a truce. And in this truce, because I can't stop myself, it's okay to bend down and put my lips over hers and kiss her.

Fuck, her lips are soft and perfect. Her tongue is sweet from the spritzer, just as I imagined. I can't stop myself from moaning at how good she feels. I hug her closer as I put more pressure in our kiss. Her arms wrap tightly around my neck. She's just as into this, allowing me to kiss her harder. Damn, I can do this forever. My legs may give out and we may drown in the middle of this lake, but this girl may be worth my demise. Howls and clapping from behind us slice through our bubble, reminding us we're not alone.

Casey goes rigid, instantly pulling away from me. Back is the uptight version. She offers me her fiery eyes one last time before pushing away and swimming back to the boat.

I wait a few seconds because Big Jim Jr. needs a moment. Before I double back, I spot a hot pink top floating in the distance.

Fuck.

Seventy hours to go.

CHAPTER SEVEN

Casey

"It was out."

"It wasn't out. It hit the corner. In bounds."

"Bro, it was fucking out!"

Us girls are sitting on the ginormous balcony overlooking the guys below in a heated match of pickleball. Apparently, the owners, who Mick's agent rented the house from, are professional pickleball players. From the gold US Open trophies and framed photos of them alongside famous people, I would say they are pretty darn good too.

Mick and Jim practically throw themselves at one another, claiming partners, but Jason puts a stop to it, arguing the two were getting too good, and puts Jim with Jerry. Having no idea what the crapshoot pickleball even is, us girls sit around relying on Google and Urban Dictionary to explain it to us. Turns out, it's kind of like tennis, but played on a smaller sized court, like badminton and paddles instead of rackets. Also, they use a whiffle ball. And if you live your life by the trusty bible of Urban Dictionary, it's the shit.

LAKE REDSTONE

The game started off pretty easy, them going over the rules, but once it started to heat up, so did a few tempers and the drive to win.

"What are those guys arguing about now?" Poppy asks, setting her drink stuffed in a pink "getting white girl drunk" koozie down and sitting forward to peer over the railing at the ridiculous, state of the art, built-in pickleball court.

After getting kissed like I've never been kissed before in the lake, with no top on, might I add, I swam to the boat, and hid in the back the rest of the day. I claimed heat stroke even though we'd only been on the lake just over an hour. Thank God Jim stayed in the water and away from me. I mean, who the hell does he think he is?

Hot. A good kisser. Hot. Built like a steel rod. Hot. Don't forget the steel rod below. And those tattoos. Those eyes. That smile!

Mother of pearl! How is it someone like him is single and available for hire? He *has* to be a gigolo. Male prostitute. The way he's causing my insides to go all gooey and warm, he's had to have had lots of practice. Yes, that has to be it. Guys like him simply don't exist in real life. Well... they do, but they're taken or way more expensive than my measly fee of five hundred dollars. I also need to stop being so abrasive and enjoy myself. When was the last time I actually felt this attracted to a guy? *Never, girl. Never.* I agree with myself. It's been never since a guy has made my belly do that girl crush swirly thing, causing my insides to feel like they're being attacked by butterflies. If anything, I should be embracing the fact that this guy, real or not, is showing me the attention I've unsuccessfully set out for since I grew boobs and learned what feelings for the opposite sex were.

"Who the hell knows? Jerry's probably cheating again,"

Katie says, breaking into my thoughts, taking a big swig of her beer shoved in a neon yellow, "I don't get drunk, I get awesome" koozie.

"It was fucking out, man! If you'd stop smoking so much weed, maybe you'd be able to see where the actual lines are," Jason snaps, and we all sit forward. The two men are at the net going at it.

"I'm not fucking high, man."

"Dude, you swung at a piece of fuzz floating in the air."

We start to laugh, and they look up, realizing they're causing a scene.

Katie stands and leans over the railing. "Why don't you boys all whip it out and sword fight to the death to see who wins."

I spit out my drink, and June giggles next to me. Jerry gives his wife the stink eye, while Jason smiles dreamily at his June. I sigh, sipping my drink as I get lost in their personal moment.

Gosh, do I want what they have. To get lost in each other's eyes, no words needed. Love so strong, they feel it through their steely gazes. He's probably telling her through his telepathic stare that her hair looks beautiful ruffled up in her ponytail and she makes the best sugar cookies on the planet. She's probably silently telling him he's an amazing man and father and tonight she's going to—

A whiffle ball buzzing past my ear snaps me out of my haze.

"Fuck it, but next time, I'm not fucking around. Let's change teams. Jim-Bob, you're over here on skins," Jason says, nodding for Mick to change sides.

"Oh, man, your model hubby isn't gonna be happy," I tease Poppy. "He has to put his shirt back on. No more model pecs to distract us." Poppy laughs, knowing her husband. Indeed, Mick pouts as he throws his muscle shirt back on.

That's when Jim takes his off.

And the four of us choke and spit out our drinks.

Hot.

Tattoos.

Steel rods everywhere.

"Casey, you're one lucky girl," June comments, right as Jim looks up and catches me gawking. He winks at me, causing a row of panties to drop—mine, most importantly—and tosses his shirt to the side. The game continues with more arguing and Jerry swatting at nothing.

We girls, on the other hand, catch up and drink.

"So, Case, I have to admit, I don't remember Jim-Bob from my anniversary dinner," June says in between sips of her margarita, tucked nicely in a tie dye, "drunk wives matter" koozie.

"Me either," I reply, because I've had a few too many and honesty is the best policy. I take in the expressions of my friends. Confusion all around. Oops. Maybe honesty is *sometimes* the best policy. "I *meant*, I had such a good time, I barely remember the night, let alone my boyfriend." Phew. Saved myself on that one.

"Who cares. He's super-hot and really nice. Good catch. So, fill us in. Marriage worthy?"

I choke and sputter, abusing alcohol for a second time in only minutes. What is happening to me? Treating booze like a redheaded stepchild when I only want to love it. Wait, what is wrong with these women? Marriage? I'm preparing my soliloquy to win my alcohol back and they want times and dates when I'm marrying my fake boyfriend and popping out his fake boyfriend spawns? Should I spill that I didn't even get his last name? What if it doesn't sound good with Casey? *Can't be worse than Kasem.* The memory of this same conversation comes shooting to the frontal lobe of my brain. *Titsworth, Pecker, Quakenbush, Bonerz, Hardick, Wang...* Okay, so the conversation was at a bachelorette party. But still—all point to no marriage.

I wish my friends wouldn't make such a big deal out of it. So, it's been a while since they've seen me in a stable relationship—little do they know—but words like *keeper*, *marriage*, and *can't wait to see what your babies are gonna look like* instantly come spilling out? I imagine, if Jim were real—figuratively, because, you know, super real and playing pickleball shirtless in a display worthy of all the drool—and we actually had a relationship, and he loved me, if he was kind and supported me for who I was, didn't judge me for being me...

A small amount of weight I constantly bear on my shoulders frees up imagining all the ways I wouldn't have to pretend to be someone I'm not if someone like Jim were real. All the horrible blind dates the girls set me up on would be a thing of the past. The lies pretending I'm way more mature and intellectual than I really am. And I don't need him to be rich or successful, or smart or fit. The fit part definitely helps. As I watch him take a swing at the ball, his body, a shimmering mountain of muscle and flesh, flexes all over. *Lord almighty, he's got it all.* I can't even stop my own mouth from filling with saliva. I lick my lips—shoot, what were we talking about? *Jim...I mean, perfect guy.* Oh yeah! I merely want him to be honest. And funny. Listen to my dumb stories and maybe even laugh at my lame jokes.

And don't get me wrong, I've searched high and low for my very own version. I've just never had luck with guys. I didn't have a high school sweetheart or love at first sight encounter at a bar. I wasn't saved by my prince charming, or, in Poppy's case, her saving her prince. I just always concluded I was never at the right place at the right time. Let me add in ever. Never ever. I was never ever in the right place.

I also just wasn't as lucky as them.

"Well? Has it been discussed? I wouldn't let him out of my sight if I were you."

Five hundred dollars for seventy-two hours? I'd have to rob all of Illinois to pay him for a lifetime of company. Not that I wouldn't mind keeping him for longer than the weekend. *Swing, flex, sweat, grunt, oh my. Focus!* Let him out of my sight? Pfft. Sure, easy for the happily married one to say. And that's always the downfall. My best friends all have perfect marriages. Yeah, they fight, but in my eyes, it's all silly nilly stuff. Well…aside from that one time with Poppy. Days before their wedding, she threatened to leave Mick. It wasn't because he installed a stripper pole in their basement behind her back for reasons I, personally, never want to know—Poppy actually thought it was romantic—but because he was trying to learn a stripper move off YouTube to impress her on their wedding night and ended up breaking his tailbone two days before their two-week honeymoon in Maui.

"Marriage is the last thing on our minds. Jim is so busy—"

"Oh, so it's just Jim now?" Katie busts in. Poppy laughs. I can't keep my lies straight.

"Whatever. You get what I'm saying. It's just not on the table, and I'm not sure it'll ever be." I can't say it's because

I've only known him for seven hours and he'll be out of my life in less than three days.

We're interrupted by hollering, announcing the end of the game. Thankful for the disruption, we all return our focus to the men in time to watch Mick and Jim chest bump. We take the side stairs and walk to the first level to join them. Jim, with a wide smile on his face, catches my eyes on him and aims that crooked boyish grin at me. As if this wasn't a sham, his reaction to me is so natural as he walks right up to me and plants his lips on mine.

"Did you see me kick some ass, babe? Man, how come I never knew about this game?" he huffs, wiping sweat off his forehead.

"Um...because you're too busy with work," I lie. A rich business investor wouldn't have time for pickleball, right?

He smiles again, gives me another kiss, then smacks my booty. I jump at the unexpected gesture. "Well, looks like I'm gonna have to cut back on work. This game's awesome." With a wink to die for, he transfers his attention to his new besties.

"What is it with guys?" Katie says while staring at the bromance we're all observing. "They can just meet for the first time, and within minutes, soulmates. I basically hate everyone I've met since third grade. Except you guys."

June and I laugh. Her statement couldn't be truer. "Who knows, but it looks like we all might be sleeping together so those four can cuddle," Poppy says, grabbing some empty beer cans to toss in the trash. "Which is fine with me. Mick has his shoot tomorrow, and he gets cranky before 'em. He can have his diva attitude with his new boyfriends instead of me."

I take a peek back at the guys as Mick flexes and Jim

feels his muscle. I shake my head with a smile. Guys are ridiculous. They jab at us girls and our love for lip gloss and wine, but put a group of men together and they will complement each other's armpit hair when enough liquor is involved.

"Let those two feel each other up. Let's start dinner."

With that, I follow Poppy inside, leaving my fake boyfriend with my best friends' husbands in hopes they don't exchange blood vial pendants during the next sixty-four hours.

"No way, man! Pearl Jam's acoustic set is way better than Nirvana's bootleg tapes."

Everyone has migrated onto the upper deck, all hands occupying koozie stuffed drinks. Jerry is manning the grill while he and Jim talk music.

Jim practically falls over his chair, knocking over the small table full of empty bottles. "Are you insane! Nirvana's bootleg sold a shit ton more than Pearl Jam's, first off, and second, the acoustics are pure mint. He played them all on a specially made Callahan. There's no way it tops Vetter's Rutter guitars, even though they are mint pieces. No way."

Jerry stares at Jim in awe. "Man, how do you know so much about music?" A few seconds pass before he answers. "Just a hobby…" He shrugs and gets quiet.

"Jerry! You paying attention to those burgers?" Katie barks from inside the house.

"Yes, woman! Get off my back." He grunts, returning to mind the grill.

Katie walks out holding a tray of dip and chips. "He's

gonna burn those burgers. He always does this. He starts yappin' and burns the burgers."

"Dammit, I'm not gonna burn the burgers—*shit*," he cusses as a flame explodes from the grill.

"He's gonna burn the burgers." I laugh, taking the tray from Katie and placing it on the outdoor table. The sun is going down, giving a beautiful orange cast over the lake. Down below, you can see the boats lined up with a few still out, and hear the laughter of kids playing and music echoing across the water. I lean back in my chair and sip on my cocktail, admiring the view and secretly admitting to myself I was wrong for putting up such a stink about this place. It certainly is beautiful. I've always wanted to own a home on a lake. Have that escape when you need it. The quietness of the water. Peacefulness when life gets a little overwhelming.

"What's got you all quiet?" Jim takes the empty seat next to me.

I turn to him, ready to give him some award-winning lie, but the truth falls out. "Just thinking about how beautiful it is out here. Wish I had more of that in my world."

He doesn't mask his questioning stare. "You wanna elaborate on that?"

"Nope. It's exactly what it means, JB."

"JB now?" He chuckles. "You've given me more nicknames than all the jaded girls in high school. I found myself in the girls bathroom stall with Sara Henderson once and saw all the nasty names they wrote about me—hey, where you going?"

I stand mid-sentence and walk inside. I thought maybe if I was honest, I could get an honest answer back. Always a joke with everyone. "Hey, what'd I say?" Jim follows me into the kitchen. Ignoring him, I drop the empty plates and walk into the back of the house to the bathroom. I go to shut the door, but he's behind me, slipping in and shutting it with him inside.

"Uh…I'm going to the bathroom. Can you please get out?"

"No, I want to finish our conversation. Plus, you said I stay over at your place all the time. I've clearly watched you pee."

Jesus!

"No, *you* said you stay over. And news flash—you're fake and have never seen me pee! So, please, get out." And people wonder why I hit. My hands are feeling restless. I'm fighting the urge to tackle him through the door to earn back my privacy.

"No."

"No?" He clearly enjoys being hit. A sadist gigolo. That's who I'm dealing with.

"Yeah, no. What got you all upset back there? I thought we were having a moment?"

A grumble deep in my throat releases, and I cross my arms over my chest. "Having a *moment*? Me confessing I wish I had something more real and honest in my life and you following up with how you were a whore in high school and talking about all the chicks you hooked up with isn't having a moment," I huff.

"There you go."

"There I go what!" Oh my god, this guy is so exasperating.

"Finally, you let me see a piece of the real you."

I sigh so loud, I wake the dead. "Jim, what are you talking about?"

He steps forward, and my breath catches. "You want something real. Right?" I think about his question, then offer him a silent nod. "And honest, right?" I nod. "Okay, answer this honestly and I'll give you something real."

I'm losing my cool with every second he doesn't give in and leave me alone. "Answer what?"

"Why'd you really need to hire me?"

Shoot! He catches me off guard with that one. I open and close my mouth, trying to search for the right answer. But there isn't one that doesn't portray me as deceptive. I was a fraud and wanted my friends to see me in the same league they all played in. When I set up that ad, I never thought about having to explain myself to someone. "What kind of question is that?" I throw back at him.

"A simple one. Answer it."

Drats! I want to take my fist to his nuts. Wasn't it obvious in the ad? "Because I lied to my friends about having this great guy, and when push came to shove, I had to produce him."

His smile grows. "You think I'm great?"

Oh, son of a… "No, but I'm paying you to be." Which he's failing at. Since he's spending less time being great and more time being on my damn nerves.

"Why does he have to be rich, working a boring job, and doing god awful boring things to be great? Is that what you define as great?"

All his fact pointing is grating on my last nerve. And it's because he's hitting the one nerve that's making me realize how right he is. Why did I make my fake boyfriend all these things? If that guy truly showed up at my door for a date, I'd set myself on fire to get out of it. Even now, hearing him replay all the attributes I demanded, he sounds like this super boring, stuffy guy. Yuck! And here I am getting offended when he's right! What is it I thought was so great about the person I made up? Am I high maintenance? Is he insinuating I am because of the lies I told? Realistically, I don't have a strict checklist. Only a few must-haves. He must be faithful, kind, true, fun, not smell bad... Okay, maybe this is getting long. Whatever. But I am *not* a snob who only wants a man with money and prestige. My army of defenses kick into high gear and my wall goes back up, me on top with my metaphorical pitchfork jabbing down at him.

"You know what? Yes. That's the kind of guy I want. Rich, super smart, and snobby as can be." I choke on my next rant of words when he moves in closer, my head lifting to keep eye contact. He towers over me, waiting for me to finish, but I can't even remember what we were talking about. "So there. You got your answer. Now, get out."

"You didn't give me a chance to return the favor."

"Oh yeah? What possible favor do you have for me?"

Bending down, he covers my mouth with his and kisses me so passionately, the tingles down to my toes threaten to buckle my knees. He grabs me with vigor, snuggling me into his arms, and whispers, "Damn, you're sexy when you're worked up." My cheeks burn when he tells me he wants to take me right in this bathroom, not caring who hears our passionate screams of—

"Hello? Earth to Casey."

"Huh?"

I snap back into reality. Did I just...?

"Where'd you go?"

Crazy town?

"Casey, did you just fantasize about me kissing you?

You're licking your lips, and I think you may want me to—*dammit!*"

I'm normally not this violent. But I need him to stop. I'm also not very good at being called out since I punch him in the thigh and push past him to avoid any realization that I may actually be attracted to my fake boyfriend.

Fudge.

I can do this. Sixty-two hours to go.

Jim / Bob

I walk back outside with a smile on my face. What *isn't* smiling is my stinging thigh. Damn, she has a strong punch. I probably should have gotten a background check before I agreed to do this. Possibly a police record. If I make it through this weekend alive, I'm gonna suggest anger management.

I scan the balcony. Everyone's filling their plates with homemade pasta salad, chips, and burnt ass burgers. I find my girl over at the picnic table, fighting with a bottle of wine. A small part of me says to go over and help her, but my bruised thigh tells me to stay away. I watch in amusement as she brings the cork to her mouth, using her teeth to wrestle it open. *Damn, she's hot even when unstable.*

There's no doubt my little hellion was having some girly fantasy about me in the bathroom. Being the lead singer of a band, I have a good sense on women. Enough to recognize the way her eyes dilated as they dropped to my mouth. The way her plump lips parted just a sliver. She wanted me to kiss her. She was hoping. And it's a damn shame she had to punch me and run off. I would have had no problem fulfilling her fantasy.

"What's put that cheesy smile on your face?"

I turn to my right to find June standing next to me, holding a plate of food. "Oh, just thinking about how lovely my girl is," I say. We both bring our attention back to Casey, who's gotten the bottle open and lifts it to her lips, forgoing a glass. "Just so lovely," I repeat as she proceeds to chug it, wine dripping down her chin, with no sign of stopping in sight.

"She truly is." June giggles and takes a bite of pasta salad. "Casey's always been the carefree one. A live-in-the-moment kinda girl. Not like most of us who live off kid schedules, desperately lacking adventure." She angles herself to face me. "I'm glad she's finally found someone who can truly see her for her. She needs that." Her sweet smile guilts me. Realistically, she hasn't found someone, because I'm only a decoy for her friends to think she's happy and in love. But that lost look in her eyes as she stares off in thought tells me she's far from happy. And she may want to castrate me. I guess it's my lucky day. Instead of ripping off my manhood, she's drowning herself in wine.

"Jim-Bob, can I ask you a question?"

Yeah, just Jim.

I'm sure this is where I blow it by sticking my foot in my mouth and saying the wrong thing. Something dumb like how she likes her eggs or some shit. Dammit, I'm gonna fuck this up. In the short time I've been here, I've grown to really like her friends. I may have a new bromance with Mick and his steel muscles, and Jason invited me to a football game, which I hope he still takes me to once the cat's outta the bag. "Uh…yeah. Have at it." I'm going with scrambled.

"I'm not talking down on your profession or anything—sounds like you're very successful—but it's odd to me. You see, Casey, for as long as I've known her, has never been a fan of businessmen. Let me rephrase, high-profile men. She can't stand them. It's strange she's okay with you being one. And even to work with you. It's out of character for her."

I'm going to assume June is not dumb and is starting to smell the deceit seeping from my guilty eyes. I'm also going to assume scrambled is definitely not the right answer here. "Yeah, about that...we don't focus much on work. We prefer to keep that separate." Sweet, innocent smile. Kind eyes. Ones I'm positive are trying to search into my soul for answers. Dammit, she's scaring me.

Like losing a game of chicken, I pull my gaze away. I'm not sure if she accepts my answer. I'm gonna go with no, since she continues to stare at me. And why the hell would Casey say I was rich as all mighty if she didn't even like those kinds of dudes? My girlfriend is a horrible liar. *Fake girlfriend, man.* "I mean, work schmerk. Who really defines a man by his work and money anyway?" *I'm pretty sure you do, asshole. You also hate snobby rich fuckers.*

"Hmmm...okay. I never caught the name of your company." *Fuck. RIP future Mick bromance, season tickets, and the chance of meeting the Bears entire cheerleading squad.* "Hmmm, again, it's just strange, after what her dad did and all, she swore she'd never find herself with a man—"

"Finding who with a man? Who we talkin' about?" We both whip around to Casey standing in front of us wearing a cute maroon mustache above her upper lip.

"Oh, we were just talking about jobs and—"

"Aaand—who's gonna get stuck scraping all those

burnt patties off the grill. Gotta say, your girl was dead on with the outcome of those poor burgers." We all glimpse at the table as Katie—

"*Ouch*," we say in unison as Katie throws a burger at Jerry, splattering mustard all over his face.

"Did that patty just bounce off the table?" I ask, stunned.

"Maybe I'll stick to the pasta salad," June says.

Casey claps her hands. "Great! So…hey, Jim…Bob, whatever, can I talk to you for a second. Alone?"

"Alone? Yeah…can't June just stay?" Having a mediator might be safer.

"Uhhh…I'm gonna go see how Jason's fairing on his dinner. I'll leave you two alone," she says right before ditching me.

We're both silent, Casey waiting until June is out of earshot before she sets those nervous eyes on me. "Listen. First off, I'm sorry."

"For?" I face her, my puppy dog eyes in full effect. Gonna make her work for this apology.

"For punching you in the leg." She shrugs, the purse of her lips and drawn eyebrows telling me she's not one to easily apologize.

"You mean when you punched me because I called you out for wanting me to kiss you?"

"What, no!"

"Wait, so you didn't want me to kiss you?"

"No! I mean…that's not the point. I shouldn't have hit you."

"Do you want me to kiss you now?"

"Yes. I mean, *no*! Ughhh…stop confusing me. I just wanted to tell you I'm sorry. I'm not normally this…edgy. I don't normally hire strangers to play my boyfriend and lie to my friends. This is very unlike me, and I want you to know that. I've clearly never done this before and don't know how to act. I just want to get through this weekend, okay?"

And I want to know what happened with her dad, what made her hate rich guys, and why everyone around her thinks she needs to be saved. She may be staring back at me with the fake smile she holds for all her friends, the one that says, *I'm okay, no need to worry about me*, but behind the facade, there's a story she hides deep down, one even her dearest friends don't know about. I stare back at her, wondering if it's a sad one. Is there a reason she lets everyone believe she's so happy-go-lucky when I don't think she's happy at all? Is she so worried about pleasing the people around her, she doesn't find pleasure in herself? And for someone so head strong, why would she care? Why does she want the approval of these people who are supposed to be her friends no matter what?

"You're going all creepy again, staring at me."

I am. But I can't seem to pull my eyes away. She's like a beautiful train wreck. And it may make me just as crazy, but I dig it. Every little thing down to her impressive eye-rolling skills.

We may only be an arrangement to each other—a seventy-two-hour farce—but I'm going to spend the rest of the weekend figuring out how to make whatever we have grow and flourish into something real. I just need to determine how to get on her good side. And stay on it.

"You know what? You're right. I haven't been very cooperative either."

Her eyebrows rise. "Really?"

"Well…yeah, the whole name thing, work, kissing you or not kissing you." I watch her eyes dilate and drop to my lips. Sweet baby Jesus, my prayers have been answered. "I'm simply saying, I'm willing to be more of a team player. Play the part I'm here to play." I don't say I wish this wasn't a farce and I'd like to pursue getting to know one another on a real basis.

"You will?"

"Kiss you, yes." Her cheeks flush, and the urge to kiss her becomes overwhelming. *Down, boy. Take it slow.* "I'll also play nice." I stick my hand out. "Hi, my name's Jim-Bob. Nice to meet you. Can we pretend we're in love and date for the next two days, give or take a few hours or so?" There's a pregnant pause before she finally relaxes. She reaches out and shakes my hand, the warmth of her smooth skin waking the monster in my pants.

"Casey. Nice to meet you. And thank you." Our hands stay locked longer than a normal handshake, until the warmth of our entwined fingers trigger her and she pulls free. "Well… we should probably eat something. Once everyone's done, it's going to be on."

"What do you mean it's going to be *on*?" I didn't get the whole gangbang, swinger vibe from anyone.

"Game night. It's our thing. If you didn't figure it out during pickleball, my friends are very competitive. No one likes losing."

A devious smile breaks across my face. "Well, babe, I rock at all games. It's a good thing you're dating a winner." I wink at her and reach for her hand. Before she has a chance to swoon, I pull her toward the food table. We've got a competition to win.

Casey

"A praying mantis!"

"Snakes on a plane!"

"Sperm donor! Jesus, what the hell are you doing!" Katie yells at Jerry who's on his third failed round of charades. Everyone is laughing their asses off while Katie looks like she's about to murder her husband.

After dinner, we all migrated to the lower deck for an intense game of charades. The sun set, leaving the moon to shimmer across the lake, the warm air continuing into the night. Jim and I stuck to our truce and started acting more like lovers and less like enemies. We found ourselves snuggled together in a lounge chair, me tucked on his lap. Everyone else is huddled around the massive picnic table.

"Time's up," June yells.

"Honey, it was 'go fly a kite.' How could you not get that?"

"Dude, are you even here? Earth to Jerry! You looked like you were having a seizure up there. How the hell was I going to get kite out of you making a triangle and hula dancing?" I buckle over in tears laughing while June tries to politely hide her giggles.

"It was a good effort," June says, handing the bucket to Jim. "You two are up."

I sigh, then follow it up with a huff. This is our third round of failure. Whereas Poppy and Mick guessed "elf on the shelf" and "M&M's" within seconds, Jim and I bombed hardcore. But who the hell would get a naughty police officer, which I think was meant for Poppy, and Moby Dick? I got the dick part since he was thrusting his junk at me, but come on!

I can't imagine this time is going to go any better. Jim is just as competitive as everyone else and with two losses under our belt, he's looking a bit edgy.

"Who's picking the clue?" June asks as Jim shakes the bucket with all the ideas people wrote down and crumpled.

"I got this," Jim assures me as he reaches in, determined to pick a winner. He unfolds the piece of paper and his eyes light up. Oh, great. The same award-winning grin he's gotten with the last two. Another topic he swears we're gonna nail but suck at miserably. He aims his wicked smile on me, and my stomach takes a dip.

"What?" I ask, now worried. Why is he smiling like that?

"Oh, baby, we're winning this one, hands down."

Yeah, just like the last two. Got it. Did I also mention every time someone loses, they have to take a shot of tequila *from* the bottle? And I'm not talkin' a quick swig. I'm talkin' spring break, Cancun style, throw your head back while your opponent pours booze straight from the bottle while blasting an obnoxious whistle. Katie and Jerry are half in the bag with their two losses too, but June and Jason seem to be fairing all right even though June weighs barely ninety pounds soaking wet. I'd say Poppy and Mick are the most sober, but every time Poppy turns her head, Jason pours tequila down his throat.

"All right, all right." Jim drops the bowl on the coffee table, and June prepares to flip the sand timer.

"You two lovebirds ready?" she asks, followed by a cute little hiccup. Jim crumples up the paper and waves his hand to start the time. He positions himself so we're facing one another, and my insides instantly feel funny. Tingly? *Ew, what's happening right now?* Tequila has never been a friend of mine, and that hasn't seemed to change. A layer of goosebumps spread across my body, and I'm scared to admit how hard my nipples just got. His smile threatens to eat me alive. He doesn't seem to care that we're surrounded by other people. And tequila me doesn't either.

"Ready to win?" he whispers low, the vibrations of his voice warming my lady bits. My lips part, wanting to answer him, but nothing comes out. June flips the timer, and Jim gets to work. He goes for my arms, raising them above my head, then nods for me to keep them there. His hips start to sway in slow motion, his hands caressing his abs as he begins lifting his shirt, exposing his stomach. My gasp isn't the only one heard around the room as his shirt works its way up and up. "Sweet Jesus," I muffle, getting a chuckle from June, and an "Amen," out of Katie.

"Not Jesus, keep going," Jim says, keeping his eyes trained on me. His shirt continues to rise, exposing six, rock-hard abs. His hands go flat against his skin, brushing over his pecs. "Babe, come on, you gotta guess!"

"Time's halfway," June says, her voice sounding strained.

"Uhhh…" My brain is mush. And then his shirt is over his head and hitting the floor, and all that wants to fall from my lips is, *"Come to momma."* His hands cup the back of his head, his hips thrust into me, and my tongue falls out and rolls to the floor.

"Fifteen more seconds," June pipes in.

"Babe, guess something!" Jim says, working his hips in a circular motion, bending his knees.

A laughing Poppy nudges me from behind and whispers in my ear. "Girl. Use your words." Easy for her to say. She's used to these strip teases.

Say something, Casey. Anything.

"Dog walker. No shirt, no service, uh..." Most doable guy on the planet...

Son of a biscuit, I don't know!

"How does she not know this!" Mick chimes in, his expression riled. He starts mimicking Jim's moves, and Poppy slaps him on the shoulder to knock it off. "How does she not know this! This should've been mine!" he yells, raising his own shirt.

"Ten, nine, eight...."

Both of Jim's hands cup my body, starting from my raised arms, and he strokes me fully up and down.

"Uhhh...stroke me. I'm a pole. Stroke the pole. Um... dancer...pole dancer? Wait—!"

"Ding! Time's up!"

"Stripper! He's a stripper!" Mick yells, then rips his shirt off and begins performing his pole dancing moves. Poppy takes an elbow to his bare chest to stop him, while Jim and I have a stare off.

"How could you not have gotten that?" he asks, annoyed.

"How was I supposed to concentrate with you half naked bumping and grinding on me?" I snap back.

He takes a menacing step toward me, our bodies so close, I can feel the warmth of his breath against my lips. "I was playing the *game*. You know, where I act, and you guess?" Another step, and my stupid hard nipples press against his bare chest. "I set you up perfectly. Pole, dancer, I even took my shirt off for special effects."

"Yeah, how does someone not get that?" Mick grumbles, throwing himself onto the nearest lounge chair.

"Seriously, Mick?" I direct my narrowed eyes on him.

"What, since you have your stripper degree from YouTube, you're the expert?"

He lifts his head, flexing his pecs. "It makes me knowledgeable in the dance field, so yes."

Oh, give me a break. Supermodel Mick and his high and mighty head. I roll my eyes twice over until they roll back forward to Jim. He's still staring at me, but he's lost the frustration in his eyes. "What are *you* looking at?" I snap, wanting to swipe that now smug look right off his face. I also wish he would back the hell up so my nipples would stop trying to carve their initials into his pecs. Ugh…

"Why the look?" Jim asks, pushing me more to want to murder him.

"Obviously 'cause she's mad she doesn't know a good dancer when she sees one," Mick says, giving Jim a fist bump. That's when my shoe meets Jim's shin.

"Ouch!" Jim squeals, going down to nurse his bruised appendage. "What was that for!"

I go to clutch him by his shirt, but since he's not wearing one, I fumble and wrap my hands around his neck, pulling him away from the group. "What's wrong is you're *supposed* to be on my side. Not against me!"

"How am I against you?"

"Seriously? Fist pumping the enemy is not being on my side."

He frowns, not understanding. "But he's an amazing dancer. Did you see the way he swayed his hips?"

I go for round two of shin abuse—

"Okay! Okay! I get it. What do you want me to do?"

"Tell him he sucks and you can beat him."

His facial expression morphs into shock. "I will do no such—*ouch*! Dammit, that hurts!"

"And so will the next round if you don't stay on my side." He looks back at me with the saddest puppy dog eyes. "Seriously?"

"It's just…I like him, and he, Jason, and I are really bonding, and that would be unbrotherly of—*shit*! You're insane." He turns to the group, all leaning over in their seats trying to listen. "Mick, your moves suck. And I challenge you to a dance off. My girlfriend, who I'm in love with and would sacrifice anything for—even my bromance—thinks this is what's best—"

I flinch in his direction to shut him up.

"Hell yeah, did someone say dance off?" Jason jumps into the ring. He picks up the bottle of tequila, pouring a hefty amount into his mouth. He turns the bottle on June, then Katie and Jerry. I stand there with my arms crossed, waiting for Jim to follow through. But he's stalling. He waits for the bottle to come to him and takes a huge swig. When he pulls back and sees my searing eyes, he goes for another pull. After the third one, I snatch it out of his hands.

"Knock it off!" I tap my foot on the ground. Jason laughs and heads inside.

"Where the hell are you going?" Jerry calls out, and Jason waves his hand for us all to follow.

"Come find out," he replies, and everyone jumps from their seats to follow as he walks down a hallway covered from floor to ceiling with koozies.

"What's the deal with the koozies, man?" Jerry questions while he stops and swaps out a "Don't worry, beer happy" koozie for "I got killer crabs in Maine."

Jason swigs at the tequila. "What do you mean? Whoever has this much dedication must be a legend. Did you see the glass case? Dude has some sick koozies in there. If it was unlocked, I'd snag that 'Field of Dreams' one in a heartbeat."

We let Jason lead us through the koozie museum and up a set of stairs until we pop out by a wooden door, a sign *The Rodge Lodge* above the entrance. When he pushes the door open for us all to enter, we find ourselves speechless, standing in a state-of-the-art gaming room. The entire area is filled with any and everything gaming. From the dart board on the wall, to the pool table. Pinball machine, karaoke machine, and—

"Holy shit," Jim spits out as my eyes follow his. I peer down, realizing we're standing on a dance floor. And should I mention it looks like it lights up?

"I think I just died and went to heaven." Mick ogles the place. "You think there's a pole somewhere?" He spins around with hope in his eyes as he scans the room.

"Welcome to The Rodge Lodge."

"How exactly do you know so much about this place?" Jerry walks off to a shelf full of old vinyl records.

"I read the book."

"*What book?*" everyone asks in unison.

Jason shakes his head and takes a deep swig. "The Lake Redstone book, man! It's on the table. It's the history of the house. The owners—I guess the guy is some sort of dental genius—invented a tool that modernized oral surgery. Made a butt-ton of money. He and his wife travel the world, hence all the koozies. Homeboy was at a conference up in Washington state when they were invited to play a game of pickleball. Turned out, both him and the missus were masters at it. Got picked up by a huge sponsor, and now they literally travel and play for huge sporting events like the US Open. Guy's even on the pickleball association board."

Mick smacks his hands together. "Pretty impressive." He picks up a remote, and with a single click, beams of neon color blast from the Plexiglass squares, bringing the dancefloor to life. "Enough chatter. If I wanted to know more about the owners, I'd invite them to Sunday dinner with the wife and kids. Now, I believe there's a competition I need to win." Using the remote, Mick slides the poor thing, like a stripper prop, down his chest and starts rotating his hips in a slow, circular motion.

"All right, Magic Mike. Let's see what you've got. I've learned a few moves myself that have gotten me some high ratings." June blushes. Awe! My sweet little June and her man get naughty. That's my frisky girl!

"Fine, it's on. But I get to pick the song. Clearly, I would be the best in recommending the perfect dance music." Mick walks over to the stereo system, and we all take our seats for the show. Jason is starting to stretch, and Jim has a somewhat worried expression on his face. Oh, come on. He can't be that bad at dancing! Mick takes his phone out of his back pocket and shoves it into the phone slot.

"Let's go, cowboy! Stalling? Afraid Jim-Bob and I are gonna whoop ya?"

Mick grumbles, still offering us his back. "Pfft! Have you seen my hips move? J. Lo would be jealous."

"Then what's the problem?"

He continues to fiddle with his device, lifting and smacking his phone back on the base. "Dammit."

Jason sighs and goes in search of the problem. He grabs Mick's phone, and after a short struggle, wins it over. "Dude, what is this?"

"My phone. Give it back."

"No, man, this is 1995's phone. Does this thing even work?" He holds up a tiny iPhone. "How cute, Mick has a baby phone."

Mick tries snatching it back, but Jason lifts it high and messes with him, waving it back and forth. "For real, what is this? Your mom called, she wants her iPhone 4 back."

We all bust out laughing as Mick struggles to win his phone back. "Does this thing text? Little phone for a little guy?"

He finally snatches his phone from Jason. "For your information, the newer phones make my butt look big. This one fits perfectly in my back pocket."

"Whatever you say, iPhone 4."

"Shut up."

"iPhone 4."

"I swear, I'm gonna kick your ass."

"*iPhone*—"

"Oh, Jesus! Hey, Alexander Graham Bell, put your fossil phone away and let Jason set his up. We have a competition to win. Right, Jim-Bob?" God, these two kids could go at it for hours. I turn to Jim, who doesn't look ready to win. "Dude, come on. It's dancing. You've danced before, right?"

"Uh…yeah, but not against a legend."

I roll my eyes. I'm just as competitive as the next guy. Or girl. And there is no way Jim is going to lose this for us. I know Mick. He plays dirty. I'll just have to play dirty too.

CHAPTER EIGHT

Casey

Me and my gosh darn dreams.
Always in bed with someone.
Getting nothing.

I'm in a canoe with my old high school math teacher. Sounds gross, but when I was fifteen, he was super hot. As he prowls toward me, my heart beats rapidly against my chest. My body temperature rises, my skin warm to the touch. Clammy almost. When he approaches me, he uses his hands to spread open my legs, but they won't budge.

Open your legs, Casey. He wants in!

But no matter how much I demand my conscious to let the hot teacher in between, my legs stay closed. As if they're being restrained by something. I fight harder and harder, while trying to tell him not to leave. He begins to back away, and I panic, because I really want to see how talented he is. He had such big hands, so my fifteen-year-old curiosity always got lost in the what ifs of down below.

"Don't go," I call for him, but he continues to back

away. "Don't go, we can do this! If we subtract the isosceles from the triangular math equation, we can totally do this!" *What the…?*

I work my mind around the obstacle and hop to my feet. If he can't come in, I'm going there. I steady myself, a smile of satisfaction on my face. I start to bunny jump toward him, but he stands, leaning backwards. "Where you going, hot math teacher?" I purr, taking another hop closer.

He leans back farther. "Hey, careful," I say, worried he's going back too far. Can't have my dream sexy guy fall out of the boat. A hop closer. More leaning. "Seriously, you're gonna fall." I begin to panic. His back is stretched so far, he's starting to transform into Keanu Reeves in The Matrix. Damn, he's like Gumby…

"Hey, that can't feel—"

I jerk awake just as my teacher is about to snap in half off the canoe. I'm sweaty, and clammy, and my stomach decides it wants to expel everything inside it. Throwing my hand over my mouth, I groan, breathing through my nose to calm my erupting stomach. Everything is blurry, but I can confirm I'm in a bed. Trying to concentrate, confusion fills my still drunk brain as I take in my surroundings. The four key W's simmer in my head in major need of answering. Who. What. Why. Where.

Why am I in a man's t-shirt? Which smells glorious, by the way.

My blurred eyesight allows me to confirm I'm not in my own bed. Further investigation tells me I also have no pants on. Great. A bit of panic mixed with a large dose of confusion surfaces, until my brain takes pity on me and tiny bits of memories flood back. Lake house. I'm at the lake house with everyone. A small sense of relief calms my still swirling belly, until more questions arise. How did I get up here? I don't remember going to bed. Did I drink too much? That's a silly question. Moving on, I scrape my brain for pieces of last night. Everyone was drinking. Tequila waterfall. I groan, and my hand goes back over my mouth.

There were the Frisbee burgers, charades, The Rodge Lodge, and tequila, so much tequila…

"Oh God, kill me." My hands slide up my face, covering my eyes. My fingers dig into my eye sockets to help the throbbing in my head. *Why, Casey, why!?*

"Why what?"

My eyes shoot open so fast, I almost throw my hands out to catch them from falling out of their sockets. I scream, ready to bash whoever the intruder is in my room. That's when Jim lazily pops his head up from the floor. "Jesus Christ! You scared the hell out of me!" I hiss, grabbing the blanket and pulling it up my legs, but the sheet is tangled around my ankles. *My legs are trapped… Hmmm… make sense now. Sorry, hot teacher.*

I lean to the side and see Jim with a pillow and a thin blanket laying on the floor next to the bed. He also appears to be—

"Why are you *naked*?" We…did not—*did we*?

"'Cause you're wearing my shirt."

My eyes shoot back down to the heathered grey shirt, a lithographed guitar with *Limited Infinity* sketched below it. It's super comfy, and damn, I nonchalantly inhale. It smells good, and—

"Wait, why am I in your shirt. Don't tell me we—"

"Had wild passionate sex until you passed out of pleasure overload?"

Oh my god.

"No, we didn't. You banged on the headboard, wanting to let the entire town think we were having wild, passionate sex, then puked. *Then* I proceeded to put you in the shower, held you while you beautifully sang Eminem between yacking, then passed out. I couldn't figure out your bag, so I put you in one of my shirts."

No, no, no, no. Be patient. He's gonna also say he's kidding.

Say you're kidding...

He's not gonna say it.

"You're not kidding, are you?"

"That you sang beautifully? Yes. It was like listening to a dying animal."

I pick up a pillow and toss it at him, which he avoids by flexing his biceps to block his head. "Okay, sorry. You were amazing. But also...yeah, all true."

Why!!!!

I fall back onto the bed in hopes it swallows me whole. How is this guy still even here? I've done nothing but bite his head off and embarrass myself. He *has* to think I'm senile. But cute, though. Does he think I'm attractive? I hurriedly thrust my fingers into my hair, brushing it out of my face. What resembles a chip falls out, and I quickly toss it, then lick my thumb and scrape dry drool off the side of my lip. I get a sneak peek at my reflection in the mirror and bask in the horror.

Oh hell.

I give up.

I should allow him to tap out—give him an out and let him run as fast as he can away from me before I do any more damage to my already sinking reputation. That I even thought I could go an entire weekend pretending to be dating a random stranger and not pull any of my typical shenanigans was a joke.

If I let him leave, I'll surely have a lot of explaining to do, and the whole, "let's all feel sorry for Casey's drama" is going to be worse than the truth *and* this tequila hangover, but after the foolish mayhem I pulled last night, I can't force him to stick around the rest of the weekend.

I sit back up. "Listen, I'm gonna save you the trouble of giving me some lame excuse of how your grandma died or work suddenly needs you for a huge emergency and you need to leave. I wouldn't have signed up for this either. So, it's cool to bail." If I'm lucky, he'll be in such a huge hurry to get the hell outta dodge, he'll forget to ask for his shirt back, because this is super soft and—

"No, I'm good."

My head whips around. "Wait, you are?"

He shrugs. "Yeah. I actually had a great time last night. Minus being vomited on, of course." I grunt again and cover my eyes. "But hey, on the plus side, I did get to see you naked." And then my eyes go wide. His laugh reverberates throughout the room. "Just kidding. I didn't look. Well…I kind of didn't look. I had to wash puke out of your hair, so I had to keep at least one eye open."

How mortifying!

Why can't I just grow up—drink a normal amount and say my goodnights like a decent human being instead of blacking out and always waking up with half my clothes missing? Or, in this case, all.

I blame this on Jason. Damn him and his obsession with wanting to be a college shot girl. Images of liquor being poured down our throats like a waterfall of nothing good flash through my muffled brain. "Oh god, what did we do last night?" I grunt, holding my head together so it doesn't crack in half when my brain explodes.

"Well, there was a lot of drinking. Jason sure does make a fine shot girl." I squeeze my eyes shut, wishing the storm brewing in my stomach to stop. "And that sure was some dance off, not gonna lie." Dance off...dance off... *No! Go away images!*

Hollering and laughing fill The Rodge Lodge as Mick gives Poppy his award-winning lap dance. "Damn, Mick, didn't know you still had it in you! I'm about ready to shove some dollar bills down your G-string," Jason howls, buckling over in laughter. Jerry falls off his chair, holding his stomach, and Katie spits out her drink.

"I'm the real deal right here, my brother. Now, let me show the officer what these hips can really do." Mick winks and grinds on his wife.

I throw myself at Jim, who's seated in the chair next to them. "Pfft! That ain't shit, Micky boy!" I holler.

"Jesus," Jim grunts as I throw my leg over him and grind into his lap. He fumbles with his beer, but loses his grip, spilling all over us both. "Babe, a little warning—"

"No warnings needed, babe. We need to show them how it's really done." I roll back and forth on him, trying to be seductive, but I'm also tanked.

Jim leans into me. "How is it really done?"

"I call bullshit!" Mick yells, grinding harder into Poppy.

"Bull patootie nothing, we do this all the time!"

"We do?" Jim whispers.

"Yeah, we do," I growl, working my hips in long strides over his lap. My hands dig under his shirt, meeting solid abs and chest. Sweet Mother Mary and baby Jesus.

Jerry starts to laugh. "I don't know, Case, your man looks pretty scared right now."

I peek down at Jim, his expression pained. "Oh, come on. I'm not bad at this," *I hiss, working harder to sway my hips back and forth over him. My fingernails dig into his bare chest, and I ride them up, wrapping them around the back of his neck.*

"Casey, you gotta stop," he whispers, trying to hold my hips in place, but I fight him. No way I'm letting Mick win. "Jesus, Case, you really have to stop," *he groans, his eyes half closed.*

"Fuck no—can't. Gotta show him up." I divert my attention to Mick, who's about to do a headstand over Poppy's face. That cheating bastard. I need to step it up a notch.

"You all right over there, Jim-Bob?" Jason asks, chuckling into his beer.

"Just dandy," he grunts.

"Dude, suck it up!" I bend down and whisper in his ear, "I'm not paying you to look miserable."

"Not sure if you're paying me to nut in my pants from you dry humping me either," he groans again. My eyes shoot down to his crotch and the large tent in his pants. Oops. Hollering has my attention back on my competition. Mick is shaking his junk upside down into Poppy's face. Dammit! I take a quick second to consider Jim's situation. But the laughter throws me into major competitor mode, and Jim's minor inconvenience takes a back seat. I jump up, climbing and standing on the chair.

"Shit, what are you doing?" Jim asks.

"Raising the stakes," I say, conjuring up my childhood headstand expertise. It can't be that hard. Simple task. Hands down, legs up.

"Casey, no…"

Hands down, legs up.

"I don't think this is a good—"

My hands go down, and I swing my legs up…accidently meeting Jim's face and knocking him out.

"Oh god." A heavy wave of mortification hits me viciously as my belly threatens another eruption. "I'm *sooo* sorry." He starts rubbing at his nose. Can I be any more of a hot mess? The image of him with Kleenex shoved up his nose to stop the bleeding the remainder of the night has me covering my face and shaking my head. "I don't know what came over me. I just—"

"Wanted to win. I get it."

"Yeah, and instead, I almost took your head off with my horrible stripper moves." We stare at each other until we both burst out laughing. "Like, really? I haven't attempted a head stand since I was, like, twelve!"

"About the last time I got dry humped by a girl." Oh my god! My hands go back up.

"Kidding." He chuckles.

I peek through my fingers. "Really?"

"Yes. I actually got dry humped by a girl in college once. It ended just as horribly." I pick up another pillow and throw it at him. He dodges, grunting as it nicks his nose.

"Oh geez, I'm not winning any points here, am I?" He strokes his wound. Even with a bruised nose, it doesn't go unnoticed how attractive he looks. His wild hair is all ruffled and sexy, his muscles and tattoos on full display. *Dammit! I'm ogling.* I pull my eyes away to stare at a piece of invisible dust on the wall. Sounds of movement come from the floor where Jim starts to get up, and a small jolt of panic surges through me. My eyes fail to stay away, and I catch him just as the thin blanket covering his hips falls as he stands. Hands fly back over my eyes in fear I'm about to get an eyeful. Thankfully—*or regretfully*—he's covered in a pair of shorts as he sits on the edge of the bed.

"Don't worry. I'm sure the money you owe me will cover the plastic surgery for my new nose." New nose? What kind of shady doctor does he have to reconstruct a new nose for a measly five hundred bucks? Which *also* reminds me—I don't even *have* five hundred bucks! There's a sliver of hope maybe he responded to my ad before the price change and he's here for the fifty bucks. My own nose crinkles at the scary thought of him getting a new nose for fifty dollars. "What's that *ew* look for?" Jim breaks up the disturbing image of him with a sketchy putty nose.

"Oh…uh…nothing. Just—"

My words are cut short. Jim makes an unexpected move and jumps up, throwing his body over mine. I fall back, my head hitting the plush pillow, eyes wide as he leans over me, his lips merely a hairsbreadth from my own. "Go with it, 'kay?"

Before I can reply, his lips fuse against mine. Shock, confusion, excitement—all shoot through me at once. His lips are warm and perfect against mine. My body temperature shoots up, and a few short seconds is all it takes for me to sink farther into the mattress. Two quick knocks sound on the door, and Katie pops her head in with an invitation.

"Well, well…at it again, are we?" My eyes enlarge as I stare in shock up at Jim. He eases up, pulling away just a smidge, allowing our eyes to connect.

"Can't get enough of her." He winks at me, and for a split second, I lose myself in his words. Fake, but I let them soak in as if they're real. He smiles down at me as if *I* am real—*we* are real—and this, us molded together, warm with that energetic buzz, is something we've been feeling for a lifetime.

"Well, calm it down. We need Casey to be able to walk today. Mick said it's a long walk to the waterfall shoot. Also, breakfast's ready, so you might wanna get up."

Just as fast as the moment bulldozes through us, it's swept away. Jim bends down, brushes his lips against mine, then climbs off me. Katie coughs, hiding her moan, as she gets an eyeful of Jim in all his shirtless glory. I side-eye my friend, because she shouldn't be ogling my fake boyfriend, then admire the goods myself. He must be one of the top-rated gigolos in the state, because he sure is lovely.

"Got it. I gotta use the bathroom, then I'll meet you all downstairs, cool, babe?" He blows me a kiss, and like a love-sick teenager, my lips part in anticipation for that air kiss to float and smack me on my eagerly willing lips. *God, what is wrong with me!* I'm still staring at him. Those eyes. That sexy hair. Muscles and muscles and—

"Earth to Case?"

"I do."

"Huh?" both he and Katie say at once. *Crap-sicle. What did they ask me? Rewind, brain...ah! Bathroom, breakfast—got it.* "Yep, got it. Meet you downstairs." He smiles at me in a way that melts my insides. Like the perfect grilled cheese sandwich, the gooeyness of the deliciousness just melting out of the two toasted slices of bread—am I comparing the way my insides feel to food? *Sigh.* What I wouldn't give for that smile to be real. He walks past Katie, who doesn't even attempt to hide the fact that she's staring at his butt. I nod, agreeing it is a nice piece of meat. Rare, plump to the touch— "Okay! You can stop staring now," I grumble, strangely jealous. I need to get some or eat. Both seem just as important right now.

"It's impossible. So, not sorry. Speaking of not sorry,

how are you doing this morning? Heard lots of banging going on. You gonna be able to walk after all that action? I saw him in his wet bathing suit. He's a lady bruiser."

"Lady bruiser?"

"Yeah, ya know—monster down there. Large and in charge. Beat up that—"

"Jesus!" I toss the last remaining pillow on the bed at her. "I got it. And no, I'm fine. I'll be able to walk just fine." Since I didn't have any sex whatsoever and have no idea if he really is a lady bruiser, though there's no mistaking he has a full house down there. My cheeks flush, giving Katie the wrong idea.

"Oh god, you lovesick horn-ball. You can fill me in on all the details later. But for real. Get your ass up. Mick's on the prowl making sure he's not late for hair and makeup."

I nod, and she shuts the door, leaving me with my thoughts of big bruisers and the fake butterflies still swirling in my belly. I throw myself back into the mattress and press the comforter to my face to muffle a loud groan. What have I gotten myself into? Just like everything else in my life, I didn't think past the first layer of the issue. I show up with a fake boyfriend, but what about the rest? I didn't think that maybe, just maybe, he would turn out to be an okay guy. Attractive, kind, goofy, cuddly—shoot, the list goes on and on!

Then, there are the lies. I didn't think how much this would affect my friends if they found out. How do I send Jim on his way in two days and tell everyone we broke it off? He wasn't the one, and don't ever attempt to contact him? My own mood plummets thinking about him being in the wind, and I've only spent around twenty-four hours with him.

More groaning.

Suck it up, Casey. You made this bed, now you lay in it.

Which I also can't do because Poppy yells my name from downstairs.

"Coming!" I huff and throw my legs over, but not before getting my foot caught in the sheet and tripping off the bed.

CHAPTER
NINE

Jim / Bob

After a cold shower and thoughts of my grandmother naked, I head downstairs to find the crew sipping on coffee and eating breakfast.

"Hey, there he is!" Jason comes up and smacks me on the back. I play it cool and only puff out my chest slightly. I'm really liking these guys. Bromances are a real thing. My eyes find Casey, who's shoving a danish in her mouth. Crumbs fall down her chin onto her cute little bathing suit cover-up thingy. She's opted out of her hot pink lollipop bikini for red and white kissy lips. My mind goes to that naughty place, and I picture my lips being where all those patterns are. *Shit*. I force my mind back to my grandmother.

"You hungry, bro?"

"Very." I lick my lips at how perky her breasts look in that top. The way they bounce as she laughs at something June says.

"Yeah, I was meaning like a fucking donut or

something." Jason laughs, smacking me again on the back. "Man, you've got it bad, don't you?"

I pull myself out of my daze, not realizing I just blamed my hunger on my girl. Fake girl. She is *not* mine. This is a paid relationship. As in not real with money involved. My shoulders slump slightly, and I nod to Jason. "Yeah, I'm thinking about keepin' her," I joke, knowing that's a lie. Come Monday, I'll be back to the norm: running the bar, playing in the band, and wondering where exactly it is I should be in my life.

Jerry walks by and hands me a donut, and I shove it in my mouth to keep myself from repeating my thoughts out loud. I continue to stare at Casey, dying to know what's going through her head. Parts of last night replay in my head. The comment June made about Casey's dad, for one, eats at my curiosity. It also brings up the hate I have for my own father. How money only ruins lives. I could have had it all, but I walked away from it. At thirty-two, I may be living on nickels and dimes, but I'm not under the claws of my asshole father.

I wonder if she dealt with the same shit.

Did she have a son of a bitch of a father like mine, who tried to control me with his power and wealth? Ruin our family because he was selfish and went outside his marriage for pleasure, killing my mother in the process? It's been years since I've spoken to him, but the mere mention gets my blood boiling. Not once has he attempted to reach out. Show a sliver of interest in my life. A life he frowned upon. But I'd live a poor man's life any day over being his puppet. He may not have control over my choices anymore, but one thing he, to this day, still holds power over is the way I deal with life. Just like him, I keep people at a distance. Trust is non-existent. I learned from a young age those who could be trusted were near and far. My father lied to me my entire life. He lied to my mother, and even after her death, that trust was tainted. But in the end, it made me who I am.

It was during the last year of high school, out of the blue one day, I picked up a guitar and realized I had a calling. I started to play, sing, write music. Not too long after, I joined a band. It didn't pay the bills, but it soothed the loudness in my head—the anger I refused to let go of whenever my mind went to that dark place. Instead of the ritzy jobs my father tried to place me in, I picked up bartending jobs where I played.

Being propositioned by chicks came along with being in a band. I had my fair share of un-memorable one-night stands, but I was over it. It had been over a year since I took a girl home and gave in to meaningless sex. I just wasn't into it anymore.

I had been online trying to search for any entertainment gigs I could find when I ran across Casey's ad. I first scrolled through it and laughed. The things people will pay for. The things people will do to get paid. I shook my head and continued, hitting up some dude who was willing to pay a solid three grand for a band to play at his kid's graduation party. But then the ad was updated. I got notified since I'd clicked on it previously and saw the price increase. My eyes practically fell out of my sockets at the hike. I re-read the details, and thought how terrible could it be? I responded and that was that.

Had I been worried I'd be walking into a shitshow? Fuck yeah. The internet is a scary place. Half the crap is false, and nobody is who they say they are. Did I think I was walking into my own death? Yep. This could have been some creep wanting to saw me into pieces or steal my organs.

Did I expect to find a hot little brunette with an attitude and spark that almost blinded me? Fuck no. I'd be lying if I said I was disappointed. Far from it. On the outside, she was everything I pictured in someone I wanted as my girl. But then, she spoke and yelled and hit, and for a moment, I was second guessing my choice. She was hot, but it didn't mean she still wasn't a serial killer. The thought sat heavy on my mind on the way up to the lake. But the sweet scent of her hair as she slept on my shoulder kept the weird thoughts at bay. I told myself I could make it through the weekend, take my money, and use it to get some new equipment for the band, new stools for the bar, and it would be worth it. But now, peering around the room, I can't imagine them not being my friends after this is over.

Casey must feel my eyes on her because she looks my way, wiping raspberry jelly off her lips.

"All right, everyone. It's time," Mick starts, addressing the room. "I know you're all excited. Watching a shoot can be a very intense experience."

Jason bursts out laughing, and Jerry throws a donut hole at Mick's head.

"Hey! I just blew out my hair!" He swats away the powdered sugar on his forehead. "Let's all get on the boat and head over. I want you all to know you'll be treated like VIPs there. I've already told my team who you are."

Poppy shakes her head and reaches for her beach bag. Everyone else starts gathering their things. I wait to see what Casey will do. That's when she slides off the stool and begins to limp toward me.

"Oh, you've got to be kidding me," I laugh. Gotta give my girl credit. Faking a limp due to her soreness from the big guy. My chest fully expands with pride, and I smile wide as she makes her way to me. I pull her into my arms. "I'm flattered and all, but don't you think the limp's a bit much?" I snuggle her into my chest and kiss the top of her head.

"Flattering, I'm not," she grumbles. "My foot got caught on the sheet and I tripped out of bed. I think I pulled my groin." I start to laugh, and she slaps me in the chest. "It's not funny! It hurts like hell."

I look down at her sad little pouty face. Damn, she's cute when she's whiny. "Oh yeah?" I say, swiping a piece of hair off her cheek.

"Yeah."

She whimpers when I bring my hand to her thigh. "Relax. Let me massage it out." She starts to protest, but the second my fingers dig into her sore spot, she moans and leans into me.

"Oh yeah. Feels good."

Probably not as good as it feels to have my hand on her warm, smooth skin. "How's that?" I ask, keeping my dirty thoughts at bay. For once, my monster downstairs isn't trying to poke at her and I'm genuinely concerned with helping her out.

"So much better. Thank you." She pulls away from me, and I release my grip on her. "How'd you know how to do that?"

"I'm on my feet a lot. My muscles tend to cramp up sometimes. Plus, dehydration is a sign of muscle cramping. A good bartender taught me that once."

"Oh." There's a small pause before she asks, "And what do you do that you're on your feet all day?"

I guess this is where I tell her my truth, which is nowhere near a rich investor with rich tastes and even richer aspirations. I don't get why I care so much what she thinks of me. It's not as if this will go past our weekend agreement. Then again, the thought of us getting together after all this for a drink sometime sounds kind of nice. We only live a quick twenty-minute bus ride away from each other. It wouldn't be hard to see each other more than once or twice.

"You gonna hold out on me, or am I right and you're some kind of gigolo?"

Wait—what? "Gigolo? Uh...no. Actually, I'm—"

"You two coming?" Katie's voice interrupts my response. "Everyone's already in the boat, and Jerry's taking bets on if you two are going for round two on destroying that headboard, *which* Mick made sure to point out is some sort of antique the owners were gifted by the Kardashians or some shit."

Casey's mouth drops, while I laugh. "As in *the* Kardashians?" she squeals.

"Yep. That was my reaction. He also said to tell you if you break it, you buy it."

"Uh...what? I don't have the money to pay for that. What is it, like, a billion dollars?" Stress floods her features, and I take hold of her hand to ease her worry. She passed out way before any damage was done.

"Whatever you say. But hey, love is priceless, right?" Katie chuckles and backtracks down the hill.

"Tell them we are *not* destroying that headboard!" Casey yells to her back.

Katie doesn't bother turning, just lifts her hand to wave. "Will do. Considering my bet was you two in the shower again. You two make some strange ass noises by the way."

She opens her mouth to deny, but I pull her into my chest and press my fingers to her lips. "We'll be right there," I yell as she slaps my hand away and whips around, now sporting her angry face.

"What the heck? Now they're gonna think I'm some sort of perv! And why the hell are you smiling?"

"For one, those strange noises were you trying to rap to Eminem while yacking. So, unless you'd rather them know *that* over thinking we're in love and can't keep our hands off each other—even if we enjoy making strange noises—then I suggest letting it go."

She stands there in silence, her eyes doing all the talking. She's pondering her choices, her brows creased. She might also be remembering hanging onto me naked in the shower while putting her fake microphone in my face to back up her lyrics while she puked.

"Ughhh… Whatever. Let's just go." She snatches her beach bag off the ground and storms out of the house while I follow close behind, humming "The Real Slim Shady."

The sun is like a ball of fire, sizzling my skin, even with the breeze as we sail across the lake to Mick's photoshoot location. Everyone is snuggled up with their significant others. Even Casey is on my lap. My fingers find her sore spot, and my thumb brushes along her inner thigh. I lean forward, taking in the fruity scent of her suntan lotion, and ask, "How's the groin?"

"It's better. Thanks," she replies, pushing up her sunglasses.

I nod and lay back against the chair.

Another question strikes me, and I lean forward again.

"Why'd you think I was a gigolo?"

Her body stiffens. "I...uh, I thought—"

"We're here!" Mick shouts. Everyone's eyes focus on a small landing with a trail that leads up a hill. People with cameras and lighting equipment are everywhere. Forgotten is my curiosity of why my girl thought I was a male prostitute. In its place, the excitement and curiosity for what the hell we're about to walk in to.

Mick docks the boat, and we all jump out. Assistants grab our things and help us up the long path. Mick starts barking orders, and everyone follows his lead as if he's God. I'm in complete amazement watching a flock of hair and makeup people chase after him as he makes his way to a chair with his name across the back. When he sits, he's attacked at all angles with brushes to his hair and face, someone plucking his eyebrows—

"Jesus, he's like—"

"Ridiculous?" Poppy comes up next to me.

I turn to her and nod. "Yes. I mean no! He's...amazing." I'm serious, if nothing comes of Casey and I, I may try to pursue him.

"I get what you mean. I was like you in the beginning, but I'm used to it now. They call him the Fabio of his time. Romance industry eats him up." I turn back and watch a woman blow a single strand of his hair in place.

"Excuse me, Poppy, we're ready. If we can have your group follow me to the waterfall..."

Poppy nods and waves for us all to follow. I give one

last glance at Mick, who's having his pecs massaged with oil. Dammit, he's my new idol. I jog to catch up to Casey. When we make it to the waterfall, Casey starts to stall.

"Wait, we're supposed to climb in the water with him?"

I shrug. "Guess so." I grab her hand to climb down. We need to make sure to get a good spot.

"Yeah. I'm not so sure about this."

I turn back. "Why not? It's fine. Come on." I'm starting to get impatient. Camera crews are taking up the good spots.

"It doesn't really look safe…"

"Babe, it's fine. Trust me." I try to tug her this time, because now we're going to be forced into the second row. Katie and Jerry pass us and get in the water no problem, while Jason gets smart and carries June. "Here. I'll carry you down." She continues to hesitate, but I finally get the okay and lift her in my arms, steadying myself as I make my way into the water. Right then, Mick appears. He has a whole crew behind him, holding a towel, umbrella, and spritzer.

My hero.

"You realize it's creepy the way you look at him, right?"

I snap out of my haze. "Huh?"

Her arms wrap around my neck as I coddle her, possibly squeezing her butt a little tighter than necessary in case I accidentally slip. "What's it with Mick? You keep giving him the googly eyes."

I catch sight of Mick. He's swinging his hair around as flashing lights bounce off his oily chest and the rock wall of the waterfall. "Do I have to really explain?" I laugh and shake it off. "I'm kidding. I think you have some great friends. I'm just in awe, I guess. You're lucky."

I wish I had a close group of friends. A gang. A tribe of sorts. I consider my bandmates friends, but we don't have inside jokes or know each other's favorite restaurant, allergies, or any childhood memories kind of cheesy shit. I have my favorite bartender, Judith, but she's not one I can sit down and have a beer with and share all my thoughts and aspirations. This group? They have that. I see it in the way they all laugh with one another.

"Lucky?"

"Yeah, Case. Lucky." I set her down. I wish I would have shut my mouth because her goofy smile turns down. Great. Now she feels pity for me. "And I'm glad for you, 'cause *my* awesome group of friends are the same—"

"You two watching this?"

Jason breaks into my lie, and we both bring our eyes to the photoshoot. Mick is sprawled on a rock, throwing his head back as the water splashes against his chest. The photographer is cheering him on.

"That's it. Feel the sun on your chest. Let the water seduce you. That's it. Chin to the gods feasting down at your beauty. Fantastic!"

Everyone stares.

My mouth drops open.

Jason's brows shoot up.

Katie, June, and Casey become speechless.

Poppy stares in appreciation at her man.

"How…have…we…*never* come to one of these before!" Jason says, keeling over in a fit of laughter. After a few seconds pass, everyone else joins in an eruption of laughter. The photographer snaps a billion photos a second while Mick flips himself onto his stomach, resembling a mermaid on an abandoned rock.

LAKE REDSTONE

"That's it! Show the rock who's boss. Be one with the water—yes! Flip that hair, gorgeous. Flex—yes, flex! Beautiful!"

We're all transfixed to the sight when an assistant dressed in zoo gear wades through the water, holding a—

"Dude, no way! That's not what I think it is, is it?" Jerry asks.

"Is that a—?"

"Snake? No way. No amount of money and fame is worth that thing on me," Casey says, shivering in my hold.

"Oh hell no," Jason says and we all watch in horror as the zookeeper starts wrapping the huge snake around Mick's neck. The lights start flashing, and the photographer goes berserk. I swear, he's about to blow a load at how excited he is snapping each pose.

We all fall silent and watch the shoot play out.

Until it goes to shit.

Mick slips on the slick rock, and the snake slides off his neck, disappearing into the water.

Everyone freezes.

A few uncomfortable moments pass until someone speaks.

"Um…is that supposed to happen?" Katie asks, her voice filled with hope that it sure as fuck was.

"Yeah, I'm not sure," Poppy says, sounding a hundred and fifty percent sure it wasn't. It doesn't help that the assistant looks about ready to puke and the photographer is white as a ghost.

Then it happens.

Complete and utter mayhem.

The photographer starts screaming, along with the assistant and lighting guy. The spritzer crew takes off, and all our heads follow the zookeeper as he takes a leap off the rock and dives into the water.

"So, should we…uh…"

"Yeah…"

When his manager screeches, "Run!" we finally kick into gear. Katie and Jerry take off toward the shore while Jason picks up his screaming wife and throws her over his shoulder.

"Case, go." I nudge her, but she doesn't move. "Casey, we gotta go! Fuck knows where that thing went!" She still doesn't budge. The color has stripped from her face, and I think she's in shock. Great. I spring into action, picking her up and booking it.

The rocks below are slick, and I almost slip. I fumble with Casey in my arms, which triggers her to come out of her zone—and start screaming.

"Fuck," I grunt when she fights against my hold, nudging me in the balls. I almost drop her, but push through it. I have to climb up a little ledge of rock to get to solid ground, but something slithers against my leg.

No, no, no, no…

I step on the rock and scoot over to reach the next rock. My only thought is to get the hell out of this water.

I try to keep my cool, but then I see it.

The devil's creature.

I consider myself a man. A tough, no-bullshit, I'll-kill-for-anyone kind of man.

Except right now. My inner child threatens to scream like a girl and take off. I spot Jason at the edge of the lake and think quick. "I'm gonna toss you to Jason."

It doesn't help that she latches onto me tighter, seconds away from choking me. "No way! You'll drop me! I won't make it!" Her grip strangles me, and instead of trying to save us both, I'm trying to wrestle her arms from around my neck so I don't pass out and doom us both.

"Babe, listen. I'm gonna toss you. He'll catch you. Unless you can walk." Wrong thing to say. I'm going down. Never saw my life ending by being choked to death by a chick—and not even sexually related. I start to cough.

"Case! I'm here! I got you." Jason steps in, trying to help. Casey starts shaking her head erratically, knocking me in the nose. I lose my balance for a quick second, and she starts to scream harder.

Something slithers past my leg again—and I start to fucking lose it. My own panic sets in, my muscles burning from holding her squirmy body, my legs in the same position, trying to keep us steady on the slick rock. It's now or never.

"Babe, it's okay. I've got you. Just relax. I won't let you go." Her eyes are wild, staring into mine. "It's you and me, okay?" She nods back and forth, her movements jerky. I guide my hand up and grip her waist. "Damn, you're beautiful like this. All flustered." Her eyes dilate. Her grip on me eases. "Would it be wrong to want to kiss you right now?" Her lips part, and I feel her chest inhale a small breath of air. "Pretend it's only you and I, would you let me kiss you?"

Her body succumbs, like Jell-O in my arms. She unclenches her death grip around me, her eyes now at half-mast. Her lips part even more, ready to answer me.

That's when I toss her.

She goes flying, her ear-piercing shriek waking the dead. Thankfully, Jason's football skills are on point. He catches her just as something wraps around my leg and I fall under the water's surface. I thrash my legs out and reach for anything to take to my ankle and bash the thing off me, but when my hand disappears into the murky water, the only thing I retrieve is a fistful of seaweed. Well shit. That's not good. Neither is the feeling of a slithering creature hugging your calf.

I'm two seconds away from screaming like a frightened little girl. What are the chances if I toss myself at Jason, he'll catch me too? My eyes search out the group. Tons of hands waving in the air, open mouths screaming something, but I'm deaf to it all. The only sound I hear is the thumping of my heartbeat. I guess now's a good time to mention I'm scared to death of fucking snakes. I still have nightmares from when I lost a bet to Stu, our bass guitarist, and he made me sit through fourteen hours of snake movies during one of our tours.

I'm a goner.

This is it for me.

When I die from a snake attack, I hope whoever plays my character makes this part look way manlier than what's really happening. There's sudden tightness around my ankle and I prepare to lose my leg along with my pride and life.

"Oh, son of a bitch," I groan. Time is flashing before me. I need to man up—now. With my luck, my made-for-TV movie would be a bust and everyone would remember me as the sissy who squealed like a pansy and let an anaconda take him out.

Suck it up, bro. What would Steve Irwin do? Fuck! He'd probably hug the damn thing! Regroup. *Think, think...* Crocodile Dundee. That guy slayed snakes with his bare teeth. Problem is my stomach revolts at the thought of biting into the slithery creature of death.

Back to the hopes of the heroic movie.

Shouts from the zookeeper catch my attention, my eyes shooting toward the waterfall. His mouth is open and moving, but I can't understand him over the other shouting.

"What?" I yell, wanting to tell him I'm kinda fucking busy right now.

He yells again, and I try to decipher what he's saying. "Snap his neck on the rock?" Jesus, a little morbid don't ya think?

He shakes his head and shouts again.

The pressure tightens, and it's now or never. My adrenaline kicks in, and I swipe away a bead of sweat running down my face. I'm normally a lover of all things, but I have to remember this thing is out to kill me, so I need to not hold back. If that dude insists, death by snapping and bashing it is. I inhale and exhale in three short gusts, stretching my neck. Searching deep inside myself for my inner snake slayer, I exhale in a loud howl and go ape shit, taking my hands to the slimy creature and gearing up to destroy.

CHAPTER
TEN

Casey

"Catch, bro." Jason tosses a can of beer to Jim, then follows it as he dives off the side of the pontoon boat and swims up to where everyone is floating in a circle on foam noodles. Every time there's a riff in the water, I panic. Even though we're far from that stupid waterfall and that psycho rabid snake, I can't stop picturing its slithering skin disappearing into the water. My body shivers at the thought, even with the blazing sun beating down.

"Man, that toss was killer. How'd you learn to throw like that? No, wait—don't tell me. You're in the Olympics. Shot put. The way you manhandled that snake, I'd say you wrestle alligators in your sleep," Jason says, laughing.

I keep my eyes trained on Jim, waiting for his response. A small part of me is anxious because I can't have him blowing our cover, but the bigger part of me is more curious how he managed to lift me above his head with the strength of a bull and throw me five feet. I didn't put too much thought into it at the time, because I was clearly too busy screaming bloody murder. Once Jason had me safely in his arms, my concern shifted from my safety to Jim's. When my eyes caught the commotion, the way he handled himself was…was…so freakin' hot! Not only had he saved my life from being bit and swallowed by Hell's spawn, he slayed the demon creature with his bare hands!

My tummy does a little fluttery thing at the thought. He was like my knight in shining armor protecting me. Okay, so what if we learned after the fact it was just a trained rosy boa with zero venom and had been to more than a thousand shoots without a single mishap.

Still…

Snake.

Scary.

No thanks, Satan. Not today.

I see the guilt in Jim's eyes knowing he killed the eighteen-year-old harmless snake, but in my eyes, he's a hero. In Mick's producer's eyes, a very expensive misfortune.

"Nope. No gold medals for World's Most Expensive Snake Killer." His attention shifts to Mick. "Which I'll pay for."

Mick shakes his head and takes a swig of his beer. Should I mention Jim's translation of the zookeeper yelling, *snap its neck on the rock*, was actually, *stand still and he'll unlock*? "Don't worry about it, brother. It's part of the deal. Insurance and set fees. They prepare for that stuff. Virginia was getting old anyway."

Virginia? It was a *she*? And *she* had a *name*? Poor Jim, who's visibly distraught with guilt. Using my legs, I swim closer to him and pat his shoulder, giving him the comfort he deserves. He *did* save my life.

"Okay, so spill, what the hell do you do?" Jason asks, and the direct question sets me on edge. God bless it! Why do my friends have to be so damn nosey? I open my mouth to reply with something super over the top, but Jim beats me to it.

"Nothing exciting. But I used to be a bouncer in college. Got used to throwing out crazy drunks way bigger than her."

Crazy drunks...hey!

My legs kick out, and I splash him. "I am *not* crazy... or drunk!" And for the record, I've been watching my figure and making better dieting decisions. You'd be surprised how many less calories are in a Corona Light.

"Bouncer to successful investor. That's a story right there." Jason raises his beer. The rest follow, and Jim and I share an awkward stall before raising our drinks. I wish my friends would stop staring at him like they're so enthralled by all things Jim. It makes me uncomfortable. It also makes me feel like a big jerk. They're all starting to really like him. I heard Mick telling Poppy he wanted to ask Jim to go on his next safari tour because he thinks Jim would enjoy wrestling the animals. I heard Jason tell him he got the tickets they talked about and would make plans when they got home to go to said game. I even heard Jerry ask Jim to set up a time after our weekend trip to talk music and take a tour of his vinyl record collection.

How am I going to rip this guy out of their lives in less than a full day and not feel like a total jerk about it? I'm going to have to face the music. I should tell them all. But I can already picture their faces. Disappointment. Anger. Sadness. Always pity for poor Casey.

And how would this make Jim look?

Just as big of a lying jerk as me. And I can't do that to any of them.

"Jesus, Jerry!" Katie's squeal breaks me from my thoughts, and I see everyone swimming in opposite directions.

My first response is panic. That goddamn snake resurrected and has come for revenge. My chest starts to collapse, and I try moving my legs to swim away, but my body freezes in terror. That's when Jim wraps his arm around me and kicks his legs out, swimming us outward into the lake.

"Hey, relax." His low voice soothes me instantly, pulling me into his chest. I can't reply, but I watch as Katie whacks her husband over the head with her noodle and swims back to the boat.

"What happened? Why is—?"

"Jerry pissed in the lake."

Ew. "Like right there?"

Jim chuckles, and I can feel the vibrations of his chest against my back. "Yeah. Apparently, when you're high, you forget the difference between being in a chlorine filled pool and a lake."

"So, no snake?"

His mouth is so close to my ear, the warmth of his breath heats my lobe. "No snake."

Phew. My breathing begins to relax. Then I realize how close Jim is holding me. For a split second, his lips ghost over the back of my neck, and the sun starts to disappear from my vision as my eyes slowly close. I wait for his mouth to touch my flesh.

"I really like your friends," he hums, teasing me.

"They really like you," I tell him, because it's the truth.

Instead of pressing his warm, wet lips and sucking until I explode—sorry, I've gone into fantasy mode—he adjusts me in his arms, so we're nose to nose.

"Can I ask you something without you kneeing me in my balls and killing any hope of me having kids?"

I want to knee him in the balls for saying that to me! But his sweet, innocent look tells me I've been taking a lot of swings and maybe I should play nice. I nod. "Yes, I promise."

Sorta...

"Why do you think your friends will look down on you if you aren't really dating someone?"

Dammit, wrong time to promise no physical abuse. Why did he have to go there? I have no idea. Because they'll have the same reaction they do every time they critique my life. They'll pity me.

"Because they won't see me the way they would if they thought I had the fulfillment of a man in my life." His expression is still tender, but his brows go up. "I've always been the single one. If you haven't figured it out by now, they're all perfect, and happy, and established. And unless you're blind, deaf, and dumb, you've realized I'm far from that. They pity me. They think because my goals aren't to be successful, married, or have a dozen kids locked up behind my white picket fence, I must not be happy. And *that* means they set out this unrealistic goal of trying to *make* me happy. It's too much."

Even the thought of spewing out twelve kids gives me the heebie jeebies. Especially after hearing half their stories about drug-free water births, natural, blah, blah, vomit. My crotch clenches shut as we speak.

"I get it. But I don't think they pity you. I think they see a charismatic, carefree girl who doesn't let life pass her up. I don't think you need to lie about having a man in your life. You only have to be truly happy."

"I am happy," I say in defense. My knee starts to aim.

"All right, all right. You're happy. Whatever you say, boss." He goes silent for a second, but he wants to say more. "I just wanted to let you know that even though you have some anger issues, you're an okay chick. Possibly more. It's still to be determined if we make it out of this discussion with my balls intact."

I stare at him, less concerned with attacking his balls and more focused on what he just said. "You think I'm an okay chick? You barely even know me."

"I know enough to see you have a spark that lights up any room you're in. You may be a hot mess, but if I had to define it, I would call it a beautiful disaster. And I would be lying if I said after this is all said and done, I wouldn't want to call you sometime and take you out on a real date—be the real us and learn about the real you."

Have mercy…

Did he just…

"Breathe."

"I am breathing," I snap.

I wasn't breathing.

He just asked me out. I think. Asked the real me out—not the fake me. My heart beats faster. My cheeks flush. Still being in his arms, he's able to sense the shivers cascading over my skin.

"I'd even be the one to pay this time," he follows up with a mischievous smirk.

"What?" I ask, then it hits me. "Oh, the money I owe you." I roll my eyes as his laughter vibrates into my chest.

"I may want to wine and dine you on off-business terms, but you aren't getting out of paying me for my services here. I've endured a lot of abuse. Earned that cash." He laughs again as he closes his eyes when I splash him.

"All business, aren't you?" I say, fake pouting. "Weekend isn't over yet, pal. I'll be the one to decide if you've earned your keep."

His eyes light up, and my stomach spins. "What?" I ask, nervous.

"If it's about earning my pay, then I should probably get to it." His head moves forward, his lips gunning for mine.

Excitement rushes through me at the thought of his lips against mine. I've been secretly aching to kiss him again since last night. And now, as we share this moment, me tightly wrapped in his arms, it's the perfect—

"Hey, lovebirds!" *What the... Dang-it!* We break apart to see a fancy speed boat nearing our way, a man in a swimsuit and robe leaning over the side, a cigar hanging from his mouth. "You the group staying at The Rodge Lodge?"

"Huh?" I ask, confused.

"The Rodge Lodge. Larry and Sherry Rodger's place. Aren't you the kids renting it out?"

The Rodge Lodge...oh yeah. "Yeah, that's us," I reply.

The guy pulls the cigar from his mouth and blows a huge puff of smoke into the sky.

"That's what I thought. Heard the rap music playing from the boat. Same beats I heard last night echoing off the lake. Got an enticing invitation for you folks. One you don't want to say no to." I'm pretty sure Jim and I both come to the same conclusion. Swinging is not on either of our bucket lists. "See that house on the hill? Biggest one on the lake? That's mine. And I'm inviting you and all your friends tonight for a party."

We both adjust ourselves to stare in the direction the man points. "Wow, that's a huge place you got there," Jim says.

"Like I said, biggest on the lake. Huge party. Bring yourselves. And maybe some of those fancy koozies they have stocked over there. Preferably blue, with a signature on it."

I'm a bit weirded out by the man. Who wears a king's robe in the middle of summer on a lake? We both smile, thank him for his offer, and tell him we'll see him tonight, then he's gone.

Mick propels toward us, and Jim helps me climb into the boat. "What was that all about?" he asks as Jim hands me a towel.

"Some guy apparently knows the owners of the house we're renting. Invited us to his party tonight."

"Who?" Jason asks.

"Didn't catch his name, but he lives in that house." Jim points to the mansion on the hill.

"Oh shit, *that* house?" Jason exclaims, and all eyes fly to him.

"What do you mean *that* house?" I ask.

"The house on Bunker Hill. Read about it in the Lake Redstone book. All sorts of rumors about that place. It's been said people have gone missing there. Some say it's haunted. When I was taking care of my morning duties, I googled it. Photos of celebrities drinking the finest whiskey. No joke. Pictures from Brad Pitt and Jennifer Aniston to Michael Jackson."

"Oh, stop." June waves her hand. "You're just messing with us."

"Nope. Look it up yourself. The house is owned by some archeologist. Found a shit ton of fossils back in the eighties. Cashed in. Now he lives in the house and hosts extravagant parties on the lake. Strange he invited you after admitting we're staying at The Rodge Lodge. Swore there was something about them having beef with each other."

"Um…can we go back to missing people?" I ask. I feel like that's an important factor.

"Like dead people haunted?" Katie chimes in.

Jason takes a swig of his beer. "Like weird shit happens up there. Unexplained stuff. People go, and some don't return."

Yeah, hell no. I'll be just fine sitting at the lake house watching Jerry get high and play with the air.

"What kind of whiskey?" Mick asks, curiosity glowing in his damn eyes, and if I'm not mistaken, interest.

"Mick, no. Not a chance," I argue.

"Why not? Seems kind of fun to me. No one's gonna go missing. And if we get some expensive whiskey out of the deal, no harm, no foul."

My life ending because some crazed lunatic axes me in his mansion on the hill doesn't seem like "no harm, no foul" to me. "Yeah, I'm out," I say. Final answer.

"I mean, it could be fun. It says here they have a state-of-the-art music museum. Tons of signed memorabilia from musicians who've visited the place."

Jim's ears perk up. *Dammit, no!* "What kind of musicians?" he asks.

"Who *cares*?" I smack him. "Ones who are probably dead, like we'll be if he wins and lures us in."

"I'm in." My eyes whip to June. All my friends have gone mad!

"Poppy?" Jason asks. Thank god she is a smart person and will *definitely* say—

"I'm in too."

What!

Katie and Jerry both repeat the same answer, and I'm stuck standing there gaping at my friends as if they've all lost their damn minds.

Mick claps his hands together. "It's settled. Party tonight on Bunker Kill—I mean, Hill."

I'm once again on the boat after going back to the lake house, showering, eating dinner, and slamming a whole lot of wine in order to get myself to agree to this. The sun is long gone and it's pitch-black outside, the bright moon as our guide. I tried my best to talk everyone out of this idea, but it turned out to be pointless. The more I fought, the more everyone wanted to go.

Ghosts.

Fancy whiskey.

Music museum.

Who gives a hoot! I was outnumbered. Hence why I'm sitting with a scowl on my face. My eyes catch Jim, who's sporting a carefree smile. I aim my scowl at him, but he winks at me, overpowering my anger. My glower drops a smidge and turns to a solid pout. I shake my head, so he doesn't think his cute little endearment fazed me, and stare back out onto the lake.

Thankfully, it's a short ride before we're docking at the

bottom of the hill. The house is huge. Complete darkness surrounds the perimeters, but the entire hilltop illuminates in a glow of lights. With my attention swept up in the house, I don't notice everyone is already off the boat. Jim reaches for me, offering his hand to help me off. I'm hesitant, because even though the house looks inviting and bright, it still has that major Addams Family feel to it.

"Babe, it's gonna be fun. I promise." He can't promise that. He has no idea the bloodbath that's waiting for us. "Listen, if you're feeling uncomfortable, we'll leave. I'll fake a stomachache—huge IBS issues—and get everyone back to the lake house."

I'm not sure if I find his dedication gross or romantic. I lean toward romantic—because, why not?—and allow him to take my hand and escort me onto the dock. We head up the hill, following a rock formed pathway. Outside the glowing lanterns lighting the path, it's complete darkness. Even though it's a warm night, there's still a chill to the air. The trees in the distance whistle, and glowing eyes gleam from the bushes. I squeeze Jim's hand harder and walk a little bit closer to him. We head up two by two, us being the last. Now, I'm wishing I got off the boat sooner so we wouldn't be the last couple. This leaves us vulnerable to get taken from behind and hacked with a chainsaw. I pick up the pace and pull Jim along, passing Katie and Jerry.

"Dude, if I knew I was gonna have to walk half a mile to get to this place, I would have opted for a better pair of shoes," Katie gripes, tugging on Jerry to keep up. I decide not to mention "along with easier to escape in when we all have to run for our lives." Jim regards me curiously, but I shrug and keep walking. I've always loved Katie, but better her than me. I've never been to Paris or sky dived. She has—it's only fair.

By the time we make it to the top, Jerry is wheezing, and I've broken into a sweat. We all take in the house, which is gigantic, still screaming, *Addams Family lives here!*

"I knew it. The lights are a ploy," I say, studying the mansion, two strange stone creatures sitting on each side of the pillars at the bottom of the steps leading to the front door. Jim squeezes my hand, assuring me everything's gonna be fine, when the front door opens and the owner steps onto the wrap around porch. "Stop this insanity *right* now." The man from earlier today comes out dressed in a vampire costume.

Hell no.

I'm out.

I go to leave, but Jim spins me back around.

"Welcome, welcome. I'm glad to see you've made the right decision."

"Which is what? To die?" I mumble, and Katie kicks me.

"What was that?" the man asks.

Jim tucks me into his side. "She said she could use a glass of wine." He steps forward, shaking Gomez's hand, who introduces himself as—weird—Herman.

Smiling, he opens his arms to our group. "Well, you've come to the right place. My wife is a wine lover herself. Hope you like a deep red."

And...I'm out.

Jim grabs me as I pull a one-eighty to run and pulls me forward, forcing me to walk up the stone stairs.

Or not...

As we step over the threshold, I search behind me and see nothing but excited faces. My friends are idiots. Am I seriously the only one with my head on straight? I mean look at—

"Ah, hello! You must be the young group staying at The Rodge Lodge." An attractive older woman approaches us, dressed to the hilt in black, all but her lips, which are painted a blood red. My mind automatically assumes it's the blood of their previous victims. *Since when did I become so morbid?* Since I walked into an episode of the Addams Family.

"And you are?" The woman sticks her hand out, waiting for me to take it. I'm too busy staring back at Morticia, so Katie does the honors, pushing me to the side.

"Hi, I'm Katie. Great place. Super…gothic-chic," she says, surveying the place, admiring the décor. I give Katie my side-eye. Gothic chic? The place is like a tomb for dead things. The house opens into a large room with floor-to-ceiling glass windows, hence why the darn place was glowing from the outside. But on the inside, gothic wouldn't be my word of choice. A dreary cemetery is more like it. Besides the large living room and kitchen, I spot an obnoxious number of hallways and stair passageways. *Where the heck do all these lead to?* Probably death traps. I stay close to the group, making sure I don't fall through a secret trap door when something catches my attention. Herman begins introducing us all to their other guests. While I vaguely hear introductions for *Lurch*, *Uncle Fester*, and *Cousin Itt*, I walk off until I find myself in an enclosed hallway, the walls covered in hanging glass cases filled with strange…

"Is that a *head*?" I gasp, leaning in closer, trying to figure out if it's real.

"An old artifact."

The intruding voice startles the color right out of me. I spin around to see Gomez standing a bit too close for my liking. "Dug right out of the deepest part of Ancient

Egypt. Found it myself while doing work in the most secluded desert." Yeah, where my heart is now since it just exploded out of my chest.

"Wow, you dug up...a head?" My voice is a bit shaky. He looks like he's mentally measuring the circumference of my head. Frack, he's probably wanting to see if it would fit in one of these glass cases.

"I did. I was on a trip in Cairo. Thirty-seven-hundred-year-old burial site. Her head was wrapped in cloth. History tells us after her death, they took the ancient steps of mummification. Preserved her. She's a beauty, isn't she?" My mouth wants to say something, but it's too busy catching flies as it hangs open. "Now, come. Let's get you that wine."

He extends his arm to lead the way back into the large kitchen area. I take one last glance at the mummy head, hoping I look a little better when my head ends up next to hers.

"Shots! Shots! Shots! Shots!" Jason shouts as Wednesday—or, to be fair, Herman's daughter, Redelle, passes around a tray of shots. Besides having black hair, she also looks nothing like The Addams Family's daughter, since she stands at a solid six foot plus. The daughter of a linebacker would be more fitting.

Speaking of the Addams Family, it's funny how one minute I'm fearing for my life, and the next, I'm taking down mystery shots with Uncle Fester, *who*, in fact, turned out to be a cool dude. Kind of strange and keeps staring at my chest, but he keeps refilling my wine, so it's all good in my book. I take another swig of my 1943 Chateau Cheval Blanc red blend and scan the crowd for Jim. After having to fend off Red, who kept trying to personally feed him shots, he snuck off to use the bathroom, but has yet to return. I place my empty glass on the counter and walk off in search of him. I'm light on my feet as I take a left down the dark hallway leading toward the bathroom. After spending the last couple hours drinking with Gomez and his family, I'm less worried they're going to have my head on a platter for tomorrow's dinner. Black is technically my favorite color, so the dark decor does kind of do it for me. Gothic chic to the core. I giggle at my own agreeance to Katie's earlier comment and sway on my feet, pressing my open palm against the wall for support. A painting of a medieval graveyard shifts on the wall, and I grab at it before it plummets to the ground. "Yowzers, that was close," I mumble, picking up the pace and heading farther down the low-lit hall.

I'm not even sure what I'm doing, or why I'm searching Jim out. What do I plan on doing once I find him? Ask him if he needs any help? Make sure he washes his hands like a good little boy?

I burst out in a fit of giggles. *Okay, grow up, Casey.*

Got it.

I shake it off, putting my mature face back on. The hallway seems to never end as I walk past a handful of doors, opening each, but none leading to the bathroom. I tell myself I should knock, in case he's doing his thing, but the thought of getting a peep show has me practically throwing my body into each door.

Pervert.

Never said I was anything less.

LAKE REDSTONE

I chuckle again as I pass a double door entryway. It's closed, and I'm about to continue walking when the soft strumming sound of a guitar followed up by a low, husky voice filters through the slit beneath the door. There's a melodramatic tone to it, sad yet beautiful. Knowing I might miss out on Jim and his peepshow, I stop and quietly lean in to steal a peek at who's inside.

What I wasn't expecting to find was Jim.

My breath catches when, to my surprise, I see him standing in the back corner, of what seems to be the music museum, holding a guitar in his hands, strumming along the chords while quietly singing. My lips part slightly as I take him in. His voice is beautiful. Melancholy. His fingers glide back and forth as if he's a master. I'm not familiar with the song, but it seeps into my ears, warming every part of me, down to the tips of my toes.

I'm completely transfixed on his lips, watching him, until a soft hiccup betrays me, and he lifts his head to my presence. "Woops sorry...I, uh..."

He chuckles, placing the guitar on a stand next to him. "By the glaze in your eyes, you want more than just my autograph."

"No, uh...wow. I didn't know you could play," I say, still in a trance.

He shoves his hands in his pockets and peruses along the wall, taking in all the signed photos and memorabilia. "Oh, you know...one of the many things I do, when I'm not jet-setting to Paris or eating fancy steak while gobbling up billion-dollar investments."

Okay. I felt that jab.

I walk into the room and stop next to him as we both face the wall. He's admiring a signed Bon Jovi record. "I used to have a huge crush on him when I was a kid," I say, trying to break the tension.

"You and me both," he replies. I almost give myself whiplash jerking my head to face him. He chuckles and moves on to the next framed record. "Come on, who didn't? It's Bon Jovi. That long hair? The way he made sweet love to that mic. *You give looooove a bad name*," he sings the title. I stare at him. More like at his lips. Jesus, where did that voice come from? "Looks like that song did it for you too."

I snap out of my haze and smack his arm. "I was more of a 'Living on a Prayer' kinda girl." Which is a lie. I'd sing that song to my Bon Jovi poster so hard, I'd cry simply thinking about being his girlfriend.

Jim raises a questioning brow but doesn't say anything further. He brings his attention back to the wall. "Motley Crue."

"Hedonists," I spit out, knowing the insane backstory of the band and their pleasure-seeking addictions. This time, it's Jim's turn to look my way in surprise. "Yeah, yeah. I know my music too, show off. I was huge into them in high school. This one time, I got suspended for refusing to take my fishnet stockings off during gym class. Coach sent me to the principal's office. Long story short, the school secretary left the intercom unattended and *someone* started singing, 'Shout at the Devil' to the entire school."

His eyes light up, a smirk so sexy across his face. "You?"

"I still claim my innocence…" I wink and face the shirt with all the band's signatures.

"Always been trouble I see."

I shrug. "I guess so." Also still waiting for it to pay off. You know, the whole live free or die trying motto. I'm living all right, but the whole payout seems to be lost in the mail.

We move on and stop at an autographed Neil Diamond record. In unison, we both sing the chorus of his most famous hit, 'Yesterday'. We cut off, our eyes landing on one another, and bust out laughing.

"My favorite song!" I say.

"Mine too."

"I mean, *Saving Silverman* has to be one of the best films to come out of 2001." I laugh in return. He holds the humor in his eyes, a glint of approval in the way he smiles back at me. There's no hiding the spark of attraction that's buzzing between us. We'd both have to be fools to think we can continue to hide the fact that we're attracted to one another. I'm sure if we touched right in this moment, we'd both get shocked.

"So, uh..." I start, not sure what else to say. What I don't say is kiss me senseless, because I fear if he did, the high voltage sparking between us, I'd probably electrocute him.

"This place is pretty cool." He breaks the silence, raking in all the memorabilia.

"Yeah, Jason wasn't lying when he said they had a music museum. Crazy to think he had all these famous musicians here."

He nods and continues walking, his eye catching something in the corner of the room. I follow him. Soft explicit words fall from his lips as he reaches down to pick up another guitar. "Holy shit," he curses, his fingers brushing against the mahogany wood.

"What?"

"I can't even. Do you know...?"

"Semi-music history genius and all *Saving Silverman* quotes, yes, but a mind reader I am not," I say.

"Babe," he calls me, not realizing it, but his attention is completely transfixed on the guitar. "Look at the signature."

I lean forward, my eyes having to squint to survey the autograph. "Is that—?"

"Kurt Cobane." His voice is strained. He has yet to take his eyes off the instrument.

"You think it's a fake?"

"Not a chance. Look at his signature. The way he signed his name, there was always a distinction. Way after he died, people tried selling forgeries of his shit, trying to make a quick buck. But real fans started coming forward pointing out the imitations. It's an easy miss, but a true fan would know instantly. This bad boy…it's real." The instant his fingers brush against the tight strings, I identify exactly what he's going to play. Nirvana's "All Apologies" whistles from the sound hole as Jim works the instrument like he was born to play this exact guitar. It's when he starts softly singing the lyrics, I finally lose myself.

"You all right there, trouble?" he asks, still playing flawlessly.

"Yeah. It's just…so beautiful. I wish I was as talented as you are." And it's the damn truth. An investment banker may be rich with money, but someone like Jim is rich with talent.

"You can be. Come here." He stops playing and pulls the strap from over his head. Taking a step toward me, he lifts the strap over mine.

"Oh no." I put my hands up to stop him, but he doesn't listen. I'm too scared of knocking the guitar out of his hands, so I stop fighting him. The strap is delicately placed around my shoulder, and the guitar now rests across my chest. Jim takes a stand behind me, his chest pressing against my back. His hands wrap around me, lifting my arms and guiding my fingers to where they need to be. "Jim…" I start, but he ignores me. His breath hits the back of my earlobe as he adjusts my fingers, each tip touching a cord.

"You want to place your index finger on the second fret of the A string, and your middle finger on the third fret of the low E string." With his guidance, I do as he says, all while trying not to concentrate on how good he feels pressed up against me. His enticing scent, bold and masculine with a hint of spice seeps into my nostrils, and I lose my footing, taking him in. "You okay?" he asks, adjusting the guitar.

"Yeah. Just nervous. What if I break her?"

The rumble of his low chuckle feels like heaven tickling my eardrum. "It's a her, huh? You won't. Fender guitars are made to love you back. This model is called the Mustang. Cobane altered the guitar to be played with his left hand, instead of his right. Now, strum from the E chord all the way down."

I inhale a small staggered breath and pluck the C chord with my pinky while my index finger tugs on the E chord. A smooth melody of sounds releases from the instrument, and Jim hums.

"Now, press this finger to the F chord, and this one to the G chord." I do as he instructs, and as more music echoes around the room, his smooth-as-silk voice follows. "See, you can play just as beautifully," he says, pressing his own fingers gently over mine. Together, he plucks and strums, playing another Nirvana classic as he hums the lyrics in my ear. I'm not sure at what point I close my eyes, but the vision before me is magical. Behind my closed eyelids, I'm not standing here with Jim at my back, but in front of me. We're laying down and his fingers, as he strokes the guitar, brush along my bare skin, sending a heated path to my core. His eyes are on fire, matching the blaze in mine. His head dips and his lips, warm and plump, fuse to mine. He kisses me with a ferocity and there's nothing I want more than for this fantasy to become real.

My fingers must have stopped following his lead because he pulls away. I barely notice the strap being lifted off my shoulders or Jim replacing the guitar back on its stand. I hardly register him positioning himself in front of me, or his open palm reaching out to my chin and raising my hooded eyes to his.

He leans into me with such slowness, I fear I'll combust before he even makes contact. There's a sudden pulse between my thighs. Holy mother of pearl, he's about to kiss me. I know this is simply him playing his role, but I can't help but feel more—want more—need more. This kiss, this much needed kiss he's about to gift me, is something I've wanted for so long. The ache in my stomach is now triggered by need. The tightness in my chest caused by want. The disillusioned emotional trigger going off in my head threatens to bring me to my knees. It hits me all at once. This moment. Him. This is what I've yearned for.

"Casey?" His voice is deep, yet a gentle melody to my ears.

"Yeah?" I barely recognize my own weak voice.

"I'm going to kiss you now. And I want you to know it has nothing to do with our agreement."

"Okay," I whisper, the words barely ghosting across my lips.

"And I'm also going to enjoy the hell out of it, 'cause I've been wanting to do this ever since the first time I got a taste of you."

"Mmmm," I moan. My eyes are shut, and my lips have already parted with the hope he does more than kiss me. Deep down, I'm begging for him to completely ravish me.

He's so close, the soft rumble of his chest vibrates against my own as he chuckles. His free hand works around to my lower back, pressing me closer into him. "God, you're beautiful," he hums, his breath hitting my lips as he covers mine. Just as I remembered—warm, soft, perfect fused against mine. A soft moan travels up my throat, but he swallows it with his tongue as he parts my lips and entwines his tongue around mine. I open wide, and together, we explore, kiss after kiss, dancing around one another. His grip on me tightens, and an aroused moan trickles through his lips. There's no hiding the sparks blazing around us, the aura of our sexual connection lighting a fire between us. My hands slide up his chest, the softness of his shirt brushing against my open palms. I grab for his neck and press my lips harder against his, the thread pulling us together on the verge of snapping.

Not even in my wildest dreams would I have imagined this farce would turn into something so breathtaking. This is real. This kiss is real. The way my skin prickles with need is real. We go at each other like two crazed teenagers, until we're panting and in need of a breath.

His touch becomes more tender, his lips softer as the passion burns into small pecks until he eventually breaks away. I fight to keep my eyes closed. I don't want this moment to end—don't want disappointment or regret to radiate from those steely hazel eyes, because there's no way

I can pretend it meant nothing when it meant way more to me than I want to admit.

"You okay in there?" His voice is light, but there's humor lining it.

"I am. Just...waiting..."

"For what?" He brushes his thumb along my lower lip, and my eyes flutter open, no matter my fight to keep them closed. I search for the expression I fear to see, his eyes, I can stand here and stare into his eyes for—

"What are you waiting for, Casey?"

"To be reminded that this isn't real."

His hand is still snug at my lower back, his thumb stroking along my skin. "Do you want this to be real?" I do. Does that make me foolish? Could a guy I've done nothing but terrorize since meeting me actually feel the same way for me? "Hey." He tugs on my waist, pulling my attention away from my negative thoughts. The door to the music room opens, and we're interrupted as Herman walks in.

"I see you've found my museum."

Jim lets me go—and poof! Saved from answering that silly question by the Addams Family. Do I want this to be real? Ha! A guy I just met? Want a relationship with? Wait, who said anything about a relationship? My eyes whip to Jim. Do I *want* to date him?

"Yeah, this is unreal. All these musicians have been here?"

"Of course. The house on Bunker Hill is a legend. Many famous rock stars, actors, and actresses have dined and partied here. Sometimes I forget who all we've entertained." Entertained wouldn't be my word choice. How about lured in, tricked, slaughtered and turned into viewing art for his head gallery.

"You okay, Ms. Casey?" Herman asks, and I nod a million nods a second.

"Totally, Gomez."

Jim's brows shoot up, and I raise my shoulders in a *what?* shrug. His lips curl against his will, and he faces Herman. "She meant, *wow* impressive. She's had a little too many of those shots. Slurring her words and all."

Nodding, Herman raises his arms and claps his hands together. "Well, I must inform you, it's time to play some games."

Great. More games.

'Cause the one I'm playing with my heart isn't risky enough?

CHAPTER
ELEVEN

Casey

When we head back to the main room, everyone is trashed. Katie, in her drunk made-up language of can't-understand-a-word-she-says tells me Jason and June left. June was festering a dinosaur in her head, which I translated to not feeling well.

Their other guests have disappeared as well. Herman makes an announcement for us to follow him, and I lean into Katie as we all walk down another dimly lit hall. "Where exactly are we going?"

Katie wobbles into me, spilling her glass of wine down her shirt. "Aw, shmit." Jesus. I grab her glass so she doesn't spill any more and chug it, because darn it, 1943 was a good year. "Hey!" She swats at me and falls into the wall. Jerry saves her and tucks her under his arm, while Jim takes her place and walks beside me. His closeness is like a match setting fire to my crimson cheeks. I keep my attention forward so I don't make eye contact with him. I hope he forgets about that kiss and never mentions it ever—

"Are we gonna talk about what happened back there?"

...again.

"What? The spill? I know. Who spills three-billion-dollar wine? She really needs to get—"

"The kiss."

Dang it.

"What about it? It was just a—"

"It wasn't just a kiss to me. It wasn't for you either. I felt it. You did too—"

He abruptly stops talking when I trip and fall into the wall. "Shit, you okay?"

Nope!

"Yeah, fine."

"Here. Let me help you." He takes hold of my arm and guides me as we come to a short set of stairs leading us to a back door outside. The night sky shines down on us, and we all look around, curious to where we're being taken.

"Okay, so this 'mystery murder' is cool and all, but where are we going?" Poppy chimes in as we come to a large encased structure. I start assessing my surroundings. My creeper radar is starting to activate.

After slamming the rest of his beer, Mick asks, "Cool. What is this, some sort of bunker?"

Herman makes an about face, placing his palms together. "You are exactly correct, my hecatomb."

Mick nods in excitement, while I try to spin the in-house dictionary inside my brain. *Hecatomb...hecatomb...*

"Wait...doesn't that mean, like, sacrifice?" Katie asks.

I knew it! Well, not really, but that word sounded nothing like friend, pal, homie, or comrade. He's going to sacrifice us all! Like cement being poured in my shoes, my feet stop with not a chance in hell of being moved.

"What's wrong?" Jim halts with me, attempting to press his hand to my lower back to keep me moving.

"What's *wrong* is this is where we all die," I whisper loudly. "He's taking us to an enclosed bunker with no windows and probably no air, and I bet once the doors close, they never open. Spikes come out of the walls, and we all—"

"Case," he coos to calm me down, "relax. Nothing's gonna happen. A bunker is basically another name for a game room."

I stare at him. "Bull patootie."

His shoulders rise and fall in a carefree shrug. "Totally. It's an old military hideaway where soldiers hid weapons waiting to kill people." My mouth falls to the ground. "But we're good! No one's gonna kill us. That's just crazy."

Foolish man. Little does he know, the person who says *that* is always the first to die. I've seen this scary movie. I know for a fact I live because I see what's coming. But all my friends? RIP. Goners. One of them might as well say they'll be right back.

Jerry sticks his head through the open entrance way. "Looks cool. Gotta take a piss first. I'll be right back."

NO! I love Jerry! He's my favorite! He's been my coach through so many important milestones in my life! He fired me up at my first bull riding competition at our favorite bar, then encouraged me to fight through the pain when I broke my arm flying off. Trained me for the local fair's annual hot dog eating contest, which is a lot harder under the pressure of a crowd, then motivated me to sign up for the pie eating, when I barfed all over the contestant next to me and got disqualified. So many times! The hot pepper eating contest on Taco Tuesday, the Oyster eating competition… ew that one ended real bad.

I shiver at the memory.

I reach for Jerry's arm, but Jim stops me. My head whips in his direction, my eyes shooting murderous daggers at him. He may not care that Jerry's about to die, but I do. "Babe. Chill. Remember, if anything feels off, I'll make a scene and get us all out of here."

He may be an expert on music, but he sucks at scary movies. He has no idea that line never works in the end. I huff out a huge frustrated gust of air and fall into line with the rest of my insane, soon-to-be-goner friends.

Herman steps across the threshold of the cement blockade and flicks the light switch, illuminating the large, rectangular space. I still refuse to move, but peek my head in, my eyes adjust to the walls splattered in strange paintings and an odd array of gigantic cardboard heads of one man's face being used as dart boards. The center of the room holds a large cement island. A pub table littered with random treats sits in the corner, and off to the side is a mini fridge with a state-of-the-art surround sound stereo system.

Okay…so maybe it's not a kill room.

Slowly, but cautiously, I pick my feet up one at a time and walk into the room. My guard is still way up, and if need be, I'm prepared to use the fighting skills I learned from *The Karate Kid*.

"This is an…interesting place ya got here," Mick chimes in, heading straight for the mini fridge to snag a beer. He tosses one to Jim and cracks open another. "Gotta ask. What's the story behind the dartboard? Gonna assume no love lost for that poor chap?"

We all join in, our focus on one specific large cardboard head half mutilated by darts. As I tilt my neck to the side, I swear the eyes are stabbed out.

"Ahhh, that... He is what you would call an enemy of sorts."

Yeah, that's not disturbing at all.

Confusion masks Poppy's previous carefree expression. "Hmmm...yeah...why again do you have a bunker in the back of your house?" *That's right, Detective Poppy. Get the answers we need.* My eyes stay trained on her. If anyone can sniff out a murderer, it's Poppy.

"Because they are magnificent. The history behind them. Who would not want a creation of this magnitude in their possession?"

I can't help it. I raise my hand. Jim throws it back down. Herman continues. "Secret buildings built for their enemies. A space enclosed by cement and rock, thick enough that not a single soul on the other side could hear them if they screamed for help. It was said they built these with the intentions of luring in their prey to these small dungeons in order to obtain useful information.

"Uh...and why would they want to do that?" Good, Poppy. Keep it up.

"Because it is amazing how much you can obtain when in duress."

I watch Poppy's eyes enlarge just enough to know she's not down with that answer. "Okay...I'm gonna need a better explanation. Otherwise—"

"They make excellent game rooms."

I tug at Jim's shoulder. "We should probably get going," I say, faking a yawn.

Herman waves his hand through the air at the amenities. "And miss the best part? Do you not have the urge to indulge in all the luxurious things in here? Come, enjoy some desserts. My wife has personally made her specialty brownies. They will bring you to a whole new level of euphoria." He waves to the table filled to the rim with desserts. Jim's eyes light up and he takes a step forward to reach for one, but I slap his hand away. God knows what's in those. Probably poison or roofies or...*eggs and brownie mix, you weirdo, chill out.* "I have researched what your kind plays and have fulfilled the wishes of entertainment for you."

That's where he loses Katie. *"Our kind?"* She crosses her arms over her chest. *"As in, humans?"* Jesus, this is becoming too much for me. I'm about ready to dislocate Jim's arm just to drag him out of here.

"Yes, the floppy, flip—"

"Flippy cup." Mick's eyes brighten with excitement.

"Yes, Flippy cup. The bunker holds the perfect table. I shall supply the red cups. You play and enjoy."

And that's all it takes for Mick and Jim to light up like Christmas trees. Herman reaches for a thin remote off the cement center island and points it toward the stereo. Old school rap music booms through the surround sound speakers tucked high in the corners, and Mick wastes no time shaking his ridiculous hips to "Picture me Rollin" by 2Pac.

My eyes search out Poppy, knowing she's *not* down for this. She'll rein her husband in, because she's smart. We'll put our foot down and everyone else will have no choice but to follow. When our eyes lock, they're not gleaming with the same determination. Her shoulders go up and down. *No way.* "No, you take that shrug back," I say. She doesn't reply and takes her place next to her husband.

I turn to Katie and get the same reaction. "What? Since when did *you* become no fun?" she says and follows Poppy because she sucks too.

You know what? To heck with this. I'm outta here. If they all want to be slaughtered and end up on the wall of heads, that's their problem. I throw my daggered eyes at Jim. "I'm leaving. You can come or stay. But I'm leaving." He looks at me, then like a scaredy cat, steals a glance at Mick, who's lining the cement island with red solo cups. "Oh, give me a break!" I throw my hands up.

The door opens, and I turn toward it, hoping it's Jerry. He'll leave with me. As long as he doesn't see those brownies. Instead, Redelle walks in. She stops next to Jim, standing way too close for my liking, spiking my already sharpened mood. She's not small by any means, so when she leans into him, her head dips almost an inch to meet Jim's ear.

"If she's leaving, you can show me how you take it."

My eyes almost burst. "Excuse me?" I hiss. Jim's full mouth of beer expels all over Katie's back. "What did you just say to my boyfriend?"

"I said, if you're leaving, maybe he can teach me how to play it. The game? I've never played. Big cups. Do you fill them to the rim?"

I can't even bother to pat Jim on the back as he continues to choke on his drink. Between my mindless friends and my mindless fake boyfriend and *now* this mindless Big Red hussy, *who* is trying to hit on my fake boyfriend in front of me, may I add, I'm gonna lose it! He might not be mine in reality, but he's mine for the weekend, and I don't plan on sharing him with anyone. Just the thought of her slimy hands near him has my jealousy radar ready to snap off the charts. "You know what?" I stick my chest out on a pout, throwing my arm around Jim. "I'm actually gonna stay." Because I'm over the top, I lean in and lick his neck. Pulling back, I say, "He only likes when I show him how to take it anyway." *What?* Ugh, that made no sense!

Jim's chest rumbles in a low chuckle as I tug him toward the table away from her hungry eyes and settle in a spot next to Poppy, which ends up being a rookie mistake because it leaves the other side of Jim open for Big Red.

"How romantic, did you save a spot for me? Want to show me how you take it after all."

"I heard that!" I snap, sloping over the table to snarl at her.

"I'm sorry, I just don't understand how to play the game. Nothing wrong with asking a kind gentleman how to play it." She bats her fake spider looking eyelashes at me.

Does she think I'm dumb? "Yeah, the problem is you're not asking him how to play it!" I snap, snatching up my solo cup and chugging the small amount of beer in it.

"Hey! That's for the game. No cheating." Mick refills my cup. Bringing his hands together, he swipes them back and forth. "All right, let's pair up and get this game started." He surveys the teams as two random guests straggle in. One takes a spot next to Big Red while the other goes across from Mick. "Wait, not even teams. Yo, Katie, you and Jim gotta swap to the other side."

Ha! Take that, Big Red.

Jim turns to me, gripping me by the waist and hauling me into him. My breath hitches as my breasts smash up against his hard chest. His head dips, and I melt in his arms, unable to pull my eyes away from his soft lips. "See ya on the flipside." And then he kisses me hard and quick. He releases me, and I sway, taking a bit too long to recover. It's been so long—okay, maybe never—since a guy's kiss affected me in the way Jim's does. My eyes slowly reopen as he makes it to the opposite side of the table. And he seals the deal as he winks at me, causing a massive flutter of butterflies in my belly.

Poppy tilts into me. "You two are really cute together."

I'm still staring at him. He's still staring at me. "Yeah, we are," I reply as realization hits me. We *are* kinda cute together. He makes me laugh. He's kind. He seems totally accepting to my unstable ways—and he's *so* darn talented. The way he sang and played that guitar not only melted the panties right off me but left me with this deep level of appreciation and pride. We both share the same love for music, admittedly suck at charades, and care deeply for our friends. Ever since he confessed he'd like to go out on *actual* date once this is all said and done, in the back of my mind, I haven't stopped thinking about it. What would I wear? Where would he take me? Definitely no Mexican on the first date. Spicy food is a toss-up for me. Oh my god, a date! My belly twirls like a ballerina at her dance recital, thinking about going on my first date with the boy I have a crush on. *Do I have a crush on Jim?* Yeah, he's not real, but he is. This could all be an act. He was hired to be this way. My brows crease at the thought. What if I'm acting foolish? What if this is all make believe and I'm being naïve?

My mood, like the titanic, plummets, and that warm, fluttery feeling ices over. My eyes harden, and I pull my frigid stare away from Jim. I pick up my cup and slam back the small amount of beer.

"Casey, knock it off!" Mick complains and refills my cup. I slam it back again. Poppy fights the cup out of my hand and places it away from me.

"Babe, you okay?" I look back at Jim, still wearing that cute, carefree smile. No, everything is not okay, I want you to actually like me and wanna date me, because even though I paid you to be here, I really want you to like me.

"Yep, just dandy," I reply instead. He doesn't buy my answer because his eyes transform, holding a bit of concern in them.

"Pity. Still uneven. I'll just have to go to the other side." Big Hussy interrupts the moment as she slithers her way across the table next to Jim. Leaning in, her voice husky as she says, "So, open wide and take a big gulp? Is that how it works?"

I'm going to murder her. I grab the beer can to throw at her head—

"Okay, ready?" Mick interrupts my plan to take her out and the game begins. Mick slams his beer and flips his cup within seconds. Katie, who's across from him, does the same, and is just as fast. Poppy completes hers flawlessly, and I'm up. I'm normally a world champ at this, but I slam the beer, and instead of focusing on my form, I can't stop staring at the way Big Red keeps stroking her cup up and down. I hear her ask Jim to show her how to hold it, and my fingers clench, knocking my cup off the table.

"Come on, Case. What the hell!" Mick battles me. I huff, bending down to snatch my cup and slam it back on the table. I slide it to the tip of the table, and with my index finger, pop it up. It lands perfectly on its head, and I smile, lifting my victorious eyes to Jim. That's when I see it.

That big ol'...

"Hey, you can't dump the beer down your chest. You have to drink it," Mick complains.

My eyes see red. "That's enough! We're leaving."

I'm about to crawl over the table and slap that smug look off her face. When I try, an aching in my groin reminds me of my pulled muscle and I grunt, making my way around the table instead. I'm prepared to throw Jim over my shoulder to get him away from her, when, shockingly, he throws her hand off his shoulder and meets me halfway. His hand extends, and I thread my fingers between his.

"Not so fast." Herman's bean stock frame steps in front of me, blocking the door. The music shuts off, bringing an unsettling energy to the room. "Before you leave, there is something you have access to that I desire to possess. In return for my hospitality, I require you to retrieve it for me."

Everyone has morbid visions of how they think they'll die. Okay, maybe only me, and I swore I was going to kick it doing something epic. Like body surfing or fighting a shark. So…I'd probably slip off a bar and break my neck trying to reenact the movie scene from Coyote Ugly. But it was never anything close as to what my mind is conjuring up right now. "Yeah, you're not squeezing my head in one of those wall frames." I've had enough. I've hit my weirdo level for the day and I'm getting us out of here. My hands thrust forward, and I push past him. I reach for the door handle and put all my weight into it pulling it open. Problem is, it doesn't budge. I tug harder, but no luck. Panic shoots up my arms and down my spine as I struggle with the knob. "What the…why's the door locked?"

"Like I said, you have something I want."

The air in the room thickens. The mood shifts from carefree to ominous as all eyes capture the seriousness of Herman's stare. Jim forces a smile on his face and takes a slow step toward him. "Hey, man, it's all good. Let's just call it a night."

The cold stare Herman holds in his dark eyes tells me he's not ready to call it a night. Poppy slowly places her drink on the island. "And what would that something be?" she asks, working her negotiation skills. I'm quite familiar with them since she's used those skills to talk me down from many bar tables when I've attempted jumping from one to another. If anyone can talk this psycho down, it's her.

"A *Hootie and the Blowfish* koozie."

Mick spits out his full mouth of beer across the table, hitting the random old lady in the face. "*Koozie?*" He coughs, and Poppy smacks his back.

"Yeah, say again?" Katie speaks up.

"Larry Rodgers took what was rightfully mine. I brought him into my home while entertaining Darrius Rucker and his band. Darrius signed a koozie, and Larry unjustly left the premises with it. I want it back."

A pregnant pause silences the room until Jim bursts out laughing. He bends forward, taking his hand to his chest. "Oh man. Good one, bro. Signed koozie. You got us there. I really thought Case was right there for a sec and you wanted our heads on a display." Jim works out his fit of laughter and straightens. His eyes scan the room to see no one else has followed in on the humor.

Yep, everyone is still stiff as a bone.

"Oh…shit." Jason's eyes are focused directly at the dartboard. "That face. It's the owner of the lake house. That's Larry Rodgers."

Herman speaks up. "That autograph is a priceless artifact in my eyes. It was signed before Darrius foolishly tried to pursue his solo career. He should have never taken it. Its rightful home is in my museum."

"Yeah…so, I'm pretty certain they got back together. Why don't you just get another—"

"That's not the point!" Herman snaps.

Poppy shakes her head. "Okay, you're saying you're trying to keep us hostage for a silly koozie? Just ask for it back. Go get it. Shoot, file a police report. But this is getting a bit ridiculous."

Big Red steps forward, her watchful eyes taking in Poppy, trying to suck out her soul. "No one leaves until we get that koozie. Which doesn't seem like a bad thing." She licks her bright red lips and lurches closer to Jim with a hungry look in her eyes. Everyone stands motionless, eyes traveling from one to another, muddled, in shock, and simply unsure what to do next. We're seriously being held hostage over a stupid koozie!

"Okay fine, have it! Why do we care?" I say.

Jim, Poppy, and Katie all nod in agreeance.

Mick, on the other hand, does not. "Yeah, but if it's locked up in that case, it has to be important to the owners too. Not sure we should—"

"Shut up, Mick!" we scream in unison.

"Ah, so you've seen it. I knew that Hygiene bastard had it. Bring it to me. My daughter will escort one of you. The rest of you don't leave this bunker until I have my hands on the koozie." He points to Jim. "You. Get me my prized possession."

Hell no. The way Red's licking her lips, mentally eating Jim alive, she isn't going anywhere with my man, let alone making it out of this room alive. It's so gosh darn rude! I need to think. I've dodged bouncers, cops, godawful dates…I need to figure out how to dodge this life or death situation.

"And what if we don't give in? You're also stuck in here," I start in on him.

Herman crosses his arms over his chest. "I will stuff

you all into the tomb and wait for the next renters to fulfil my request."

My mouth isn't the only one that falls open. Brows up, crinkled, a vast variety of expressions that scream one thing.

Confusion.

All around.

"What tomb?" Someone just *had* to ask.

Herman's eyes land on the center island. So do ours. It doesn't take long for all pieces to fall into place. The cement island is far from the perfect flippy cup table, and more like a large casket. Poppy jumps back, dropping her cup.

Katie also steps away from the table. "Okay! To heck with this. Have all the koozies you want! Shit, I stole the 'Beauty is in the eye of the beer holder' one, but you can have it! Just let us go."

We're back to freaking out. The air gets thicker with apprehension, and I swear it's harder to breathe. Long gone is the cool demeanor Poppy held, and in its place, uncertainty. Oh fudge, if *she's* panicked, it's not good for any of us.

Mick looks just as freaked. He's lost in a trance of thought. His panicked eyes say he's probably thinking about how he'll never model again. I actually manage to roll my eyes and take in Katie, who now looks the least panicked as she picks up all the beer filled solo cups and chugs them. When my eyes finally land on Jim, his are searing into me. Time stops. My heart flutters a beat. His body language is relaxed. His hands rest casually in his shorts pockets. He stares at me. So angelic. So calm. So hot. God, we're all about to die and I can't help but think about ripping my shirt off and jumping his bones.

We stand there entranced with one another for a few more seconds until his eyes shift over my shoulder. When they return, his own demeanor changes. His eyes speak to me. Telling me—

The door opens behind me and Jerry walks in. "Hey. Why's everyone—"

"GO!" Jim hollers, then barrels into Herman, knocking into him. That's my cue to run. I twist, setting my foot, and push off, running out of the bunker. No one else thinks twice and jumps into action. Poppy grabs Mick. Katie pushes the poor old lady over and runs through the open door. I hear the heavy breathing and screaming of Big Red, but I don't stop. The pathway is steep and barely lit. The adrenaline cycling through me has me sprinting at an impressive pace, but I can't see where I'm going. Searching out each rock while keeping my focus trained ahead is almost impossible.

"Shit, I lost my sandal!" Katie cusses. I make the mistake of stealing a glance behind me as she trips, bumping into Jerry. The domino affect takes seconds but feels like a slow-motion scene out of a movie. Complete havoc ensues as Katie fumbles over her bare foot and grabs for anything to keep her steady. That anything is Jerry—who misses the next rock and trips sideways, falling into the abyss of blackness, taking out a bush.

"Oh my god, Jerry!" I yell, but Jim is there, catching hold for him.

"Just keep going! I got this. Get down to the boat." He waves me off as he goes in for Jerry. Katie bends down to pull her remaining sandal off and whips it into the bushes, then starts at a full sprint. Mick and Poppy are hot on her trail, and end up blowing past me, and I become the caboose of the getaway train.

LAKE REDSTONE

My feet smack against the rocks, making headway down the path when the lighting starts to flicker, then the entire walkway goes dark. I can't see a damn thing. My heart is like a hammer slamming against my chest. My eyes try to stay focused on the silhouettes in front of me until they fade into the darkness of the night. The rumble of the boat's engine ruffles my eardrums, sending a jolt through me. How did they get so far ahead of me? Jim is behind me, right? There's no way I'm all alone out here. I coach myself not to do it. Don't look back for Jim. It's the number two no-no in a scary movie. You never look back. I'm seconds away from dying of a panic attack. But I'm even closer to having a heart attack if I don't turn around and confirm the sound of shoes hitting rock behind me are Jim's.

Thump.

Thump.

Thump.

My heartbeat is like a bass drum. My lungs are putting in more work than they have since high school track, forcing quick pants of air in and out of my tight chest.

Thump.

Thump.

Thump.

I have to be close. I hit the bend where the walkway curves around a stone-built fireplace, bringing me to the last leg of the path. The lake appears in the distance, the glow of the moon shining on the boat like heaven's savoir in my eyes.

Ten more yards. I can do this. Voices travel up the hill, my name bouncing off the walls of the surrounding rock.

Eight more yards.

Six more yards.

Two…

My feet hit the dock, and I'm almost home free. Relief floods through me as I see my friends waving at me, Mick in the driver's seat, idling and ready to get the hell out of here.

Twenty more feet and—

"Case."

My heart detonates inside my chest and explodes into a million pieces as terror shoots up my throat. I scream at the sound of my name being called from the shadows and slip, throwing myself off the side of the dock. I barely have time to suck air into my lungs before I crash under the water into complete darkness. Having a heart attack and drowning would not have been my second guess, aside from shark wars, at how I die, but here we are. My body seizes, the panic causing my muscles to paralyze. Unable to swim, I sink deeper into the water, the temperature quickly dropping the lower I go. Goodbye, world. Goodbye, hours of DVR'd reality shows I'll never get to watch. Goodbye, unlimited taco Tues—

I jolt back to reality when two hands wrap around my waist. Drowning is one thing—being captured and tortured is *definitely* not on my bucket list. I go berserk and struggle as the sea monster kicks, pulling us up to the surface. As we break the water's lining, I choke out a startled cry. "Don't murder me! I don't even like Hootie—"

"Case, it's me. You're fine."

My eyes burst open wide, searching through the darkness of the night for the familiarity of his features. "Jim?"

"Yeah." I take him in, never more thankful to see him and—*wack!*

"Ouch!"

"Why'd you just pop out of the bushes like a mad killer and scare the life outta me!"

"I didn't mean to. I was hiding. Redelle almost got me up there, so I had to jump in the bushes to avoid her. But when I did, I landed on some hidden slide which shot me all the way down here. I hit the bottom hard and think I knocked myself out for a second."

Oh my god! My hands work up his chest, pushing his soaked hair away form his face. "Are you hurt?"

"No, just a scratch or two," he says, wading his feet to keep us afloat.

His answer doesn't assure me. "You could have a concussion. You could have drowned jumping in here." More panic.

He tugs me even closer against him. "I wouldn't have. I had other plans," he says.

"And what was that?"

"Saving you."

His reply comes with a big bang. If I were on solid ground, I'd be thrown off my axis. His willingness to risk his own life to save me takes the breath right from my lungs. I crush my lips to his, releasing everything swirling inside me, giving it to him, showing him every ounce of emotion I feel. I wouldn't be surprised if lightening crashed across the night's sky, drowning us in the intensity of this passionate kiss. He reciprocates, giving as much as he takes. His grip around me tightens as our lips continue their assault, struggling to stay afloat. I wouldn't care if we sunk to the bottom so long as he never stops.

"Wait, shine it over there—you have to be kidding me!" Katie hollers as a flashlight beams down on us. "We thought you two were drowning! Get the hell in this damn boat before we all die!" A life raft is thrown into the water, and Jim and I separate. We share a look, no words needed. The lust in our eyes and thick aura around us scream exactly what we want to say. We both want this.

He lets me climb up first, and Poppy immediately wraps a towel around me. Jim is up next, but then jumps off onto the dock. "No! Where are you going? Let's go!"

"Shhh...hold on. I'm going to untie their boat so they can't come after us."

Best kisser on the planet and super smart when in a life or death situation.

He disappears onto the large boat, causing panic to shoot up my spine. We all stare into the night, catching glimpses of his silhouette as he moves back and forth, until finally popping back onto our boat. Mick doesn't waste another second. He pulls out, then throttles in the direction of the lake house.

Making our way up the small hill that separates the lake and the house, a massive sense of relief washes through me. As I hit the bottom patio, I shake out my tank top, water dripping all over the floor. Poppy waves her phone, breaking away from the crowd. "I'm going to call the local police. Let them in on what a lunatic they have living on their lake," she says before disappearing.

The chilled night air combined with my wet clothes have me cold and soaked to the bone. "Oh my god, I need to go change." There's a shiver in my voice as I excuse myself to head inside.

As the patio door swings shut, I hear Jim's voice.

"Yeah, I'm gonna do the same." I peer over my shoulder as he walks through the door I entered moments before. My blood starts to warm, my heartrate kicking into gear. I'm not sure why I become nervous, but I quickly find the stairs and race up two at a time. My palms become sweaty, and my hands tremble lightly. What the heck is wrong with me? I'm acting like I've never been alone with a boy before. *That's 'cause he's not a boy.* That kiss, that strength—he's all man. I rush onto the top platform and throw myself into the bedroom, debating locking the door like a chicken. The sounds of his feet hitting the stairs has my nerves jammed in my throat. "Son of a biscuit..." I spin around in circles, unsure of what to do. Start changing? Pretend I'm sleeping? The crazy part of me measures the gap between the floor and bed to see if I can hide under it.

A shift in the air has my skin prickling the moment he walks into the room. The aura around us is so powerful, I grab for my bag to keep myself steady. I peek over my shoulder, an unevenness to my voice. "I'm just going to change. You didn't need to come with me."

Excitement and nervousness crash into me at the sound of the door closing behind him. "What makes you think I'm coming with *you*? I'm wet from saving your life. I also need to change."

Jesus all mighty, he sure is wet too. His drenched shirt is stuck to him, accentuating his muscled chest, his tattoos on full display through the soaked material. I catch myself staring and rip my eyes away and start to aimlessly dig in my bag.

"I hardly consider that saving my life. I learned how to swim a long time ago." Digging through random shirts, I bide my time to cover the complete lie in my eyes. I may know how to swim, but the panic rushing through me was like an anchor wrapped around my legs, sucking me deeper into the water. As high and mighty as I want to portray myself, I would have been in deep doodoo if he hadn't jumped in and rescued me.

"You sure? That kiss told me you were pretty thankful I jumped in for you." My eyes squeeze shut. Our lips crushing together in the heat of the moment. The feeling of our hearts slamming into each other's. I fully turn, unaware of his silent steps. He's so close now, I fear he can sense my entire body buzzing, see my heart beating at a rapid pace. He takes a small step closer, leaving only a hairsbreadth between us. I panic and give him my back, hiding my flushed face, and rummage through my bag. Two hands press against the flesh of my hips. Any response I had for him lodges in my throat. His soaked shirt presses to my back, and his warm breath assaults my flesh where my neck meets my shoulder. A hitched breath is stolen from my lungs as his lips make contact with my skin.

"Wha—What are you doing?" What a ridiculous question. I know damn well what he's doing. And it's killing me not to man up—or woman up—and whip around and offer every single part of me. He doesn't jump to the occasion to answer me. Instead, his grip tightens. His lips glide along my skin, hitting the top of my shoulder blade. I soundlessly beg him for more. His tongue on my flesh. His grazed teeth against my skin. "Jim..." His name falls breathlessly from my lips.

"Just say it. Thank you, Jim, for saving me."

"I didn't need saving," I moan, his open mouth gently kissing my bare skin where my shirt hangs off my shoulder, granting my partial wish.

"So stubborn." His teeth press down, nibbling at my skin. "When are you going to stop avoiding this attraction between us?" *Never*, I want to cowardly say. He doesn't wait for an answer. The small whimper that escapes my lips is good enough for him. "Never saw this coming either, but if it takes me stepping up to admit it, I will. Want me to admit you've knocked me off my damn feet? How about if I confessed, I want nothing more than to fall headfirst into the possibilities of what it can become? Would that get you to stop avoiding this?"

My eyes flutter closed. His hands move just a smidge, allowing his long fingers to grip and tease the lining of my hip. I open my mouth to speak, but my words are captured by the knot in my throat. "You don't have to pretend. We're alone. No one's gonna hear you." I cowardly say.

His teeth press down, this time not as gentle, capturing my sensitive flesh. My body succumbs to his words, my hips willingly twisting around to face him. Our eyes collide, and the fire blazing threatens to burn down the world around us. The way my body submits to his intense gaze has my lips parting, sucking in a strangled breath of air. No longer am I staring at the warm, easy-going man I've spent the last day and a half with, but the intensity of a man ready and able to slay anyone or thing threatening to get in his way of having all of me. His high voltage stare darkens and penetrates through me, twisting my stomach into knots. A thousand different sensations flutter through my body when his hand works its way around my neck, gripping it in a way that my knees are in jeopardy of buckling. His mouth opens, his tongue wetting his lower lip as he speaks. "I know what you're trying to do. Downplay what's happening here. So, I'll put it as blunt as possible.

I don't want to kiss you because I have to, I want to kiss you because I want to. And I want you to give me the okay to do so. Because when I start, I won't be able to stop, so I need you to be on board with this."

A kindling of desire burns, fireworks igniting every nerve-ending down my spine to my toes. His admission entraps me, his willing prey needing his hands and mouth to consume every inch of me. I snap, breaking from my self-control. Time and gravity can't collide fast enough as I lift myself up off my heels and crush my mouth to his. Just as eager, he meets me halfway, and we meet, our lips fusing together. His hand travels up my neck, his fingers tangling in my hair. A moan rumbles through me, but he swallows my small whimper and kisses me deeper. I melt into him as his other free hand clasps at my behind, squeezing my butt cheek and pressing myself into him. My legs wobble, feeling the hardness of him against me. My hands become wild, sliding underneath his wet shirt. My palms meet smooth muscled skin, and a fierce hunger builds, suddenly making me ravenous. His own moan vibrates inside his chest, and his mouth breaks from mine as he helps me peel off his shirt. I tug on my own until they're both discarded on the floor.

"God, you're crazy beautiful," he praises, going back in for more. We trip backwards and fall into the small dresser perched against the wall, shaking the mirror.

"Crazy beautiful, right? Not like crazy, comma, beautiful. I kinda haven't been—"

His tongue collides with mine, shutting me up, kissing me deep and senseless. "Both, but more beautiful." He chuckles against my lips, waiting for my retribution. Instead, my hands go into his hair, and I tug hard, forcing him closer, our connection deeper. "I'll take it. Just keep kissing me."

"I can do that," he breathes heavily, his mouth moving down my chin, his wet lips kissing along the slope of my neck. His hands cup my behind, and he lifts me, propping me up on the dresser.

We go at it like two starved lovers, unable to fight hard enough for the closeness we both desire. My conscious is smacking me knowing I could have been doing this the whole time. My hands thrust deep into his hair, and I squeeze tight. The rumble from his chest rises up his throat, and a sexy growl falls from his lips. As if igniting the flame between my legs even more, I pull him closer, stepping up my infatuation for my tongue dancing around his.

With the gentle thrust of him grinding into me, I go wild. My hands yank hard at his hair, and he pulls my butt cheeks forward, grinding me into him. I moan so loud, I almost accidently bite his tongue. My hands are needed elsewhere, so I let loose my death grip and go for his shorts. *Off. Off. Off,* my greedy mind repeats as I pop open the button and race to get his zipper down.

He's in his own race, jerking at my shorts. The problem is our clothes, wet and soaked to our skin is making it extra difficult.

"Dammit," he growls, unable to get my shorts down. I'm not in as bad of a predicament, but it still takes me some iron strength to push his shorts past his monster hard on before they drop to the floor. I go right for the gold and reach into his briefs, my hands working around him. I about die at how large he is. Maybe I should have done some exercises to prepare for this. Kegel boot camp.

I get one solid stroke in, my hand barely fitting around his whole girth, when a growl so deep reverberates in his chest.

"Dammit, you're gonna kill me."

"Same. What do you do with this thing?"

He kisses me harder, thrusting into my hand. We both moan in unison as my hand strokes up and down his length.

"Fuck, I need you on the bed." He lifts me up and hustles toward the bed. Forgetting his shorts are around his ankles, he trips, and we go flying onto the mattress. His heavy weight lands on top of me, but we don't miss a single beat. His mouth devours mine. He kicks off his shorts, and his hands work at the second button on mine, hauling them down my legs.

I can't remember the last time I was so excited about sex. Oh my god, I'm gonna have sex! Wait…I'm gonna have *sex*. My excitement crashes into my nerves, and I suddenly worry I'm making a bad call. *No, you're not. Let him do all the dirty things to you.* My inner voice isn't always the best influence. Most of the time when I listen, I end up in situations I regret. *You saw what he's about to give you. No turning back now.* I did see, and felt, and…"Oh god," I moan as his teeth bite down on my earlobe.

His hands caress my hips, latching onto my soaked panties. He raises his head so our eyes meet, and my belly clenches at the intensity shining in his. "These gotta go." He bares his teeth, his smile hungry, like a beast hunting his prey. He works his way down my torso, his movements slow, methodic, enticing, surreal, freaking insane, until those teeth are wrapped around the top of my panties.

Oh my god, he's taking off my underwear. With his teeth!

I throw my head back, anticipating what he plans on

doing next. Then I throw my head back up. Shoot, am I properly shaved? I was in a hurry. Hungover. What if I left patches? He's gonna think I'm some sort of cavewoman.

The moment he gets my panties down, I reach for his head to drag him back up, wanting to avoid any hair related topics. But he's faster and stronger. His tongue hits my warm center, and my head crashes against the bed in ecstasy.

I always pictured heaven to be a pretty place. Beautiful. Euphoric. And it is—it so is. "Oh heavens." He works me slow, until my fingers dig into his hair and I threaten bald patches. The rumble of his laughter feels even more heavenly against my inner thigh. He gets the point and starts working me hard and fast, adding a finger to throw me over the edge. When my orgasm detonates, I worry I knock him out when my pelvis thrusts forward, hitting him in the chin.

His grip latches around my hips, holding me in place as he devours me. When the last lingering tremor runs through me, he lets up. He lifts his head, his chin glistening. "You taste like heaven."

I want to laugh at his compliment and return the nice gesture and tell him his tongue feels like heaven. "Tell me what you want, Case?"

I want a million more of what he just gave me. My toes are still tingling. "I want you to stop doing so much talking and more showing."

God, I'm a perv. Dirty talking is not my thing. Being pushy and dominant isn't either. I'm fairly boring in the bedroom. But the way his voice penetrates through me, deep and sexy, I lose all sense of myself.

"Thank god. I was hoping for that answer. Getting a

taste of you made me a starved man." He crawls up my body, still quivering from that orgasm, and crushes his mouth over mine. Tasting myself on his tongue is a new thing for me. I would think I'd be grossed out, but instead I find it strangely arousing. It's effect on me heightens the already aching need I have for him.

"Fuck," he groans and sits up. "Condom."

Oh, come on! Has anyone ever used a zip lock bag and a rubber band—

"My wallet. I should have one in there." He jumps off the bed, hopping out of his briefs in the process. His wingman falls out, saluting me, and my mouth waters. His junk catches the small light from the lamp, making an impressive shadow puppet against the wall. My hand lifts to play along, using my index finger and thumb to stroke the shadow.

He rummages through his wallet, and when he turns around, I throw my hands back down. There's no denying how attractive he is. With clothes on, he's like a popsicle on a hot day. Naked, it's hitting a trench of ice-cold water in the middle of the Sahara Desert. He is what you'd call all man in his birthday suit of glory.

Like a hunky sex God, he wets his lips, scoping out his prey. My insides twirl knowing I'm his target. There's no shyness in his fiery gaze as his teeth rip open the condom packet and he slides it down his very erect, very eager love muscle. He prowls toward me, my eyes glued to his as he lifts his knee to climb on the bed. I must be dreaming. This perfect specimen of a man cannot be crawling up this bed to seduce and bring me to exultant, orgasmic pleasure. The closer he gets, the faster time speeds up. His mouth is quickly back on mine, kissing away any doubts I had. My hands go rogue molesting his abs. His are more rampant, squeezing my butt cheek, my hips, working his way up to cup my breasts. He wraps his fingers around my flesh, squeezing until my nipples turn plum in color. His mouth rips from mine, and he positions it over my nipple, sucking until I'm hard in his mouth, then biting at the tip.

My back fights to stay against the mattress. My hands find themselves threading into his wild hair. I coddle his head closer as he assaults my other breast.

"Like silk against my tongue. I can suck and taste you all day." His mouth presses against my breastbone, moving up to the dip of my collarbone. "I can live off the scent of you alone." His tongue, warm and inviting, causes a violent wave of goosebumps to break out as he sucks hard, no doubt leaving his mark.

I can't take much more teasing of his hands and mouth. My body aches in a way that begs for him to feed all my cravings until I'm full in every way. His greedy hands are back on my breasts, toying with my nipples. When his eyes lift to meet mine, they're glazed over in a sheen of lust I've never seen on another man's face.

There's a raw hoarseness to his voice when he speaks. "I need inside you like something fierce." The tension low in my belly pulsates at his words. I wrap my legs around his thick waist as he uses one hand to adjust himself between my aching thighs. One last glance just before he takes my breath away and powers into me.

God bless America.

Like fireworks on the Fourth of July, sparks ignite inside me, blasting a tremor of euphoria down to my toes. A layer of sweat forms along my trembling skin at the sudden fullness of him. I almost bite my tongue, trying to hold back the deep moan threatening to wake the dead. He doesn't pull out right away, but waits for me to adjust to him. Not realizing I had closed them, I open my eyes and connect to the flame, wild and swirling, in his eyes. The way he looks down at me creates a need so fierce inside me. I lift my head and cover his lips with my own. The rumble of his arousal vibrates against my lips as he pulls out and claims me once again. With each measured thrust, I open for him, widening my legs to give him more of me. He doesn't waste a second. Picking up the pace, he pulls out and with the strength of a bull, slams into me.

"Fuck," he growls, nipping at my lower lip. His rough hands fondle my breasts as his mouth does something magical to my neck, his tongue warm to my already blazing skin. Each thrust is a message. A vow. He's going to ruin me. And I welcome it. My legs begin to shake, tension forming low in my belly. I'm mere seconds away from the grand finale, quick whimpers falling from my lips, possibly sounding like "The Star-Spangled Banner." *God, Fourth of July is my new favorite—*

"Wrap your legs around my waist."

Yes, sir. I hope he knows any more friction is going to detonate my orgasm even quicker. My legs go around his waist, followed by another strangled moan. This position allows him to push even deeper into me, and a cry of ecstasy erupts up my throat. He suddenly flips us, and a small squeal travels up my throat as I pop up on top and find myself now in control.

"Fucking beautiful," he pants, working my hips up and down over his hardness. My hands press against his pecs, my nails digging into his inked skin. My eyes work their way up his sexy chest until I capture his eyes. Lust.

Hunger. Need. I suck in a lungful of air, feeling drunk on the rawness. It gives me the boost of confidence I need, knowing I'm causing those emotions. Closing my eyes, I slightly bend my neck back and ride him, each stroke leisured. I want to stay in control, but my orgasm is knocking at my door, ready to blow the entire house up around us. I start to work my hips faster, my lips parting as a slow moan releases.

A growl deep inside Jim's chest reverberates under my hands, and his grip around my waist tightens. He presses down on my hips, pushing his hips up until he's so deep inside me, my legs tremble around him.

"Oh, I'm not done with you yet," he breathes before flipping us again, my back hitting the mattress. His eyes find mine, no doubt showing me he's right there with me, hanging off the edge of oblivion. His hips pull back, and with all his strength, he powers into me, his mouth falling onto mine as he kisses me senseless. One, two…twenty—I lose count of how many times he dangles me over the ledge until finally, the world around us denotes into an explosive orgasm as we fly over the edge of ecstasy together.

CHAPTER
TWELVE

Casey

Unlike my usual mornings, this one doesn't have me waking from a dream where my libido gets screwed out of the screwing. The sun beating in from the window has my eyes fluttering open to see a set of real-life arms wrapped around my waist, resting against my ribcage. The warm body nestled behind me and feel of his chest rising and falling as he soundly sleeps has me sighing sheepishly into my pillow. In your face, Axl Rose and hot teacher. I wonder if those dreams would have even been as good as last night. I smirk into the pillow, trying to hide the blush spreading along my cheeks. Holy hot stallion—

"What are you thinking about?" A deep voice tickles my eardrums. Warm lips press against my neck as Jim lays a slow kiss to my skin. I close my eyes, enjoying the feel of my boyfriend's—my eyes shoot back open. Reality sets in like a freight train carrying a load of "oh my god, I had hot, crazy sex with my fake boyfriend last night and now we're cuddling" reality, ready to crash and burn.

"Uh, nothing, just…" Just that I have *no* idea how to act in this moment! Last night was hot and amazing and we both wanted it. I *sure* wanted it. But we'd been drinking. Our adrenaline was high due to our near-death experience. It's morning, and everything is…normal. Is this where we both pretend we've made a huge mistake and run to the bathroom and never return? Do I roll over and ask him for round two? Do I pretend I have narcolepsy and start to snore?

"Your tense body tells me you're about to freak out. Probably tell me last night was a mistake and possibly elbow me in the balls, in which I'd tell you it wasn't a mistake and to please spare my balls."

Oh, he's good.

"I wasn't." I totally was.

"Well, if it matters, last night was amazing. I normally don't let girls I don't know take advantage of me, but it was well worth it—*ouch!*"

My elbow meets his gut, and I twist in his arms. I expect to see pain in his eyes when I face him, but there's humor there. "I did *not* take advantage of you," I pout.

"I don't know, I'm pretty sure I remember you demanding I—*shit!*" he yelps as I take two fingers to his nipple, clamp hard, and twist. "Jesus, my poor nipple, what did it ever do to you?" He laughs, and before I can attack his other one, he flips me, my back landing on the mattress. He's up and straddling me, hovering over me, his bare chest on full display. I'm trying to muster up my angry face, but my eyes can't stay focused. "See something you like?" He continues to tease me, flexing his pecs.

"Not a single—*okay*, knock it off!" Jesus he's got a great chest. Even more so, his laugh is infectious, addictive.

I want more and more and more of it. I can't argue with what he's saying. There was no holding back last night. I felt something, and I chose to explore it. And the deeper I went, I realized I wanted so much more.

"Well, I'm pretty sure Mars can attest to the fact that you didn't have a bad time yourself. Your moaning and grunting like a wild feline was heard on seven out of eight planets." I wait for him to confirm or deny. Also, to call *me* out. I'm pretty sure the moaning was coming from me, and I sounded more like a pterodactyl. *Sue me.* It's been a while since I've had a night like that, if ever.

"Then the critics agree. Last night was totally worth it. And I'm glad it happened." He smiles down at me. That little fluttering in my belly sweeps back into action, swarming into a small tornado. "I'm also hoping you won't harm me in any way because I'm going to kiss you."

I don't get the chance to reply. His lips find mine, and he does exactly as he said, slow, gentle, Nobel Prize worthy. My heart picks up, and my hands find his chest, sliding up until I'm threading my fingers into his thick hair. My voice betrays me as a soft moan slips from my lips and I tug him closer. Our lips part, and our tongues do a beautiful dance around one another. All too soon, he's pulling away. If my grip locked around his hair is any sign I disagree with the end of this perfect kiss, I don't know what is.

His eyes find mine, holding the same glow as my own. "Don't worry. There's more where that came from."

Banging from the other side of the wall seizes our attention, followed by yelling. "Seriously! Stop. If I smell another fart, I'm going to murder you. God, did you eat a dead animal?" Another bang, possibly the sound of a shoe hitting the wall. "Sorry, I can't help it. It had to have been from those stupid craft beers Mick made me drink," Jerry argues. Another shoe hits the wall. "Oh my god, stop! Get out of here."

Ew!

We both stare at one another a second longer before bursting into a fit of laughter. The next door over opens and slams. Nothing like killing the moment with the mental picture of suffocation by death farts.

"Not sure I have enough game to get back on track after that—"

"Yeah. No one does."

He chuckles and slides his fingers under my t-shirt. I peek down remembering I'm actually in his shirt and it's somehow hiked up past my navel. "You truly are lucky, ya know?" His thumbs caress my skin, sending a heat wave down to my toes. "Some people never find that one true friend, let alone a whole squad of them."

"What do you mean?" I'm trying to ignore the building temptation to flip him and attack.

"When I was growing up, I didn't have many friends. I was an only child, so I basically spent a lot of time alone. My parents traveled a lot, so I had a nanny. She was the closest person to me, but who wants to say their best friend was their live-in caretaker? Anywho, I didn't make friends easily, and any time I did, they would get run off by my father. He wanted me to be portrayed as this intellectual kid. He didn't think hanging out with anyone less prestigious was in my best interest. We—*he* came from money, so 'no kid of his was going to slum it with the lower class.' Couldn't have the Harrison kid hanging out with heathens."

He pauses to take a breath. His story surprises me. Never would I have expected he came from money. He doesn't act like it, nor dress like it.

"I was a junior in high school when I met Jameson. He was everything my father despised. He came from a shitty family. Chose when he wanted to show up to school. Smoked more pot than Bob Marley. But he was my friend. My only friend. He gave a shit. He was there when my parents weren't. When I felt like I had no one. He may have come from nothing, but he had more passion and drive for life than anyone I knew." He stops to brush a strand of hair away from my face. "Anyway, the way you all are, it reminds me of him."

My heart is heavy for him. His solemn eyes cloud with emotion sharing this part of his life with me. "It sounds like Jameson is a great friend."

"Was. He died right after we graduated high school."

There's a shadow of pain behind his deep-set eyes. "Oh, Jim, I'm so sorry." My hands lift to cover the bare skin over his heart.

"It's okay. Long time ago."

"Doesn't mean it still doesn't affect you."

"I owe him so much. He should be here. Not me." He shakes his head. "Fuck, sorry. Didn't mean to get all depressing on you. It's...I guess I've never really shared this story with anyone."

My hands find his face, caressing his warm cheek, the days' worth of stubble tickling my palm. "Can I ask how he died?"

"Car accident. He shouldn't have been out that night. My father and I got into a fight. A nasty one. I was so sick of him trying to run my life. He never cared about my dreams or aspirations. He couldn't see past the plans he set for me. The rich son following his rich father's footsteps. I didn't want to run his company. I could give a rat's ass about money or image. He said I'd do what he wanted or he'd cut me off. So, I told him to go to hell and took a swing at him. My mom was hysterical, and I took off. Found myself at a party drinking and getting high. I passed out and some chick went through my phone and called the first person in my contacts, which was Jameson. It was close to two in the morning when he came and picked me up. I barely remember because I was so messed up. A truck driver had fallen asleep at the wheel and hit us. Broke my arm, nose, and cracked some ribs. Jameson was dead before help even arrived."

My heart cracks. His pain. The sorrow in his eyes. The reliving that night by retelling his story. I should have never asked. "Oh, Jim, I shouldn't have made you tell—"

"Hey, I didn't tell you to feel sorry for me. I just…I've never really talked about it, and I felt—"

"Thank you for sharing with me," I tell him, wanting to wrap my arms around him. Would that be weird? Are we even on that level where it's okay for me to comfort him?

"What about you? What's your story?"

Topic change. Totally get it.

"I don't really have one. Boring upbringing, even more boring—"

"June mentioned something about your own dad."

Dang it, June! "Would it be corny to admit we kind of have the same story?"

"Not at all," he says.

"My dad was pretty similar to yours. Successful. Pushed

me into going to law school. He wanted me to do anything but what *I* wanted, which was discover myself and let my cards fall into place on their own. He was never around, so he barely knew me. Had no idea I hated the thought of becoming a lawyer or a doctor. I wanted to travel, become an artist, even though I'd never picked up a brush. Thought about becoming an actress. I wanted to be whatever my heart led me to be. Daddy Dearest didn't feel the same way. The more he tried to control me, the more I acted out. Fast forward a bunch of years of rebellion later, I'm still trying to find myself and I haven't spoken to my dad in years. If you don't count the birthday cards he sends with my mom's forged signature."

"Wow," he says, then dips down to place his lips on mine for a soft, quick kiss. "Our stories are similar." Another peck. "Sure we don't have the same dad?"

"We could—wait, what! *Ew!*" I slap his side. His chuckle is deep and sexy as he blocks another whack by capturing my arm and raising it above my head.

"I'm kidding. Don't beat me. I'll do whatever you want." His smile is so darn infectious. He bends forward for another kiss, then lays next to me. Together, we rotate onto our sides to face one another. "Will you tell me more about you?"

"What do you want to know? All things will lead to disappointment. I'm kinda, as you can already see, a hot mess."

His finger brushes over my lips. "Beautiful disaster has a better ring to it."

My lips curl into a grin. "I can handle that. But for real, I don't really know what to say. I don't have any great stories. I haven't done anything to be proud of. Actually…there was this one time on Cinco de Mayo—"

"How about twenty questions? You ask me a question, and I ask you. We'll feel like we've known each other our whole lives before breakfast is even served." His legs find mine under the covers and tangle around me, tugging me to snuggle closer. "I'll even let you go first," he says, threading his fingers inside the shirt of his I'm wearing, brushing against my bare skin.

I'm a little nervous at what questions he wants to ask me. But even more intrigued at the questions starting to form in my mind. I tuck my hands under my cheek and wiggle my toes in between his. "Okay. I'll play. How old are you?"

"Thirty-two." Damn, okay. Two years older than me. I can handle that.

"What's the last craziest thing you've done?"

This one's easy. "Hiring a guy to play my boyfriend." I laugh, and he joins me.

"Fair enough. Your turn."

Hmmm…I don't know whether to go straight to the deep end or start slow, like his favorite color or— "Last time you had sex?"

"Six hours ago."

"No! That's not what I meant!" I really need to stop hitting him. He covers his head when my hand bonks off his forearm. "Answer the question."

"I did. You can be more specific in your next one. My turn. When was the last time, before me, you were with a guy?"

My mouth drops open. Cheater! Embarrassment flushes across my face as I answer. "About a year. But! It's not because I can't get a guy. I might not have much going for me, but I still have my morals intact." And considering I slept with a guy I've known for only forty-eight hours, I can use that black kettle now. "My turn. What do you do for a living?"

His brows go up. "Ahhh, don't want to know my answer?"

"Nope, it doesn't matter."

He eyes me for a second before answering. "About a year myself, even if you don't want to know, and I own a bar."

Shut the front door! "You own a bar?"

"Are you asking another question? You skipped my turn."

I roll my eyes and maneuver my legs so I take his captive. "It was rhetorical. That's awesome, how come you never mentioned it?"

"Because I'm supposed to be a rich, jet-setter feeding you steak. My turn. Do you really even like steak?"

At that, I laugh. "I actually do like steak, but I prefer a good, juicy burger. Sweet potato fries over regular, and butter pickles over dill." He smiles and nods, accepting my answer. "My turn. How do you know so much about music?"

His response is fast. "I play in a band."

Oh, come on! "Now you're just pulling my chain."

"No chain. Only the heartstrings of adoring fans. I play guitar and am lead vocals for an alternative band. Jameson got me into it when we were kids. He handed me a guitar one day and I never put it down. I manage the bar and set up gigs when I can." Why did he just get a billion times hotter? Hot, magic with his hands, owns a bar—like music to my ears! "Come by sometime and I'll give you free cover."

"Oh, wow, thanks! Going all out." I fake being annoyed.

A wave of silence falls over us. He's staring at me, making me nervous about his next question.

"What are your plans after this weekend?"

And there it is. Short question, lifelong answer. One I don't have a reply for. What are my plans after this? Probably go home and continue being a loser. Pretend I have all these aspirations when I still can't figure out my place. "I don't know. Maybe find a job. Get a haircut. I was thinking about getting a pet. But they say if you can't keep a plant—"

"What are your plans with us?"

…alive. Fraggle rock! I don't…I… "That's two questions," I say, trying to bide myself some time. I've never been one to speak my mind—in a good way, that is—so I don't know how to honestly tell him what I want to happen. That he follows through with that date he talked about. To see if this strange way we met can blossom into something real. That he envelops himself in my life and doesn't run scared soon after. They all sound like great answers, too bad I chicken out and turn the tables on him. "My turn. What do *you* plan on doing with us after this weekend?" Gah! There, I said it. I bite down on my tongue, waiting for his reply. I start counting down from ten, swearing if he doesn't reply by the time I get to one, I'm jumping ship. *Five, four, three—*

"Hmmm, I'll probably check in with work. Make sure the bar ran smoothly while I was away. Read my mail. Take a nap." Okay, I'm about to whack him. "A juicy burger does sound nice, so I'll wait the proper three to five days so I don't appear too interested, then call a girl who scared me at first, but found a way to really impress me, and ask her out on the date I promised. I'll cross my fingers she says yes, 'cause even though she's super violent, I'm starting to really dig her. She has great taste in bikinis, did I mention that?"

My hand twitches to slap his shoulder, but his comment reminds me I need to calm it. "She sounds like a real catch. Hope she picks up when you call." I throw humor back at him, and a squeal erupts from my throat as he pounces on me, throwing my back against the mattress.

"I hope so too. I'd hate to suck down that juicy burger and double order of sweet potato fries with honey mustard dipping sauce and a side of pickles all by my lonesome. And I bet she's a strawberry shake kinda girl too."

Jesus, I don't know what arouses me more: the way his body straddles mine, the hazed over glaze in his eyes as his fingers brush along the exposed skin around my navel, or the way he described that damn burger and fries. My libido votes the hot guy on top of me, but my stomach, which decides to growl something fierce, chooses the burger.

"Hmmm…your eyes tell me you're hungry for one thing, and your stomach another. What's it gonna be?"

I start the counting in my head. I need to make it seem as if I'm pondering a decision I made the second he offered it. "Well…if forced, I guess I'd be okay with feeding the appetite you see in my eyes, and if you impress me, we can move on to feeding me in another way."

His brows curve up, a pleased smirk across his face. His hands smack together, rubbing back and forth. "Well, well, well, my beautiful disaster, let Chef Jim-Bob-Bob-Jim take care of that hunger for ya."

Another loud yelp falls from my lips as he goes in for the kill, his hands and mouth everywhere I hoped they'd be as he feeds my starved appetite.

Jim/Bob

Pre-breakfast took a bit longer than expected, so by the time we make our way downstairs, the house is already alive and active. If I had to admit, I think I was more starved than she was. My fingers still vibrate at the feel of each part of her smooth skin under my touch. Don't get me started on her pliable little body that succumbed to my every demand. I've had some experiences with chicks, but none of them compare to the way Casey creates this hunger inside me. The sweet taste of her still lingers on my tongue as we make our way downstairs. It's a battle not to throw her over my shoulder and take her back upstairs and have her for lunch and dinner.

Mick and Jason are on the pickleball court having a one-on-one match. The sun gleams off Mick's chest, and I make a mental note to get out in the sun more. Maybe do more push-ups. My hands brush through my ruffled hair, debating asking him who his barber is too.

"Well, that was the longest change of clothes, if I say so," Katie says from the kitchen counter, sipping on a cup of coffee. Casey's cheeks flush, and I love that it's due to her dirty little mind going back to a visual of last night—and this morning—twice.

Poppy smacks her, placing a plate of bacon on the counter. "Morning. Missed you guys last night."

"Not really. It was like you were with us all since we heard you all night—*ouch!*" Katie throws daggers at Poppy for hitting her. I can't help but chuckle. My girl sure does make some animated sounds when she's being pleasured.

"You two want some breakfast? Bacon's ready. Got a casserole coming out soon." Needless to say, I think after our morning, we're both starved in a completely different way.

"Just in time too, I was telling Katie about the call I got his morning from the local sheriff. If you can believe this, when they went to check it out, they said there was nothing amiss! I explained again how crazy they were, but they couldn't do anything."

"Get out. Those people are psychopaths. They wanted to eat our brains for dinner!"

Poppy rolls her eyes. "Not sure it went that far, but yeah. Kinda disturbing. And for a koozie? I've seen and heard some crazy stuff on the job, but this may take the cake. Either way, they said to stay clear of the area and notify us if any new information comes to light," she finishes, handing her a fresh poured cup of coffee.

Curious what my new buds are up to, I grab for Casey's free hand and thread my fingers through hers. Bringing her hand to my mouth, I press a kiss to the inside of her wrist. Our eyes meet, and the electricity that flows between us has me tugging her into me. My head dips, and I kiss her still swollen lips. "Gonna go say morning to the guys." I kiss her again, since she seems to be stuck in the moment, which makes my chest swell with gratification. She doesn't answer, but finally composes herself enough to nod. I hear Katie's low chuckle and another grunt, assuming when I let my girl's hand go to walk outside, something went flying at Katie's head.

A shit-eating grin on my face, I snag a water from the cooler and head outside to where Jerry is laying in a lawn chair, his sunglasses covering his eyes, watching the two battle it out on the court. "What's up, ya stallion?" he asks, and I laugh as I take up the chair next to him. Cracking the bottle open, I throw back a huge swig. "Gonna have to take a few lessons from you. Maybe Katie won't be so crabby with me all the time."

"Not sure what I can teach ya, bud. Just comes naturally. The *stallion* inside me releases and they come falling at my feet." I throw my back against the chair, letting the sun hit my face.

"Well, shit." He simmers on my comment while I close my eyes and enjoy the warmth of the rays, visualizing every part of Casey's body. The curve between her hip and pelvic bone I couldn't keep my mouth off of. Her plump breasts that fit like a glove in my palm. Her perfect nipples I could spend a lifetime sucking and feasting on. Each little sound from her soft, plump lips I earned as I indulged on every single spec of her body.

Realizing I accidently gave myself a huge boner, I quickly dump the cold bottle of water over my head.

"Yeah. Already a hot one out here."

"Yep." I nod. Hell, I need to do something about controlling that guy. Now that I've had a taste, it's going to be even harder keeping him down the rest of the time we're here. Mick whacks the ball, and Jason dives, but misses, losing the game.

"That's right! Pickleball Champion!" Mick hollers, giving us a perfected Hulk Hogan muscle flex. Man, I wonder if he takes supplements. "Oh, look who's alive. Thought you two killed each other up there," he says, wiping sweat off his brow and throwing the paddle on the picnic table. He walks up to me and sticks his fist out for some bromance knuckles. "Morning, bro." He throws himself in the chair next to me. "Man, I remember those days," he starts, staring out onto the lake. "You ever been cuffed? Marry a cop and shit gets interesting. Dominant role struggle, though. That woman sure likes control." He shakes his head, lost in thought, a goofy smile on his face. "Anywho, water's gonna be calm today. Perfect for wakeboarding. Who's in?"

There's such a freeing feeling circling around me. It's been a lifetime since I've worn such a carefree smile. Laughter and shouting from inside float outside, and I hear Katie yell something about a moaning hyena followed up with a grunt.

"Sounds like the girls are getting at it. Hopefully they don't mess up that casserole. Poppy makes a mean breakfast dish. Better go get those women in check." He gets up and walks inside as June makes an exit outside. Jason guns it straight for his girl, grabbing her in his arms and laying a kiss on her temple.

"They had me at food. This hangover's kicking my ass." Jerry gets up and drags himself inside. Jason tells June he's gonna jump in the shower. Another swift kiss, and he's gone, leaving only June and I on the back patio. With her coffee mug in hand, she takes the vacant chair next to me. We both stare out into the calmness of the lake, until she breaks the silence.

"You two both seem different this morning."

"Hmmm?" I give her my quick attention before bringing my eyes back to the lake.

"Something's different."

I offer her a hasty glance. "How so?"

"Don't get me wrong. Not in a bad way. It's just… Casey's not as…uptight—nervous."

"Hmmm..." I really need to come up with a different response.

"Yeah, you two...you're acting like you've just had your first date. Not two people who've been in a relationship for...wait, how long have you been together? I forgot what Casey told me."

Shit, June's going to be the death of me. "You know, June, you can't really put a timeframe on love."

"Hmmm..."

God, why does her "hmmm" sound scarier? "Hmmm...sure does feel like forever." I smile at her, but there's no doubt she catches my unease.

"How long?"

Dammit! "Yeah...I'm not good with dates—"

"Jim-Bob."

"Two years." I plunge into my own suicide. "About two wonderful years." I watch her facial expression morph into satisfaction. Or is it sabotage? I stare back off into the lake instead. June might be the sweet one, but she's the scariest. Those silent, but deadly eyes. I sneak a peek at her sipping her coffee. I want to blurt out and ask if I got the answer right. Not sure if it's from the morning sun or my nerves, a pebble of sweat forms on my forehead. I swipe away the perspiration, feeling the intense stare next to me. She hasn't said another word, but the silent interrogation is real. Do I come clean? Fess up? The pressure to blow our cover thickens. I start to panic. Man, I'd be horrible in jail. I'd fess up in a heartbeat and get shanked by my enemies. Dammit, I'm fessing up. They all deserve the truth. What's wrong with admitting how we unconventionally met? Along the way, the ruse turned into something real. I like June. She scares the hell out of me, but I like her. Shit, would Mick understand? I feel like he's a reasonable guy. Here it goes.

"You see—"

"Breakfast's ready!"

I blow out a breath of saved by the breakfast casserole. Hallelujah! Before I commit any further verbal suicide, I bounce up from my chair. "Well, better get in line. Heard I'm in for a mean casserole," I say, then sprint inside before June can say another word.

"Okay, you hold on here. When you're ready, use all your stomach strength to push up, throwing your feet up. The board will guide you. But if your balance is off, you're gonna go down before you even get up—and hard." Jason's trying to explain the rules of wakeboarding to me. I've never done any sort of water sports before, but how hard can it be?

"Got it."

Jason slaps me on the shoulder and hands me the reins. "All right, bro, jump in. Good luck."

I search out Casey, who's staring at me curiously. "Babe, if I don't return, it's always been you, okay?" Her quick intake of breath gives me the encouragement I need. I lean into her and slap a quick kiss to her lips. The hunger in her eyes has me guaranteeing I'll be back just so I can kiss that sexy gaze right off her.

"Make sure you kiss me like that when it's your turn," Poppy yells toward the driver seat of the eight-person luxury speed boat we opted for today.

"There's more where that came from." I wink at Casey.

LAKE REDSTONE

Poppy and Katie laugh. June simply carries a soft smile on her lips. Dammit. Sweet, but scary.

Back to the matter at hand, I adjust myself toward the water, jump in, and plunge under before I pop back up. I wipe the excess water off my face, and peer up to Jason giving me the thumbs up. I return the gesture, then reach out as he tosses me the wakeboard. "Remember, tighten stomach and push up. First thirty seconds when you get your balance is key," he shouts, giving me another thumbs up. I wave him off and adjust myself on the board. "Lastly, whoever stays on the board the shortest plays on Jerry's team for pickleball when we get back." He smiles and salutes me. Determination revels inside me at the mere thought of breaking my pickleball winning streak. Mick and I are champions. I take a few breaths. The propellers activate, shooting small waves at my chest. My grip tightens, and before I know it, Mick's hitting the acceleration and speeding off across the lake. My adrenaline is spiking, small nervous tremors, but a bigger blast of excitement. I've never been huge into water sports, but it's always been something I've wanted to do. I've stage dived more times than I can count, but that's about as adventurous as I come. To be honest, I wasn't even planning on getting on this thing. I was just fine staying on the boat with Casey nestled on my lap. She was helping me cover up my semi boner caused by her cute little white bikini with fringe hanging from her top. But then the girls had to start making bets. And then everyone's manhood was on the line. I'd hoped Casey would beg me to stay on the boat with her and not risk my life for such a silly competition, but then I heard it: *"My money's on Jim. He's got a grip like a bull."* Holding onto her sexy hips while she rides me is one thing. Holding onto the grab while skiing across water at thirty miles an hour? I was tempted to fake a similar groin injury, but when my eyes met hers, there was no turning back. I saw such pride in them, I'd sacrifice my life to savor the way she was looking at me.

So, here we are, the sun bright as a ball of fire in the sky, the lake calm, besides the spreading waves caused by the accelerating boat, and me, about to first-handedly see if I have what it takes to wakeboard. My grip is tight, and I start counting down from thirty. Mick picks up speed, and I clench my muscles, readying myself to pop up. Faint hollering strums my eardrums, coaching me on as I hit my fifteen second timeframe. My legs are wobbly at first, and for a split second, I bob to the side, thinking I'm going down. Tightening my stance, I straighten out my form, slightly bend my knees, and before I know it, I'm doing it. *Hell yeah! I'm doing it!* I howl to the sky in excitement as the fresh smell of the lake hits me in the face and I glide across the water's surface. Mick does circles around the lake, my abs tightening as my body moves with the waves. After a long stretch, my arms begin to burn, and one small twitch has me releasing the grab and plummeting into the water. When I resurface, the boat is already turning around. I spot Casey first. She's standing with her hands in the air, cheering. Man, it's a good thing I'm submerged under water or everyone would get a show. I can't help but sport a shit-eating grin. Her enthusiastic cheerleading has me bursting with joy. I don't know why it matters so much, but I want to please her. Make her happy. We haven't known each other long by any means, but she deserves to be happy, and I want to be the guy to give that to her. I've already hammered out the perfect burger joint, one that makes the best sweet potato fries in town.

I've envisioned her meeting the band and introducing her to Judith from the bar. If it wasn't way past creepy and my mom was still around, she'd love her.

"Dude! That was awesome! You sure you haven't done that before? First time stud, bro!" Jason reaches down and grabs my hand to help me back in the boat.

"Nah, but that was quite a ride." I hit the deck and shake my hair out. The girls squeal from being splashed. I search out Casey, who's already walking up to me, a beer in tow. I reach out and snag her into my arms, tucking her close, my lips finding the top of her head. I press a kiss to her forehead and accept the beer. The sun forces her to squint, the canvas of beauty she offers me in those laughing eyes threatening to bring me to my knees. "Thanks, babe," I hum, staring at her. She nods, and I steal another kiss. We take up the nearest open seat, Case on my lap as Poppy gears up to go next. As if it's a natural reaction, I bring my arm around her, resting on her bare thigh. My thumb, which has ached to touch her since going out in the water, brushes along the silkiness of her skin. I would die a happy man if I got to do this on a regular basis.

Casey takes a sip of her spritzer drink and leans back into me. The sun warming her back feels nice on my bare chest. My lips find the column of her throat and suck gently. She tastes like cherry suntan lotion. A sigh reverberates from her lips, and I bite down lightly, selfishly needing more of her cute little noises. I release her flesh from my teeth and leave a small peck over the swell of my mark. God, seeing my marks on her is sexy as hell.

I lean forward and speak softly into her ear. "I like this," I say, relaxing back into the seat, taking her with me. She melts into my embrace as we silently sit together while Poppy jumps into the water. A few moments pass, and the boat is at it again, pulling forward and picking up speed. Unlike me, Poppy isn't trying to mask an *oh shit* face, and pops right up, making the lake her bitch. She glides across it like it's her job, making a fool out of anyone else on the water. My eyes widen as she does a flip, catching herself perfectly back on her feet, twisting and turning like a circus acrobat.

"Jesus, she's a machine." I shake my head in disbelief.

Casey's cute little giggle teases my eardrum, and I tickle her just to feed more into my obsession. "Stop!" she begs, but her laughter still feeds the beast inside me. "She's ridiculous, isn't she? Super smart. Unaffected by carbs, and if she ever had a one-on-one match with Chuck Norris, my bets would so be on Poppy."

Damn...

Impressive.

Poppy lasts longer than me by a long shot, eventually releasing and dipping under the water. Mick does just as good, saying his modeling shoots were where he learned how to do so many tricks. Casey passes because of her groin, as do Katie and June. Jason nails it, but doesn't last as long as Mick. If Jerry crashes and burns, Mick and I are still in a relationship—I mean, partners—pickleball partners.

"You heard what he said. Don't dick around out there. Get up fast," Katie starts in at Jerry as everyone listens in, amused by their banter.

"I know, woman. Leave me be. Throw me the damn grab."

"You're gonna fall if you don't push off, Jerry."

"I know! Go drink your spritzer. I got this."

"No, you don't."

"Yes, I do!"

Katie shakes her head, waving her hand away from Jerry as she twists around and heads to the cooler. "He's gonna crash and hurt his back. Complain all week about how sore he is. Don't wanna listen to me? Fine." She snaps a can open, and shrugs, taking a sip. "Idiot," she mumbles, taking another.

"All right, last one. Let's go!" Mick shouts, and off we go. Everyone has their eyes trained on Jerry. His beginning formation is unsteady, and for a second, it doesn't look like he's even gonna get up. His arms are wobbly as he tries to pull himself up, and we're quickly nearing the thirty second marker.

"He ain't doing it," Jason chimes in.

"Nah, he's got it. Give him a chance," Poppy says, being supportive.

A huge wave smacks him dead in the face, and he swivels on the board, almost releasing the grab. To everyone's amazement, he pops up, getting to his feet. "There he goes!" Poppy claps her hands, and Katie comes to the front of the boat, surprised.

"Well, color me shocked." She cups her palms, and screams, "You got this, babe!" She waves at him and we all watch him make his rookie mistake. He takes his hand off the grab to wave back.

"No, dude! Hold on with both hands!" Jason yells, but it's too late. As he waves back to his wife, the boat hits a small bump in the water, sending a jolt of waves to shift. Jerry loses his balance, and when the board skids over the disruption in the water, Jerry goes flying in the air.

All eyes widen as we watch him lose the board and fly

into the air. Then they all suddenly clench shut as he belly flops at high speed into the water.

"Holy shit, that had to hurt." Jason's face is scrunched in agony.

"He had to have swallowed his balls," Mick says in pain, turning the boat around to fetch him.

Katie shakes her head and takes down the rest of her drink. "Idiot."

After fetching Jerry, all parts still intact, Mick found a secluded little man-made beach toward the opposite end of the lake—the *way* other end from the house on Bunker Hill. A group of young college kids take up the other half, but don't seem to mind that we crash their party. The girls are set up in a row, each with their beach towels laid out, soaking in the blazing sun. Mick and Jason throw a football around down the way, while Jerry floats on a raft in the lake.

Walking back from the tree-line after taking a piss, my eyes search out Casey in the middle of the girls, her cat ear inspired sunglasses hiding her eyes. Even though I can't see them, I feel her watching me. I can sense it. Her body language gives her away, her legs bent, her thighs squeezing together with each step I eliminate between us. She's perched up on her elbows, listening to something Katie's saying, but if I had to guess, she hasn't heard a single word. For my own personal pleasure, I rub my open palm across my chest, working down to my navel, and smile as her thighs clench tighter. Damn, she's so sexy when she's aroused. And I'd be lying if I wasn't just as turned on playing this game. As much as I wish we were on this beach alone so I could rip that skimpy little bathing suit off and suck every single piece of her into my greedy mouth, I want to merely lay with her, get to know her, listen to her laugh, know what she likes to do, eat, listen to, what her first car was. I want to get inside her head and learn everything about her. It's been too long since I've felt the creative tick of words and sat down and written new music. Casey has broken down the blockage suffocating my fruitfulness. If I had a pen and paper, I'd throw myself into words, all birthed by the way she's brought the life back into me. Her smile is like this symphony playing in my head, each whimper or laugh forming words that create this beautiful melody, causing my fingers to ache for my guitar—to strum the strings as if I was strumming between her creamy thighs.

Every step closer I get, the heavier this mass in my stomach gets, sparking questions I never thought to have answers to. How the hell did something so unconventional turn into something pretty damn amazing?

"Dude, I think he's coming to eat you alive."

"If you two start going at it, I'm outta here."

"I wouldn't mind seeing what he has to offer—*ouch*! Man, you've become so violent in your old age."

Katie rubs her forearm as my feet hit the bottom of Casey's towel.

"Hey," I say.

"Hey," she replies, her voice soft.

"Room for one more?" I ask, dropping down to my knees. Without waiting for an answer, I start to crawl up, past her sun-kissed legs, and straddle her hips. Her eyes stay trained on mine as I work up her body, forcing her to lay back, her head hitting the towel. "Best seat in the house," I whisper, then drop my lips to hers. Gone is the girl who once tensed up when I kissed her. In her place is the compliant firecracker who takes my lips against hers just as eager as my own.

"Jesus, get a room. Oh, wait, that doesn't matter, 'cause the whole house still can hear." Poppy laughs at Katie's poke, my smile growing along her mouth. I can't help myself and deepen our kiss, mingling our tongues, hers sweet with the lingering taste of her raspberry spritzer.

"Okay, yeah. I think maybe we should give them a moment," June says, plucking at Katie's arm.

"Dude, I'll meet up with you. Curious how this plays out—*Jesus!* June, when did you stop being sweet and harmless?" Katie grumbles, huffing, then gets up as the three of them walk off to the water.

I slow our kiss and open my eyes as I pull back. "Was it something I did?" I ask, the smirk unstoppable as it spreads across my face. I wait for her routine beat down, but it doesn't come. I slide off her and lay on my side, facing her. "Favorite color?"

"What?"

"We didn't finish our twenty questions. What's your favorite color?"

She eyes me, then adjusts her body to face me. "Black. So morbid, right? But I think my personality is bright enough. Have to offset it, ya know?" I laugh and slide her sunglasses off her nose, placing them over my face.

"There. Now I can see."

"Ha-ha. My turn. The name of your pet growing up?"

"I never had one. My parents didn't like animals. I had a pet rock when I was a kid. I named it Rocky. Get it?" She shares in the humor, her eyes lighting up, accentuating the spec of hazel and green. "My turn. How old are you?"

"Older than my maturity level. Thirty." I did expect her to be a little bit younger, yet I'm pleasantly surprised we're so close in age. "Good thing or bad?" she asks.

"Is that your question?" My brow goes up in a playful inquiry.

"Actually, no. Retract that one. How often do you sell yourself to crazy people for money?"

A few seconds pass, then my chest rumbles, expelling a burst of laugher. "I can honestly say this is my first and hopefully last gig." It makes me feel good to see the relief cross her face. "My turn. Why did you think I was a gigolo?" I chuckle after asking it. Damn, she's cute when she's embarrassed.

"Well, you were so good at what you were doing. The sweet talking. The way you, ugh...this is embarrassing, but you just hit all the right points. There was no way you were only some random guy wanting to make a few bucks and be a stranger's boyfriend for the weekend."

"Good thing I was. Best random decision I've made in a long damn time."

Our expressions mask each other's. A smile full of warmth, gratefulness. Excitement for this insanely strange thing we've found. "I think I'm gonna break the first date one-oh-one rules. Not sure I can wait the three to five days to call and ask for that date I've been thinking about." Color flushes her already sun-kissed cheeks. Her eyes become heavy. She approves. I lean in and kiss her. When I pull away, a pleasant sigh falls off her wet bottom lip. "My turn. What are the chances we can cover ourselves with these beach towels and continue where we left off this morning?" I nip her shoulder, the taste of cherry painting my lips.

"I can guarantee up to second base, other than that is a bonus." My laughter vibrates against her smooth skin as I go in for another nibble. God, I could devour her right here. "When we fess up to everyone, make sure to tell them it's my impeccable charm that really won you over."

Her body tenses beneath me. "Whoa, that's not happening."

I pull back, confusion in my eyes. Continuing this ruse would make sense if we hadn't formed a real relationship. The longer we keep this lie going, the worse we both come off. And I'm starting to not feel good about all the deceit. "They're gonna figure it out sooner or later. Might as well tell them all together. It'll be fine. They like me. We'll laugh about it and—"

"Jim, we're not telling 'em."

My smile wilts. "I'm not gonna continue to lie to them." At least any more than I already have. I may have just met these people, but they don't deserve to be lied to. My conscience eats at me the closer I become with each of them. Casey should feel the same. I wait for her to agree with me, but her mood shifts in the opposite direction.

She pulls away and sits forward. "Newsflash, you already have. And telling them I hired you isn't gonna make either of us come off any better. Please, just let it be for now, okay?" For how long? Our weekend is rapidly coming to an end. Then where does that leave us? Her defensive expression transforms into pleading. "Please. Let me figure it all out." Struggling with right and wrong, I nod, and her tense shoulders relax.

"It's on, bro!"

I sit up, our focus now on the loud voices coming from the other side of the beach. Jason and Mick are chest to chest with some young guys. "What's going on?" Casey asks as I get up, catching her hand to help her up too.

"Not sure. Let's go find out." I don't release her hand as we walk across the beach to see what everyone is yelling about.

"Dude, you're injured, old news, man. I bet you can't throw past that bobber in the lake."

Jason lets the insult fall off his shoulders with a loud laugh. "It's on, Junior. I'll run across that floating water mat, do a flip, and still catch that football. Tell me who's old and injured then."

The young punk slaps his palms together. "Yeah, you got it. You miss it, we get all the booze on that fancy boat of yours."

"Deal."

Everyone starts to huddle around as Jason stretches his arms, then kisses June before walking toward the small dock, a water mat at the end of it. He positions himself, his foot digging into the sand, preparing to run out the play.

"Ready, old man?"

"Whenever you are, Junior."

"Ready, set, hike!" The kid twists, taking a step forward as he pulls his arm back and launches the football. It soars through the air, and Jason takes off down the dock, his hand shielding the sun from his eyes so he can keep track of the ball. Once he hits the water mat, like a goddamn acrobat, he throws himself into an impressive flip, twisting his body in the process, his hands out, the football falling right into his grip. He lands in the water, and everyone goes wild.

"Holy shit! That was awesome!" Their little fan club

of girls all clap and scream. I peek over at June, but she's simply smiling at her man, not a smidge of jealousy in her sweet smile.

The kid slams his hand to his side as Jason pops up, a huge grin on his face. "Looks like you're gonna stay thirsty."

"Screw that!" he scowls. "Best outta three."

Jason climbs up the ladder to the dock and struts toward the crowd. "Deal. I can do this all day."

"No way." He snaps around, his attention on me, then goes for the kill when he eyes Mick and Jerry. "These fools. Each one makes it, or we get the booze." My brows go up. Yeah, not sure how good I'd be at—

"You in, Jim-Bob? Jet-setter over here can probably do this in his sleep!" My eyes shoot to his. "My boy's gonna smoke you."

I side-eye Casey, that pleading flicker of desperation back in her eyes. Dammit. I guess them finding out I'm a fraud by sabotaging this competition is one way to come clean. "I'm in," I reply, and step forward, as does Mick.

"Totally in. Last season's swimsuit shoot had me doing this all day. Got this in the bag, baby." The kid regards Mick strangely, shaking off his comment and Jason tosses him the football. Mick goes first, preparing his stance, and with a toss, he's off, impressively flipping in the air and catching the football, tucking it into his chest as he plunges into the lake.

When I'm up, I slap Casey on her cute ass for luck, since I sure need it, and adjust my form, ready to run. I'm betting twenty-eighty on myself, but I keep that low percentage to myself. Mick and Jason are already glowing with victory. When the little teeny bopper yells, "Hike," I take off down the dock. The second my foot pushes off the dock, I suck my abs in and curl into a spin. My body follows through perfectly, and when my hands reach out, my fingers snag the football. My grip isn't on target and I almost lose it, but by the time I land in the water, I have the football tightly pressed to my chest.

Hollering booms through my eardrums as I resurface, and I can't help but scream myself. Damn, that was awesome! I swim to the dock and climb up, tossing the ball.

"All right, boys. Have fun. Sober life is the worst life." Jason laughs, throwing his arm around June. I grab for Casey, and we all retreat to our side of the beach.

"Not so fast. That dude didn't go." We all glance over to take stock of who he's talking about. Shit.

"You said best out of three, Junior."

"What? Think your friend can't do it? That's messed up."

Jason looks over at Jerry and sighs. Mick does the same, then mumbles something under his breath. Katie throws her hands up in the air. "Oh, come on! Casey just filled that whole cooler with her entire stock of spritzers."

Case whips her head in her direction. "How was I supposed to know we were going to go to battle over our stash?"

Katie huffs under her breath. "Oh, come on! Who takes up all the cooler space to begin with? Learn to drink real booze."

Casey gasps. "I drink real booze!"

The punk rolls his eyes and throws his hand in the air. "I don't give a shizzle what's in the cooler. Make him do the jump or it's ours." Why are we even bothering with this kid? He's like eighteen, and we're adults. We make the rules! "You got somethin' to say, daddio?"

"Nope. All good." Dammit! I just chickened out to a kid. I check around to see if anyone's sticking their hand out, demanding my man card. Also, nope. All are still staring at Jerry. Good.

"So, what's it gonna be? Me and my posse got some *spritzers* to murder."

Jason's gaze ping-pongs back and forth between Jerry and the punk, preparing to do some heavy negotiations, when Jerry steps forward.

"*We're* gonna murder those drinks, not you, homeboy." Katie's eyes roll up, shaking her head. Mick and Jason wear worried expressions. "Don't throw like a girl, though, ya hear me, fool?"

"Oh my god, I'm going to the boat," Katie sighs and walks off in the opposite direction.

"Jerry, you sure about this? We can just give them the coolers. We have more at—"

"No way. Those are our spritzers. I had a cranberry one earlier, and it was damn tasty."

I accidently let a chuckle slip. Jason follows Jerry to the starting area. "Okay, man, just run fast. When you're about a foot from the edge of the dock, take a light jump onto the mat. A few steps, jump, and turn, hands out. Got it?"

Jerry turns and pats Jason vigorously on his shoulder. "Got it. Don't worry." Jason's expression a mix between uncertainty and worry, he nods and steps back. We all watch as Jerry sets his stance. When "Hike" is yelled, everyone holds their breath. He takes off fast, running through the small patch of sand before hitting the dock, looking really promising at the speed he's going. The end of the dock comes quick, and we all stare in anticipation, until his foot pushes off too soon.

LAKE REDSTONE

"Dude, too soon!" Jason shouts.

But it's too late. Before even hitting the water mat, Jerry jumps, his body twisting. When the football goes flying, he thrusts his hand out.

Poppy's mouth opens in shock. "Holy cow, he's actually gonna catch that."

"What he's not gonna do is clear that water mat."

Behold everyone's amazement, the ball lands in his grip. Everyone goes berserk. Pride shines thick for my new pal. Then—*oh crap.*

"Oh crap."

Gravity kicks in, and he starts to drop.

"He ain't clearing that mat."

Definitely not clearing—*ouch*!

His body slams into the mat. With just the right landing, the middle of the mat splits open and Jerry rips through the center.

An animalistic screech blares from the kid next to us. His eyes wide in disbelief, he frantically jams his hands through his wild, boy-band hair. "He broke my mat! He broke my mat! My dad's gonna kill me!" he shrieks, his voice ear-piercing.

We have our ears covered as the kid curses. We all watch as Jerry pops up from the side of the mat. "Did I do it?" he shouts, still cradling the ball.

"Uh...not so much, man," Jason sighs.

"You broke my mat! You're gonna get it! All of you! Gonna break all your faces." He veers his murderous glare on us. "Who's first? You're all dead!"

Mick backs up. "Not it. Money making face over here."

The kid's brows shoot up, the same strange look as before, then he casts his focus on me. "You—you're dead." I debate on taking one for the team. How hard can this kid hit anyway? Jason steps forward and points to something over the kid's shoulders.

"Hey, who's the dude making out with your girlfriend?"

The kid shrieks again, deafening me in one ear. He spins in the direction of his friends, throwing his daggered stare at his posse, and screams, "What? Who's messing with my lady!"

"And...run," Jason says. Like déjà vu, I hit the sand hard, turning as we all run toward the boat. "Swim to the boat, Jerry!" He doesn't think twice before tossing the football, his breaststroke impressive as he swims away from the havoc.

Poppy runs ahead and grabs the towels.

We're all booking it through the water, and thankfully, Katie is already on the boat and starts the engine.

"Hey, get back here! Fist sandwiches! You're dead! All dead!"

"Jesus, he's an angry little guy." I laugh at Jason, ducking as the football wizzes past my head. We swim up to the boat, letting the girls climb up first. Casey slips, rushing, and I grab her ass and push her up. Once we're safely on board, we all search for Jerry.

"Hurry!"

"You got this!"

"Swim faster, you moron!"

The little thug has now gathered his posse and they're headed our way. They're vigilant in their young age and making pretty quick headway on catching us.

"Go! Go! Go!" I shout, feeling the pressure.

"We need to leave him." Casey slaps Katie's arm. "We're not leaving your husband, Jesus."

"His fault. He shouldn't have gotten us into this."

Jerry finally grabs at the ladder, and we reach down, pulling him up. Before he's fully on-board, Mick throttles the boat and we shoot across the lake. Jerry throws himself into a chair and we all huff, doing the same.

"I can't say I planned on doing so much running on this vacation," Jason says.

Casey raises her hand, her chest rising and falling in long pants. "You can say that again."

Jerry gets up and makes his way to the back to the cooler. Bending down, he opens it and fishes out a can. When he stands and diverts his attention back to us, he's wearing a goofy grin, smiling from ear to ear. Holding up the can, he says, "Celebratory spritzer anyone?"

CHAPTER THIRTEEN

Casey

I crack open a Corona, jam it into an "I'm gonna drink you pretty" koozie, and take a seat in the open lawn chair on the bottom porch. The girls are all lounging while the guys try another round of pickleball.

"No one even try getting me to leave this house for the remainder of the trip. It's clear nothing good happens when we leave."

"Amen, sister," I praise to Katie as I take a swig of the chilled beer. Katie starts in on a rant about Jerry while I rest my back on the chair, my sunglasses hiding my wandering eyes as I take in Jim. His shirt's long gone, his muscles and tattoos on display. My tongue wets my lower lip when his stomach muscles tighten as he pulls his shoulder back to take an impressive swing at the ball. The butterflies dancing around in my belly do a summersault, fluttering around. My mind can't seem to fully process how crazy this situation is. Images from our first unexpected kiss to the even more unexpected realization we're actually into each other float inside my head. He started out being a fable I made up to pretend I was in this great relationship with this great guy. But he's not a fantasy anymore.

He slams at the next ball, getting Jerry out. As if feeling my heavy gaze on him, he turns my way, and with his to-die-for signature smile, winks at me. Excitement shoots up my spine, causing my ears to tingle. My cheeks blaze with pleasure. I lift my hand and offer him a tiny wave in return. The end of our trip is rapidly approaching. Soon, we'll be back to regularly scheduled programming. But the exciting part is there's a date planned after this. I've already mentally dug through everything I own and picked out the perfect first date outfit. Which is sitting at a store, because I don't have zilch in my closet.

I get excited to eat this burger he speaks so highly about, but then panic about eating in front of him. Should I nibble? Do girls eat on first dates nowadays? Should I order a salad? Maybe I should eat beforehand so I don't get out of control and start munching off his plate when I clear mine in record time. *Dummy, you've been eating in front of him all weekend.* Right. Back to savoring that juicy burger.

I can't remember the last time I've been on a date I was actually excited for. Well, I was excited for the one Poppy set me up on a few months ago. He had made us reservations at a popular barbeque place, and when it came time to order, I'd been salivating over what I was going to get. Me and my love for food had stalked out their menu days in advance. The problem was when the waitress came to take our orders, he ordered for me! Two salads, dressing on the side.

I about died!

Then I pretended I was sick and left, meeting some

friends at my favorite Mexican place. Thank god it was all-you-can-eat Taco Tuesday. I ate 'til my regret for accepting another blind date, which I swore I'd never do again, overrode my love and fullness of tacos and guacamole.

I hope he still plans on breaking all first date protocols and calls right away. Since my weeks are pretty open—being jobless and all—I don't have anything to stand in my way of going out. Pretty open. As in, maybe I can invite him up to my place and we can start our date right then. I shake my head, knowing I'm being silly. He probably has plans. Obligations. Priorities. Like his band, his bar. This also brings a topic I wish was all around avoidable—his real life, his real job, his real identity.

My reaction to his suggestion on telling the group was rude. But I panicked. He may see it as a simple fib, but it's more. I lied to my friends, leading them on for weeks about my boyfriend. I lied to their faces, and even when I knew June was becoming suspicious, I shut her down with more lies—fake stories and feelings and blah! I can't tell them now. They'll think so low of me. And how embarrassing to face them all and admit I had to conjure up this plan to trick everyone.

Jim hits another ball against Jason and scores a point, then chest bumps Mick.

My pleasant mood trips off a cliff and plummets into a pile of betrayal and lies. Jim's really bonded with everyone. How will they take being lied to? They've all become really close over the past two days. Would they feel betrayed by Jim? Or would I come out as the horrible friend who lies and fools people?

Maybe this isn't a good idea. We're only being silly and living in the moment. Maybe it would be best if we go our separate ways. Keep both our reputations intact and that be that.

My mood finds another ledge to throw itself off. I mentally take back the outfit I had in mind, even though it was going to look super cute on me and try to convince myself burgers aren't even that great.

"What's brought that sour face on?" June sits next to me.

"I'm a fraud."

"A fraud?"

Oh, frack. I bite my loose tongue and snap out of my funk. "Uh, yeah. I can't drink this beer. I tried. Should stick to the spritzers." Lies. More lies. I love Corona. Especially on Tuesdays taken down right after a round of tequila.

"Oh, okay." She's quiet as we both stare off, watching the game. The way they all laugh and throw playful jabs at one another, as if they've been friends forever, jabbing at my own integrity in the process. When Mick and Jim win the game and go in for the biggest bro hug, my stomach pangs, feeling more like a stab straight through my guilty conscious.

"Hey, June?"

"Yeah?"

I fiddle with the bottle, tearing a piece of foam off the koozie. "Have you ever told a white lie—one you wished you would have been truthful about in the beginning, but now that the lie is out there, you don't know how to take it back?"

She's quiet for a moment, her eyes trained ahead. "I can't say I've *never* told a lie before. I tell my kids all the time how spicy ice cream is so they don't dare touch mommy's stash." We both laugh. "I think it depends on if the lie is hurtful.

People tell little white lies all the time. It's just the way of the world. I'm not sure what you're truly asking, but if someone's told a lie, and it's hurtful or will hurt someone because of it, I think it's best to be honest over deceiving."

Geez, June, way to take your metaphoric knife to my devious soul.

"Are you asking me this because you lied?" The biggest one ever. And I won't be hurting only myself when the truth comes out. Her eagle eyes burn into me, forcing me to look over. Deep down, I want to confess the crummy thing I did and be free of the heaviness burdening me. But I don't. Because I'm a coward.

"Nah, just lied on a resume. Made it out to seem like I was way more qualified. Really wanted the job, but probably won't get it now. Thought about telling the truth, but I think that ship's sailed. Better luck next time." Or in my relationship where I find a guy who's perfect for me and I don't go messing it all up with lies and deceit.

The conversation is cut short when the guys join us, Jason falling into June's lap. Jim comes at me, his skin glistening from sweat. I start shaking my head. "Oh no, don't you dare—ahhh!" I squeal as he falls into me, his perspired chest pressing against mine.

"Not what you said last night when we were all hot and sweaty, babe." He bends down and kisses me quick. No shocker, the guys all hoot and howl, while my traitorous girlfriends laugh at his joke. I go for the kill, pinching his nipples, and he groans, snagging my fingers and bringing them above my head. "Tsk, tsk. Only in the bedroom. I don't feel comfortable revealing our safe word in front of your friends." My eyes roll, fighting and losing the battle as a smile breaks across my face.

"You're ridiculous."

His lips land in another quick peck. "Ridiculously enthralled with you."

This round is less laughing and more sighing. Feeling shy that he's made us the center of attention, I bow my head so he can't take hold of my lips a third time.

"Stop," I say, low in warning.

"Stop being so smitten with you? Can't do that." We have a stare off until I can't fight it any longer. My smile breaks through, and I allow him his hard-earned third kiss.

"Okay, Jesus. You're making us all look bad." Jim's laughter vibrates against my lips. "Anyone hungry?" Jason slides off June's chair to stand.

"Starved," Jim answers, but it seems his response is meant for an audience of one.

"Good. Let's get some food on the grill. Preferably not Jerry's burgers." No one hesitates to nod and hum in agreeance. Of course, my mind is so far in the gutter, food is the last thing I'm hungry for.

"Fat chance."

"Oh, come on! We've been in the sun all day. I need to keep my shirt on."

Poppy rolls her eyes. "Seriously, we're not being skins. Just play the damn game." She gives her back to her husband as she gets ready to serve. Thank god she doesn't give in. For one, I'm not sure my game will be on point without a top on. Second, I'm still super full from dinner. Lucky for us all, Jim took over and manned the grill and made us the tastiest burgers. Not to mention the pound of ranch dip I had, along with corn salad. Okay, fine, throw in a few cookies too. My stomach is still so bloated, it's going to take an army to digest it all.

"Fine, but the winners get the losers' tops."

Poppy shoots warning daggers at Mick, and he throws his hands up. "Got it. Tops stay on." Everyone takes their positions, and Poppy serves the ball, slamming into Jim's corner. The game begins, and it doesn't take long before the relaxed smiles are gone, replaced with serious intensity across the court. Mick takes no mercy on Poppy as he whacks the ball in the corner. She takes no mercy on her husband as she slams it back, causing him to miss the shot.

"What the hell was that?" Mick barks, fetching the ball. Poppy shrugs and gets ready for another serve. The game heats up with every hit of the ball. Jim doesn't go easy on me, and I miss two incoming balls. Poppy throws her mean glare at me as the two across the net fist pump. When it's my turn to serve, I get a good slam into Mick's corner, but his paddle meets the ball with finesse, landing on our side mere inches from the net. I have to dive to get it, scraping my knees on the concrete. Jim shows no mercy and slams the ball back on our side, causing me to miss it.

"Play hard, get hard," Jim huffs, and I get up, brushing off my knees. I aim a mean stare at him, but it simply rolls off him. He and Mick are too consumed in winning. Poppy holds her paddle up, calling for a timeout.

"No way, no timeouts. Take the beating and get off the court, woman!" Mick says.

Poppy comes up to me, and we give the guys our backs, leaning our heads in together. "Okay, this may actually work in our favor. I think we can beat these idiots fair and square, but I'm not opposed to playing dirty. I say we give them a taste of their own medicine."

I like her style. "Okay. How?"

"I know my husband, and I can guarantee one thing that always makes him lose focus."

"Ew, do I really want to know the answer to this? I feel like I already know way too much about your sex life." Mick likes to share their stories when he's had a few too many. If I ever wanted to become a dominatrix, I know the couple to get starter information from.

"Hey, I see where your mind's going, and don't knock it 'til you try it. Also, not what I'm getting at. I'm talking about giving them exactly what they're asking for."

"Okay, you lost me. Last time you suggested this, it was in high school and we had to pretend we were into each other to impress Jeremy Miller 'cause you heard he was into that stuff. I gotta say, Pop, we're a little too old to be experimenting."

She rolls her eyes at me. "No, geez, I'm suggesting we give them what they're asking for—skins. Mick might be showing off to his new butt buddy—no offense—but me taking my top off will be a game killer for him. *Trust me.*"

"That's enough. Play or forfeit."

Oh, hell with it. All the fashion magazines say pot bellies are the new crave anyways. Poppy and I nod heads and break apart. But not before reaching out and caressing each other's arms. We silently share a laugh, then throw our tank tops off, leaving us in only our skimpy bikini tops.

"Jesus, what are you doing?" Mick gripes as I position myself to serve.

"Giving in to your request. It is hot out here. These babies can use some sun anyhow."

Mick's brows turn up in annoyance. Poppy takes her place on the court, and I prepare to serve. The first round is a wash since Jim has yet to be affected. But Mick hasn't lost his scowl. Two hits back and forth, and Mick finally misses, allowing us a point. There's a take-no-prisoners motto between us, and we come together for a gentle chest bump, holding together a little too long.

"Okay, knock it off. We're skins. We called it already."

"Game's already in play, babe."

Jim pats his bud on the shoulder, telling him it's going to be okay, and prepares to serve. That's when I bend my knees and squeeze my elbows in, pressing my boobs together to form an impressive cleavage shot. Right before Jim serves, I blow him a kiss, causing the ball to slam into the net.

"Oh, come on! Interference!" Mick yells as us girls share a good laugh. Jim is still staring at my chest as I snag the ball from under the net and take another serve. This time, Mick makes contact, slamming it past Poppy's block, getting a point. He puffs out his chest, going in for a man bump. Poppy shakes her head and snatches up the ball, preparing for her serve. This one lands in Jim's square, and he makes a smooth swing, knocking it back into Poppy's corner. Back and forth, they battle to knock each other out. Every swing is intense as we all watch the ball ricochet, but it's Mick's tormented face that takes the cake. Every time Poopy takes a swing, Mick grunts. On the fourth swing, he's had enough and tosses his paddle to the ground.

"That's it! We forfeit!" Jim and I throw our hands up in defense. Mick prowls over to the other side, gunning straight for his wife. She doesn't seem shocked whatsoever, wearing her smug grin as he makes it to her and throws her over his shoulder. "Damn, woman. You're gonna pay for this," he says, then storms off the court, disappearing inside.

LAKE REDSTONE

Flames from the fire crackle, sending sparks into the night sky. The bonfire is in full bloom as our lawn chairs circle around the campfire. June brought all the fixings to make s'mores while Jason brought the tequila to wash the gooey goodness down. I'm currently laying against Jim, my back resting against his chest as we cuddle together in the lawn chair. Poppy and Mick are telling the story about how they met.

"Oh my god," Jason laughs, holding his chest. "Tell the story again, how you found him hanging on the pole."

Poppy shakes her head, releasing a small giggle. "We'd gotten a distress call about a model shoot gone horribly wrong. A model had slipped off a trapeze rope and got tangled, unable to free himself. When our team arrived, Mick had been hanging upside down for some time. I guess his acrobatics weren't on par yet."

"Hey! It was my first shoot. Give me some credit!"

"Anywho, when I got there, he was pretty high up, hanging upside down in a tight speedo. They were worried at how long he'd been that way, with all the blood rushing to his head, so I had to climb up and cut him down." I can't fight the chuckle, knowing what comes next. "When I got up there, I realized his speedo was all caught up in the rope. Only way of getting untangled and down was to cut it off."

"Uh oh," Jim says.

"Hey! It was probably the best moment of her career!" Mick chimes in.

"That's still to be determined. So, I pulled out the army knife I had shoved in my belt and did what I had to do. What I wasn't factoring in was where I was positioned at the time. I was more focused on getting the poor guy down before he passed out. When I slit the knife through the speedo, the only thing that fell was his junk against my face. And did I mention he had a full-on erection?"

Everyone bursts out laughing.

"If you wouldn't have been so hot, I wouldn't have had a boner."

"You were hanging upside down about to fall and splatter your brains on the floor. Why would you even think to have a hard-on?"

"You smelled good. And talked sweet to me."

Again, everyone bursts out laughing. Maybe one of the best stories ever. Needless to say, Poppy got him down, and after having the nerve to ask for her number, she didn't even hesitate to give it to him.

Poppy and Mick start going back and forth between who loves who more as we all sit back and enjoy their cute banter. Jim wraps his arms around my waist, placing his chin on my shoulder. "What did you want to be when you grew up?" he asks softy, so no one else can here.

I take a minute, enjoying this little game we have going before I reply. "A circus acrobat," I reply, feeling the rumble of his chest against mine.

"For some reason, that answer does not shock me."

I'm not sure if that's a good or bad thing. "My turn. What was the meaning of your first tattoo?"

"It's over my hip bone. Right here." His fingers brush along my lower pelvic. "It's a line of music symbols. A quote formatted from music notes. I got it shortly after Jameson died. A notation of chords translates into 'If I die without scars, then I never truly lived.' It seemed fitting at the time. Life, whether good or bad, is a battlefield, and if you come out of it unscathed, did you truly ever fight to live?" Holy poetic Batman. The meaning in it. So much truth. Life is hard. And it hurts sometimes, and not all paths lead to a safe travel home. But sometimes in pain comes flourishment. I'm not who I am today without the faint wounds of my own journey to get here. I want to wish my friends away and bask in this moment—just the two of us. Beg him to explain every other tattoo marking his beautiful body. "My turn." Changing the topic, his voice sinks to a husky whisper. "Where would you like to go on date number two?"

His question adorns the walls of my smitten heart. My cheeks blush crimson at the mere vision of us after this weekend on not one, but two dates. Excitement settles in my core, and I swivel in his lap to suggest his bar when we're interrupted by Jerry.

"Hey, Casanova, your turn. How'd you two meet?" Our attention is stolen as everyone stares at us, inquisitive, waiting.

Crap.

Crap!

Our perfect bubble pops. I become restless in Jim's arms, forcing him to ease up on his hold. "Yeah, nothing great like Poppy and Mick's story." *Leave it be. Leave it be.*

"No, I'd actually really like to hear this one," June pipes in. I fight not to scowl at her. Since when has she been out to get me? I'm lost on what to say. I don't have this answer. And the fidgeting of Jim behind me worries me he's about to spill our dirty little secret.

"Come on, man, spill! We're all friends here. If it's sappy, we promise not to make fun of you for too long." Mick snorts out a laugh, and Poppy slaps him on his thigh. I watch Jim, heavy contemplation brewing, and my stomach takes a nosedive. He's staring at Mick, guilt written all over his face. Goddammit, he's going to tell them.

"I mean…it's kinda a funny story—"

"Yeah, can I talk to you real quick?" I cut him off. There's a flicker of confusion around the fire, but I can't allow him to do this.

"Case, it's fine."

"Yeah, but can I talk to you? Alone? As in inside?" I get up, not giving him the option to answer with anything but a yes. I tug at his arm so he moves with me, and we walk up the small patch of grass until I'm pulling open the back door. Once he's inside and the door shuts, I go to town.

"What the heck do you think you're doing?"

He fumbles with what to say until he finally spits out, "What? Mick asked, and I couldn't lie to him."

I throw my hands up, huffing loud enough to send a ripple across the lake. "Seriously? You're willing to blow this whole thing up for me because you don't want to lie to *Mick*?" I stare at him while he simmers on my question.

"Listen. I think the gig is up anyway. June is on to us, and honestly, if she looks at me one more time with that sweet, *I know what you did* look, it's only a matter of time before I panic and spill the beans anyway. And yes, I don't want to lie to Mick. He's great. Super talented. Has a great hairline. And is magic—"

He shuts up when I throw my hands up again, almost snipping him in the nose. "Jesus Christ, you're ridiculous!"

He starts to jump on the frustration train by losing a bit of his own easy-going front. "What? Why is that ridiculous? That I like your friends and don't want to lie? That it's actually eating me alive to be so deceptive?"

"Not my problem. The deal wasn't to fall in love with my friends and sell me out."

"It wasn't in our deal to end up falling for each other either, so…"

His words hit me hard. He may as well have just sucker punched me. I didn't plan this either, but I won't let him sabotage it. "Not your call. You keep your mouth shut or you can pack up your stuff and leave."

His eyes widen in shock, but there's no hiding the specs of anger that come along with it. His jaw tenses. He takes a deep breath. His hands thrust through his thick hair. "What are you so afraid of? You think so low of your friends, they'll all turn their backs on you over a small fib?"

"You know nothing about me and my friends. Stay out of it."

He takes a step toward me. "I know enough to see you're too scared to let your friends see the real you. Admit you're not as happy as you come off."

"That's not true at all."

"Oh, it's not? Do any of your friends know your real feelings about them? How you can't stand all your decisions being under their microscope?"

"Stop."

"No. Answer the question."

He steps even closer, and I thrust my arms out, pushing him away from me. "My friendships are none of your business!" I snap.

"You made them my business when you hired me to play your perfect boyfriend for the weekend! When you embedded me into your life to pretend we're so in love and perfect together. Well, now I'm fucking in it and it's not fake anymore. I'm sick of lying. I don't want to be your decoy. I like you, Casey, a lot, and I'm done playing this fake boyfriend game."

"Well, then just leave—"

"You guys okay in here?" My head whips to Poppy.

"Fine. Can you give us a moment?"

"No, we don't need a moment. We need to be honest."

I throw my burning eyes back at Jim. "No, *we* do not."

"Uh, can we go back to the hiring part?" Katie chimes in, standing next to Poppy. My eyes slam shut at her question. How much did she hear? When my eyes open, they hold a fierce anger toward Jim.

"Actually, this conversation is over. We're done here. Everyone can go back down to the fire." I whip around, needing to push my nosy friends back down the hill, but Jim doesn't let it go.

"Why are you still hiding?"

"I'm not hiding from anything!" I shout, spinning back around.

"Bullshit!"

"Bullshit?" I seethe, losing my gumption.

"Whoa! Casey knows how to properly swear?"

We both whip our heads back, and I give Katie the shut-up-or-ship-out death stare. Bringing my attention back to Jim, I continue. "You know what I'm hiding from? Judgment from every single person who has all these great things in their life and won't stop comparing it to the ones who don't have shit. I'm sick of being compared. Sick of being felt sorry for. I'm sick of trying to be the person everyone expects and hopes me to be! And now, I certainly don't need you, a *nobody*, to judge me either."

There's a harsh intake of breath behind me.

"Yeah, I'm still gonna need you to go back to that hiring part."

"Stay out of this, Katie!" I lash out, my breathing heavy. But my harsh breaths aren't the only ones pounding in my ear. Jim's chest is rising and falling in thick, unforgiving pants. There's no denying I hurt him with my selfish tyrant. My lower lip starts to tremble. I turn back to my friends, finding the rest of the crew observing a few feet back.

They all heard.

They all know.

I bring my attention stare to Jim. "Happy now?"

"Far from it," he snaps back, then turns, giving me his back, as he walks farther into the house. My urge to run to him and apologize hits me hard, but my feet don't move. "Where do you think you're going?" I yell instead, staying combative.

"Doing what my *boss* asked. I'm leaving."

I gasp at his admittance. He's going to leave? My stomach tightens, nauseating guilt surging through me. How did we get here? The day started out so beautifully, and now we're at war, the beautiful bubble we've so quickly created popping in such an ugly way. My heart hurts as much as my pride. I can feel the disappointed eyes of my friends searing into my back. "Feel free to quick pay me that five grand and I'll be out of your hair, babe," he mocks, heading up the stairs.

Five grand? "Wait a minute! I'm not paying you five thousand dollars! My ad was for five hundred!" He stops and faces me. "Don't think so, sweetheart. Five grand. Check your listing. No one would sign up for this for five hundred." His insult burns into me, lashing at every insecurity I try so hard to keep buried. He dismisses the torment I expose through my stricken eyes. He doesn't even offer me a flicker of compassion, his cold stare blank of any emotion he's shown to me. Giving me his back once again, he continues his trek up the stairs.

"You're crazy. I'm not paying you five thousand dollars. You didn't even do what you were supposed to!" I yell. My callous words are far from the real torment stabbing holes inside my chest. I bite the inside of my lip, hoping he comes back. Fight with me. *For* me. Give me just a glance of compassion I need to break down the stubbornness that's ruining the only good thing that's happened to me in so long. But he doesn't. He doesn't say another word, the slamming of the bedroom door ending the conversation.

My walls go back up, my anger standing guard. I stomp my foot on the ground and grumble, until I remember my friends are all at my back. I turn to face them, my face hot. "You all enjoy the show? Next one starts in about fifteen minutes," I bite out and walk off down the hill before they witness my messy sob show.

Not much of anything else was said after our blowout. Jim disappeared one way, and I the other. I didn't bother going up to our room to see if he had slept there or packed his belongings and left. I made my way to the boat, and after crying and sulking over what a disaster my life had become—or had already been—I must have passed out.

The rays of the morning sunshine are bright, stabbing me in the eyes. I stir in the small, twisty boat chair, groaning in discomfort. The faint scent of coffee seeps into my nostrils. I ping one eye open and peek to my left to see Poppy sitting next to me, sipping on a cup of joe. "Morning," she says, her tone friendly.

"Don't."

"I wasn't planning on it."

I shuffle in the seat and sit forward, my bones aching from being crammed in the chair all night. "Is he...?"

"Yep. Slept on the couch. Shame. If I knew your room wasn't being used, I would've moved up there. Mick's snoring was out of control last night."

He didn't leave—which means I have to face him, and I said some horrible things.

"Is he up?"

She nods "He is. Grumpy. Not even giving Mick the googly eyes. He was trying to call a ride, but Mick offered to take off early instead. So, if you're done sleeping like a bum on this boat, let's pack up and head home, 'kay?" She pats me on the shoulder, gets up, and hops off the boat.

"Hey, Poppy?"

She peers my way, her caring smile making me feel even worse. "I'm sorry. For last night. What you heard."

"No need to apologize to me. We all do crazy things. But I think you may want to use that apology on someone else. Don't let your pride cloud what can be your future." And with that, she heads up the hill.

My pride. Which is me not being brave enough to admit my faults. When we were kids and Poppy and I would bicker or get into fights with neighboring kids, our parents would always say, if you're the one who messed up, it's time to fess up. While Poppy would always do the right thing, I would suddenly find a piece of fuzz on the wall, refusing to take any sort of responsibility. Even now, twenty years later, the thought of having to gear up and fess up has me in search of that piece of fuzz. How am I supposed to face my friends now without them looking down on me?

I wish I could throw myself over the boat and drown into the deepest part of the lake to avoid the confrontation with Jim. With my friends. Avoid admitting I'm a liar and a fraud. Not only did I say some cruel things to Jim, I referred to my friends as insensitive and uncaring. I was upset, and some of those emotions translated into some hurtful words.

I stare up at the house. It's alive with everyone in and out, packing stuff into their cars. I throw the beach towel off me and stand, knowing I can't avoid life and live on this boat forever.

I hop off and make my way up. I spot June first. She smiles at me, but it doesn't meet her eyes. She's disappointed. Jason is throwing a cooler into the back of their SUV and ruffles the top of my head as I walk by. Jerry is sitting on a lawn chair, sleeping, while Katie organizes the extra coolers. "Hey, you want any of these leftover spritzers?" she asks as I pass.

"All yours," I reply, heading inside. My heart is starting to beat hard and fast. I'm scared to see him. Worried at the way he'll look at me. The way he did last night when I threw those harsh jabs his way. When I make it upstairs into our shared room, it's empty. His stuff has been cleared out, only leaving my belongings scattered around. I slowly pack, my mood slumping with each pair of clothes I jam into my bag. When I'm done, I head back outside where everyone is waiting to leave. Hugs and goodbyes are passed around, but I skip them and climb into the back of Poppy and Mick's car. A part of me was hoping Jim would ride with someone else, but when I slide in, he's already in the backseat, his head pressing against the window. He appears to have already fallen asleep. Which is good for me. I don't know how to start off. What I should say. So, I get lucky, and say nothing at all. Poppy and Mick climb in and we make our four-hour trek home.

Unlike Jim, I don't sleep a wink. I spend the entire ride staring out the window, going back to everything I did wrong. He's right. I should have never lied. I shouldn't have put him in the position I did. Remorse sits heavily on my mind. I want to wake him up and tell him, but I also didn't want to make another scene in front of my friends. I think he knows that too. A part of me feels he's faking sleep. He had as much interest in going at it with me with an audience as I did. So, I let him pretend to sleep the whole way.

I pull up the ad site where the whole stupid thing started, and low and behold, I had set the price to five thousand dollars. Looks like drinking margaritas and updating the ad with one eye open turned out to be a very costly mistake. For my heart—and my wallet.

I do the only thing that's right and quick pay through the app. I transfer my emergency fund money and hope it's enough to cover the cost. I hear his phone ping, notifying him of my payment as we pull up to my apartment.

"We're here," Poppy says. Jim wastes no time. Opening his door, he hops out.

"Appreciate the hospitality," is all he says before jogging down the street toward the bus stop. I jump out as well, calling for him, but he doesn't turn around. The bus has impeccable timing. He jumps on as soon as it stops, disappearing into the sea of passengers.

My shame only gets worse realizing Poppy and Mick witnessed the whole thing. Poppy calls my name, but I don't bother stopping to address her. Without going back for my backpack, I escape inside my building.

CHAPTER FOURTEEN

Casey

Three weeks later...

Man, life is good.

Hot though, because this sun is scorching my skin. I'm blaring the words to Bon Jovi's 'Livin' on a Prayer', possibly sounding like a howling dog in heat, while sunbathing on the roof of my building. The good thing about being unemployed and half the tenants at real jobs, no one is around to yell at you for blasting eighties music and singing at the top of your lungs.

They also probably get paychecks and feel pride in themselves for not being losers.

Well, they're all also sober, so I win. I take a sip of my third margarita, which is super tasty since I added half a can of lime spritzer to it. An incoming call interrupts the best part of the song, and I decline it. I get back to bellowing more lyrics when my phone rings again. "Seriously, no manners!" I sit up and pull my shades down to see Poppy calling for the forty-billionth time. I give her the end button like I've done every time she's called, and drop my phone, setting my shades back in place.

When I threw myself into my apartment that day, a few things happened. I got mad. How dare Jim sell me out like that. I paid him his money, he should have apologized for selling me out. I even went as far as trying to call him to tell him off. It was then I realized I didn't even have his number. So, I opened the app, but his profile had been deleted. I huffed and puffed until the anger shifted to sorrow.

I shouldn't have put him in the position I did. I shouldn't have put anyone in it. I need to grow up and accept I'm not going to be like everyone else—be happy with who I am, and not worry so much about what people think of me. If my friends were my friends, they would accept me for the loser I am. And all I had to do was pick up the phone and tell them that. Apologize for betraying their trust and hope they accept it and move forward from this disastrous situation.

Then again, I'm a coward. Disappearing and no longer having friends was a lot easier than sucking up my pride. I couldn't face Poppy. I definitely couldn't face scary June. I bet Katie would take it the best, but still, the questions on top of questions they would ask. I want to avoid those.

So, I'm avoiding everyone.

Poppy and I had a great run, but she'll find a new best friend. Same with June and Katie. And I'll stick to being the same ol' me, running my life like a wild freight train with no working brakes headed straight for a steep cliff.

I denied the aching feeling in my heart when little things would trigger thoughts of Jim. Meat, mostly. How the hell does raw meat in a local grocery store scream, "I really liked you and I messed up, so start getting emotional right in this store and throw the hamburger buns at the dude waiting in line next to you"?

Let's not mention the way he's tainted music for me. All the words of every song that plays sing through my speakers, out to get me, every verse a lyrical jab. Why do so many people sing about being wronged? Like, I get it! I'm a huge jerk!

Days went by, and weeks, and it all still felt like a million pounds resting on my shoulders. There's no denying my guilt is totally deserved. But the regret is what's pulling me down. I missed our first date, or what was to come of it. I miss his laugh. His smell, his lips. I miss how he made me feel human, not like such a screw up.

I miss *him*.

I resorted to drinking because at least that didn't make me feel like such a disappointment. But then it made me feel like a disappointment when even *that* would betray me, my emotional side taking the wheel and turning me into a blubbering mess—and nothing on Google would tell me how to turn back time. My now only friend, Olivia, from the coffee shop suggested witchcraft, but I'd probably turn myself into a toad before conjuring up a spell to make Jim fall at my doorstep begging me to take him back.

Okay, that's over wishing. At least show up at my doorstep so I can beg for *him* back.

But even though I'd be willing to suck up my pride, the damage is already done. He's gone with no way to find him. And trust me, my drunk Google searches are top money. He's in the wind. I bet Jim isn't even his real name.

My phone rings again, and I shut it off. I don't need music to enjoy myself. I have the sun and the peacefulness of myself. I toss my phone into my beach bag and snuggle into my chair, allowing the rays to warm my face—

"So, Poppy *is* telling the truth."

My body jolts so hard, I throw myself out of my chair. My sunglasses fall off my head, and I knock over my drink. "Jesus! How'd you get up here!?" I gasp at Katie, who's standing a short distance from me.

"Guy in four-B always had a thing for me so he let me in. Followed the loud music and garbage. Seriously how many pizza boxes can one collect? And what's the deal with the suitcases?"

"I'm waiting for a large money transaction to go through. When it does, I won't be able to cover rent forcing my eviction to the streets. I'll need those boxes to build a box house and—wait why are you here again?"

"Checking to see if it's true. You've been end buttoning the world while wallowing in your own self-pity. Looks fun, not gonna lie."

I pick myself up off the ground and adjust my glasses. "Well, it's a lot of work, so if you don't need anything important, I'm gonna get back to it." I crawl back onto my chair, but instead of finding the exit, she takes a seat at the bottom, pushing my legs out of the way. She picks up my drink and sips what's remaining in my large glass.

"Spritzer. Nice. So, listen. I get it. We all do. You told a little lie. Okay, a bunch. I mean god, you had the whole Bob thing going for a while—or is it Jim-Bob? Just Jim?"

Ugh. I throw my shades over my eyes and lay back. "Just Jim."

"Good to know. So, I can't lie to you. Everyone was a little hurt at what you did. The guys really liked Jim. I think Mick felt the break-up more than anyone." I shake my head, adjusting my eyes that roll in the back of my head. "But that doesn't give you the right to avoid everyone as if we're the ones who did something wrong. We get it. You lied. But *you* lied. Not us. We don't deserve your cold shoulder."

Okay, geez, make me feel even more horrible. "I wasn't avoiding you all. I just didn't know what to say."

"I'm sorry for lying, guys. Wanna go out for pizza?" Okay, yeah, that sounds simple. And basic. "I heard what you said. I get it. It can't be easy sometimes. But, ya know, you forget sometimes too that the way you may look at us, we look at you. Yeah, I have a great husband and kids... well, sometimes great husband, and my kids are demons, but there are times when I envy you. I wish I was as carefree as you. That I didn't threaten everyone's life every two seconds because people aren't doing chores or I'm pulling gum out of the dog's fur for the third time in two days. That someone besides me knew how to do laundry or turn the lights off or not piss all over the toilet bowl." She turns and pats me on the leg. "Being happy isn't having the family and white picket fence. Being happy is being okay with who you are. None of us ever thought because you aren't at the same place in your life as us, you weren't happy. We all have our days we wish we were in your shoes. I've never tried to set you up with someone or push anyone on you because I thought you needed a man. I just wanted you to find love. You deserve it. You're so kind and giving. You'd make Satan smile with one of your corny jokes. But no one's intentions have ever been to make you feel like you have to be someone you're not."

I thought I was in the clear until the single tear falls past my sunglasses, exposing my true emotions. I try to fight the second, and the third, but I lose. Katie wraps her arm around me as I cry.

"I'm sorry I lied to you guys. I just didn't want you all to assume since I didn't have someone in my life, I was unhappy."

Katie breaks away. "And we're sorry for ever making you feel any other way but loved and appreciated just the way you are."

We share a smile and an understanding.

"Be honest. How mad is Poppy at me?"

Katie shrugs. "On a scale from one to you puking on her date at senior prom, I'd say, you may want to brush up on your ass kissing skills."

Son of a nutcracker. Poppy didn't talk to me for weeks after that debacle. But there was no reason for her date to break up with her afterwards. No love lost for a guy who dumps you over a little vomit.

"Listen, we're all going out tonight, and it would be awesome if you joined. Everyone misses you."

I shake my head. "I don't think that's such a good idea, I have—"

"Don't give me some bullshit excuse. I know you have nothing planned but getting margarita drunk and feeling sorry for yourself. Plus, I was only trying to be nice because you look all fragile. But I'm not asking, I'm telling."

Geez.

"I wasn't. I had other stuff like—"

"No more lies. Get up. And for Christ's sake, shower. You smell like a Mexican hooker."

LAKE REDSTONE

Katie sticks around while I shave and shower, as ordered. Probably more so I don't escape back up to the roof. I slide into a pair of ripped jeans and a band shirt I may have snagged from our lake weekend. I considered it my parting gift. I tie the end in a knot, because I still have to be fashionable, and slip on a pair of red Converse. We head out and take the bus up town where everyone is meeting. Katie fills me in on everything I've missed while playing possum.

I feel like a huge jerk while Katie tells me how Jason was inducted to the football hall of fame at the college he attended. She also didn't spare my feelings when telling me everyone but me attended. Mick's photoshoot from the lake landed him in Esquire magazine, signing a ton more modeling contracts. Said if I didn't want to have Mick's face in my head when reading any of the latest romance books, don't bother picking any up, because he was about to be everywhere.

She lays the guilt on thick by telling me she got a promotion at work, bumping her up to a higher-grade level at school. They'd all gone out to celebrate. Another round of calls I'd avoided.

By the time we make it to the bar, I feel like I have a neon sign on my forehead blaring "worst friend ever." I let Katie walk in first, just in case anyone starts to throw tomatoes at me. My nerves are on overdrive. I dig my nails into my palm, threatening to break the skin just to keep my composure. I don't understand why I'm so nervous. These have been my friends for eons.

We're cleared by the bouncer, and Katie pushes inside through the graffitied wooden door. We step into the low-lit bar, my ears immediately piquing at the chatter and laughter. Loud conversations competing with the alternative music playing from the jukebox. My nervous vibe shifts as I soak in the laughter and smiles. I'm already digging the place as we make our way through funnels of groups. My eyes catch the bar to the right, bottles glowing behind a brightly lit shelf, all my best friends, Jose, Jim, and Tito aligned in a perfect row.

I'm intoxicated by the smell of spirits and the popping of bottles, creating an easy feel inside me. Okay, so I enjoy a good bar, what can I say?

Conversations swirl in the background as we cross the dancefloor toward a cluster of tables off to the side of the small elevated stage. I spot all my friends seated around a table, leisurely sipping on their drinks of choice. It's impossible to avoid the next round of nerves that run through me. This can all end badly. It's possible I'm about to find out I suck as a friend and everyone's done with me.

I make one last ditch effort to run, but Katie seizes my arm. Our movement catches Poppy's attention. "You're alive!" she says, catching everyone's attention. All bodies twist, curious eyes landing on me.

I wave in all my awkward glory. "Fancy meeting you all here."

Jerry gets up and pulls a seat out for me. He goes in for a hug before allowing me to sit, whispering in my ear as we embrace. "Good to see you, trouble."

I squeeze a little harder than needed back. Man, I've missed them all too. "Same," I reply, then break away. The hugs and hellos are shared amongst the group before I take my seat and a waitress comes to take my order.

The light conversation continues as if it was never interrupted by my arrival. No one makes a move to mention anything from that weekend. When a few more minutes pass, I start to get fidgety in my seat. Why aren't they yelling at me? Telling me how much I suck? Shunning me for being deceitful and taking away my friend card? Their easy-going chatter is starting to frustrate me. If someone doesn't yell at me soon, I'm going to explode!

"So, then this punk tries to resist arrest, and I wasn't havin' it, I pulled out my—"

"Is anyone gonna say it?"

All eyes land on me. Okay, this is uncomfortable. I should have kept my mouth shut. The avoidance was a lot easier than the attention.

"Say what?" June asks.

Man! They're really going to make me work for it, aren't they? I take a deep breath and release. "That I'm a liar and a loser and I had to deceive you all by bribing a stranger and bringing him in the midst of our lives as a decoy to make myself look better and for you all to like me."

There's a long pause as everyone stares at me, their expressions blank.

And then everyone bursts into an explosion of laughter.

"Good one, Case," Jason laughs, then stands. "Gonna take a leak before the band goes on."

Mick stands as well and joins Jason.

"Same," Poppy says. "Gonna hit the bar for a round of shots on my way back. Everyone in?"

Everyone agrees, and I sit in my chair dumbfounded. Did I dream up this whole thing? Am I dreaming right now, and this is my subconscious playing tricks on me? I turn to Jerry, who's sipping on a beer, and poke him.

"Ouch."

Okay, he's real.

"What was that for?"

"Why aren't any of you mad at me?"

He shrugs. Just. Shrugs! "What's there to be mad at? You lied, big whoop. Everyone lies."

"Yeah, but my lie was ruthless. Savage!"

He offers me another shoulder shrug. "Last month, I lied to Katie about forgetting our anniversary. Told her my surprise was for the following day since I knew she would be expecting something."

"And was it?"

"Hell no. Totally forgot. Work was getting so hectic, my mind wasn't on anything but. Had to scramble to throw something together under her nose. Spent a ridiculous amount on a hotel, flowers, jewelry. Had to dip into my secret golf fund too."

"Did she figure it out?"

"Nope. Was beside herself and gushing over what a great husband I am." We both share in a laugh knowing Katie would have castrated him if she knew the truth. "So, you see, sometimes lies are necessary. My intentions were in the right place, and that's all that matters—unlike Jason with darts."

Confusion lathered in curiosity pings, and my eyebrows go up. "Jason?"

"Yeah, he lied to me and said he was okay at darts. He's actually fantastic and took twenty bucks from me. Lying bastard."

I sink into my chair, chuckling into my beer. I take a sip, feeling some ease to my worries. "Thanks for making me feel like less of a jerk. I truly didn't set out to hurt anyone by lying. I just...wanted to fit in, I guess."

It's his turn to rotate to face me. "Fit in? Let's not get crazy. If you weren't you, we'd probably like you less. We don't want you to fit in. You're unique and crazy and impossibly remarkable. In your own beautiful way, of course. You'd be disappointing us more if you ever changed that." I start to cry. "Hey, come here. Why the sad face? I promise no one's mad."

"I appreciate it, but it's not just that. It's the way I also treated Jim. I was so horrible to him. He hadn't done anything wrong except actually like me and want to be honest about it. I said some horrible things."

Jerry throws his arm over my shoulder and snuggles me to his side for comfort. "Have you tried telling him that?"

"No, he deleted the app we met on, and it was the only way I had to contact him. Plus, I'm sure he wants nothing to do with me."

Jerry shrugs in agreeance. "Ouch!" He releases me, cradling his stomach. "Man, still so violent."

"You're not helping my weeping heart here."

"Ahhh…" His lips curl into a mischievous smile. "So, your heart is weeping, is it?"

Drats. I just let that confession slip. My mouth opens to spew more lies about being emotionless and how nothing fazes this girl, but then I realize that same mind set is what got me into this predicament in the first place. I take a deep breath knowing what I'm about to say may ruin my cool kid factor. Jerry may laugh at me and realize I'm not such a tough cookie after all.

"Just spit it out. You look like you're trying to pass a kidney stone or something. Which let me tell you—"

"I really liked him!" There. I said it. "The way he saw me…no one's ever looked at me that way before. Like he dove deep inside all my crazy and still saw something beautiful." He saw past my insanity and still wanted to pursue whatever was happening. The way he held my hand... it was powerful, yet so gentle. He made me feel wanted and claimed, yet held me like a treasure, afraid to break me. And his kiss. It was as if he was pouring all of himself in each beautiful press of his lips against mine. He wasn't giving me this side of him because I was paying him to. He was giving me this side of him because he wanted to show me he didn't see a hot mess girl who had lost her way. He saw a beautiful disaster. "I messed up. I found a guy who made me feel weird and funny and weak in my knees when he kissed me, and I went and messed it all up because I suck and ruin everything good in my life!" I suck down my beer before anything else spews out of my mouth. I also hear if you hold your breath it fights against an obscene waterfall of tears about to cascade down my face.

"Well, that was a mouthful." Jerry leans back in his chair, taking his own big swig of beer.

"Right? And worse, I'll never know if we would have worked out because he's like a ghost and I have to suffer with this empty pit in my stomach because I was really falling for him."

Jerry grumbles, and I turn to him. "What? What was that grumble for?"

"Uhhh...if we're being honest here, I have something else to confess."

I aim my full attention at him. "What?" My hand twitches, and he jumps.

"Okay, crazy! Keep the violence to a minimum. Now, you can't just be mad at only me 'cause I'm the only one in front of you. Consider that when you try to use force, okay?"

What the hell is he talking about? "Spill," I growl.

"We all kept in touch with Jim."

"*What!*"

"We had all exchanged numbers that weekend! Poppy told Mick to stay out of it, because she was on your side, but couldn't take the lovesick puppy bullshit he was pulling and Mick ended up betraying her and calling, *which*, may I add, is another great story."

I sit up straight. "Wait, so you've been *talking* to him?"

"More like hanging out?" He states as a question.

"Jerry, it's a statement not a question!"

"Hanging out! He's a super cool dude! Down to earth. And if you care to know, he's not mad at you. We talked about it—*ouch*! Goddammit! You are crazy."

About to be certifiable. They've all stayed in touch with him? He and Jerry talked about me? My mind is spinning like a rogue roller-coaster about to fly off its track.

"Shit, please don't hit me again."

"Ugh, I'm not. What did he say?" Did he hate me? Super mad? Maybe misses me and thought I was such a great kisser he forgot how nasty Nelly I was to him? Gah! He can't answer fast enough!

"Well, he really liked my vinyl record collection. Complimented the—"

"About *me*, Jerry!"

"That you were a huge headache." He ducks as my eyes widen. "And that you were stubborn. And violent, which I agreed, *Jesus*. But he also said you were like a hidden treasure inside your crazy beautiful mind. He actually called you a beautiful disaster, but I think crazy fits—*stop!*"

"Okay, sorry, but stay on course." My heart is beating out of my chest.

"He said close to the same thing. He was rocked by the way you two hit it off. In his own crazy way, he started making plans with a girl he just met. He liked you."

"Did he say how much?" I spit back.

"We're dudes, we don't talk about feelings or that mushy shit."

I sit back in my chair in mild shock. While I've been at home sulking, my friends have been hanging out with the one person I would have answered if he had called. This also means he's had access to me this whole time. If he really wanted to try to fix what I broke, he could have reached out. But he didn't.

I take down the rest of my beer, my mood about as sour as the taste in my mouth. I want to be mad at all my friends for betraying me. But how can I? I brought this great guy into their lives. Like a glove, he fit perfectly in our circle. I've never seen Mick so smitten with anyone before. I was getting worried Poppy might actually have some competition. Jason has never offered tickets to anyone, and it took a whole hour before he made a man date to take Jim to a game.

I wave my white flag, silently admitting I can't and have no right to be upset with my friends. Who wouldn't want to hang out with such a great, talented, sexy, great kisser, smells amazing kind of guy?

"Well, I'm glad you all kept in touch." A single brow raises in disbelief. "I am! Promise. He's a great guy. It's not his fault how things went down. It was mine. I'm glad for you guys." I offer him a generous smile. On the outside, I'm sure I look happy. But on the inside, my entire soul is deflating like a balloon being stabbed by the reality of my poor decisions.

LAKE REDSTONE

"You know I love you, right?"

I smile, raising my hand, but this time, gently pat Jerry on the shoulder. "I know you do."

"It'll all work out. Okay? But you really need to get your hitting under control."

My brows scrunch together. "Come on, my hitting is not that bad—"

"Uh oh, she knows, doesn't she?"

We twist in our chairs to the rest of the group returning, Poppy holding a tray of shots.

"Are you mad?" June asks, taking the seat next to me.

I face her, offering an honest smile. "No, June-Bug, I'm not mad. More so jealous you all get to hang out with him. I'm the one who messed up. I just hope he realizes how lucky he is, because I have some pretty awesome friends." June moves closer, and we hug it out. I feel Poppy's arms go around me, and Katie squeezes in as well.

The lights start to flicker, and the already low-lit room becomes dimmer as the band begins to walk on stage. I give my back to the stage and grab a shot from the tray. Once all are spoken for, all seven hands stretch forward and meet in the middle for a toast.

"I think it's only fair I make the toast since I'm the one who brought us all here tonight," Jerry says, raising his shot.

I stretch my hand to meet in the middle. "Here's to those who've seen us at our best and our worst and can't tell the difference. To those absent and those new, may the roof above us never fall and may we as friends never fall out. Here's to you and here's to me, the best friends we'll ever be. And if we ever disagree, well, fuck you and here's to me."

In unison, we all belt out a hearty laugh and clink, tilting my head and throwing back my shot as the band begins.

"Evening, folks. We're Limited Infinity." The shot goes down, and right back up. I choke on tequila as it burns up my throat. The familiar, smoky tone wakes my entire body. Everyone has their eyes on me. Watching me. Taking in the tenseness as my hand trembles, shaking the shot glass gripped in my palm.

That voice. The way it felt humming down my sensitive skin with each press of his full lips. I close my eyes and disappear into the shadows of my self-doubt. Did he know I was going to be here? Will he burn with anger at the sight of me? Be happy I'm here? I open my eyes to Katie, who's shaking her head at me.

"You're being a pussy," she whispers, nodding for me to face the music. Literally. She's right. What in the heck am I doing? Grow a pair! Turn around!

I don't put any more thought into it. I steady my feet and rotate my body so I face the stage. The feeling of being knocked off my feet kind of freakin' hurts. The moment our eyes lock, that buzz between us threatens to toss me on my butt. His smile guts me, and when he laughs at my obvious unease, I sway on my already tottering feet.

God, his enigmatic laughter. Remembering the way his chest vibrated against mine when he laughed. I don't know what else to do but stare back at him, wishing he could see the guilt in my eyes. His hair is dark, wild, and thrown around. He's dressed in a dark pair of worn jeans, sexy boots, and a band t-shirt. Oh God Bless, we're wearing the same shirt.

"Before we get started, I wanted to play a new song for ya'll. Something I've been working on the last three weeks.

It's still raw, just like my heart, so bear with me. I wrote it for a girl. You see, this girl was like no one I've ever met. She was really violent, actually."

Laughter surrounds our table. My mouth is so dry. I part my lips, but I can't seem to find the moisture to lick them.

"We met under unusual circumstances. Two strangers colliding in an unexpected way that turned my world upside down. Her laughter stabbed at my heart, cracking it open. Her beauty starved me of each breath. Her gentle embraces and the feisty hold she had on me sparked a fire that enveloped every part of me." He pauses a moment to play a few chords, sending an angelic tune into the crowd. "You see…this girl? The first moment I locked eyes on her, I couldn't stop myself. I may have stolen our first kiss the first time we met, but she's the bigger thief here, because she stole my heart."

"Now, I'm gonna take a chance and bring that girl on this stage and show her just how crazy I am about her." He lets go of the mic, and with his guitar still strapped over his shoulder, he jumps off the stage, heading in my direction.

Oh, son of a monkey. My heart palpitates out of my chest as he ambles toward me in slow strides. His black boots smack against the ground, his steely hazel eyes capturing mine, burning with intention. His fingers don't miss a beat as they strum along his guitar, the rhythmic melody playing flawlessly throughout the bar. My skin starts to tingle, and heat flushes my cheeks. All my fears and wishes crash into a beautiful cacophony of excitement.

Each quick breath I inhale is harder and harder as the separation between us shrinks. Loud sounds of bottles opening, patrons drinking, fans yelling…it's all white noise to the thumping of my heart. I can't stop staring at him. He holds my vision captive. He isn't just staring at me. He's reaching into my soul and showing me, and pulling on that tether that binds us, showing every ounce of emotion he holds for just me.

When he makes it up to me, I'm dizzy on my feet. "Hi." One word, laced with a myriad of emotion.

"Hi," I force out, my voice thick.

His smile grows as his eyes travel down to my shirt and back up. "Nice shirt." And I die of embarrassment, silently begging for the floor to collapse under my feet, shooting me into oblivion. He reaches for my hand, and I panic, feeling the stares of everyone in the joint. "Wait, what are you doing?"

"What does it look like? I'm trying to win the girl."

Thump.

Thump.

THUMP.

That's the pounding of my heart about to explode. I took science. I clearly understand where the Earth's axis of rotation intersects with the sun and tilts and—oh, *whatever*! What I'm trying to say is time just stopped. Stood still for a fraction of a second the moment those five auspicious words left his mouth. And in that spec of a moment, the knots in my stomach release with the promise in his stare. As time collapses, I fall hard and fast. But the greatest part is the way his piercing hazel eyes gleam with life, as if they're telling me *his* story.

He's falling with me.

I accept his hand, mine shaking in his hold. Keeping focus on his strong chin and lustrous smile for strength, he helps me from my chair and guides me back to the stage. A sudden squeal erupts from my throat when he wraps me in his arms and hops onto the stage. He sits me on a tall bar stool and pulls a second stool next to me so we're facing.

He leans in, his voice husky, almost a whisper. "Hi, my name's Jim," he says, reaching out to shake my hand again. My cheeks flood with color. I run my tongue over my bottom lip. I stick my hand out to shake his. "I don't think we ever properly met. So now, I want to introduce you to the real me." He holds my hand longer than normal, slowly releasing, the tips of his fingers tickling the inside of my palm.

Placing his lips back to the mic, he says, "This one's called 'Beautiful Disaster'." My heart halts. The world disappears. It's just him and I. He brings his warm fingers back to the guitar, creating a soft tone with the stroke of a few strings. And then, with a voice rich and smooth like velvet, he begins to sing.

"If I had the chance to tell you, I'd confess.
You're stuck in my head.
The disaster in you made me a beautiful mess.

You stripped my heart of its self-doubt,
And gave me purpose. Became the light in my darkness.

The words I crave to say to you.
Your fire fed the beast inside me. Blazed open my soul,
You make me my own kind of crazy.

I'm at the edge of falling for something beautiful.
Give me the words I crave to hear.
That you're at the tip of this journey too.

Jump with me. Fall for the unexpected.
Say you'll try. Walk blind with me.
We may crash and burn,
But the beautiful scars you leave behind will be my peace.

This is my song to you,
My beautiful disaster."

By the time his fingers slow on his guitar, I can barely see through my swollen, tear-filled eyes. My throat is raw with emotion. He pulls the strap from over his head and places the guitar on a stand next to his stool. His foot hits the stage, and he leans forward, turning off the mic for some privacy, then brushing his thumb across my tear-stained cheek. I lean into his embrace, aching for the warmth his touch brings.

"You were supposed to fall at my feet, or at least try to rip my clothes off, not cry." His chuckle, silvery and light, he nudges my chin to look at him. "Why the tears? Am I that bad?" My natural reaction is to take a whack at him, but he chuckles louder, catching my wrist mid-slap, and pulls me into his lap. I fall into his hold willingly. My head finds solace in the crook of his neck, my nose inhaling his manly scent. "I'm sorry I left. I should have made you hash things out with me. I owed you that much."

He must be the crazy one. He's apologizing to me? I pull away, my eyes searching his. "I'm the one who should be sorry. I'm the big ol' jerk who said stupid things and lied and honestly *am* crazy." I wait for him to argue that last part. Still wait… "You're supposed to tell me I'm not crazy."

"But you are. You do hit a lot." My hand twitches. Darn it! They're all right. I do have a violent streak. "But

I'm willing to let you rough me up, in and out of the bedroom, as long as you say you'll see where this can go. I should've never walked away from you that day. Tell me it's not too late."

Before I wanted to save the world and fly across a trapeze, I wanted to be someone's person. What the hell does that mean, right? I wanted to be Cleopatra to Mark Antony, Helen to Paris, Juliet to Romeo. Okay, so all those love stories ended viciously and in death, but the passion! The sacrifice both were willing to endure to be together! That's what I spent my young years yearning for, daydreaming of, and now into my mid adulthood years craving. I wanted someone who was willing to fight hard and love harder. Every true love story was founded not on perfection, but faults. And I knew I would never be perfect. I wanted someone who would lose their breath for me, because of me. Was it pathetic how many times I've watched *Jerry Maguire* just for the "you complete me" scene? Or the Notebook to watch Noah pour his heart out to Allie, bleeding the words, "You are, and always have been, my dream"? Possibly.

And in this moment, with him holding my stare, waiting for my answer, I feel like Julia Roberts in *Notting Hill* when it's time for her to confess or walk away from what could be the best and greatest love of her life. This is where I stop looking from the outside in on someone else's fairytale romance and start my own story. This is where I fight.

I straighten myself on the stool. "I still have one question left."

"What do you mean?" He asks, a slight hint of amusement in his tone.

"Our twenty questions. You got the last one in, but I didn't. So, it's my turn."

He smiles and nods once. "Okay." He leans back on his stool, giving me the floor.

Dang-it, this all looked so much easier on the big screen than doing it in real life. I clear my throat. My hands are suddenly clammy, and I wipe them on my jeans. *Get on with it, Casey.* Okay. Tell him how you feel. Here goes nothing.

"How fast can you get me that burger you promised and back to your place?" Or chicken out as always! Dagnabbit, that didn't come out as planned. I need a redo.

His eyes blaze with happiness, his teeth on full display as he grins wide. He leans slightly into me and stretches his neck to yell behind him. "Judith! I'm gonna need two burgers to-go!"

Oh my god, he's yelling across the whole bar I'm demanding food to succumb to his beautiful song! Everyone probably thinks I'm a horrible, hungry jerk! *Hi, you just wrote me this heartfelt song to show me how much I mean to you, and my answer is feed me.* "Jim, oh my god, that came out wrong! People are going to think I have some sort of burger fetish!"

He turns back to me, his smile just as beautiful and infectious as his giving eyes and addictive laughter. His voice that sunk so far into my skin and in my soul. I can't help but smile back, just as lost. "No, it didn't. You used the one word that would tell me exactly how I'm also feeling." He leans forward, finally giving me his mouth and kissing me. When he pulls away, I'm convinced my body is floating away.

"How did burger—"

"Sometimes, you're a woman of few words. When you're passionate about something, it's not how you say it, it's the way your smile lights up your entire face. Your eyes gleam with joy, excitement, happiness. You had that look when you mentioned your favorite meal. And looking at me now, I saw that same look. I knew exactly what you were trying to say."

My heart feels like it's twirling inside my chest, sparks of static dancing over my skin. And I suddenly feel as if I'm falling. It doesn't scare me, though. Because somewhere inside me, I know he's my safety. My guide. He's the stability that calms my chaos. "I think I'm in—"

His finger presses against my lips halting the biggest confession I've ever made. "Not here. I want you naked and all to myself when we both say those three words. Got it?"

I'm pretty sure at least my panties just melted off me, so undressing will be a quick task. "Right, you have to finish playing. I can wait. I'll…uh, maybe go pay for the burgers."

His head tosses back, his laugh loud and animated. "Babe, for one, I own the bar, and two, I only scheduled one song for tonight. I took a chance. And as long as Judith gets her ass movin' on those burgers, I think I won big." With owl eyes, I look around. This is his place. His bar. I should have known with all the memorabilia on the wall. The Kurt Cobane display. "So, what do you say we get out of here? You, me, and two burgers to-go?"

I can't help but share in the same giddy smile he wears so effortlessly. "I say you throw in that strawberry milkshake and we have a deal."

He shifts his neck again, and yells, "Judith! Extra-large strawberry milkshake!" Then he kisses me hard, bringing us both to a stand, me still in his arms. He grabs the mic, turning it on. "Looks like the song worked, so everyone have a good night. Limitless Infinity will finish out the set with special guest tonight, Violet here from the *Misfits*. Wish me luck!"

The crowd breaks out into howling and clapping as Jim tosses me over his shoulder and walks off the side of the stage. I can't help my own laughter bellowing from my chest as he smacks my butt, the same giddiness as his own chest rumbles with humor.

When we get to the back entrance of the bar, he flips me, allowing me a few seconds to get steady on my feet. When he tugs me out the back door to a motorcycle parked on the side of the alley, I stop, halting him.

He turns, his expression curious and anxious. That's when I stick out my hand.

"What's up?" he asks.

"Casey. My name is Casey. And I am insanely unstable and crazy and broke, and did I mention I have a hitting problem? I just wanted to introduce you to the real me. Just in case you may have sung that sweet song to the wrong girl. You can run, and I can go back in there and eat those two burgers alone."

He pulls me into him, my chest colliding with his. "Nice try. You're not getting both burgers."

Drats! "But you don't even look hungry. I'm starved!" And I can't stop thinking about that strawberry milkshake.

His mouth covers mine in a kiss, and just like those romance flicks, he weakens my knees. His soft chuckle tickles against my lips. "Babe, I'm going to work you so hard, you're gonna learn a whole new level of starved."

Jerry McGuire, you have nothing on Jim Harrison.

I nod as if I've never felt so confident in an answer in my entire existence. "You have a deal. But I get to sip on that milkshake during the warmup." Can't have that tasty treat melting on us. I mean, what a waste—

The back door opens, and a middle-aged woman shoves

two large plastic bags at us. "I must say, she sure is prettier in person. But goddamn, you've turned into a pussy. Enjoy him, sweetheart. He tends to get grumpy when he doesn't eat." Then the door slams shut.

My brows turn up. "All true. Which means I'm gonna need to eat first. We better hurry."

I allow him to take my hand and get me settled on the back of his bike, then race us through the city, knowing when he eats, it will have nothing to do with the burgers.

If it matters, the burgers don't get eaten 'til morning.

EPILOGUE

One year later...
Just Jim

"Babe, we're here." Casey snorts and lifts her face from my shoulder, the impressions of my shirt wrinkled into her still half-asleep face. She's been super tired lately, and I worry she's coming down with something. She blinks rapidly, clearing her tired eyes. "Here, let me help you with that." I chuckle, lifting my thumb and wiping away the line of drool she has trailing down from her lip to her chin. Damn, she's cute when she's groggy. She grumbles, slapping my hand away, and I laugh, looking forward to getting her alone in that room again—the room where all the magic began.

"Shoot, did I sleep the whole time?" I'm not shocked she did either. She's been working herself day and night studying for exams, and this is probably the most sleep she's gotten in the last three weeks. Casey and I have been inseparable since that night at the bar. I brought her home, and let's just say we got to know one another on a whole deeper level. She also scammed me and ate both those burgers. Damn, my woman can eat.

But she can also blow minds like no other. She may be a free spirit with no direction, but I think she just had to find her own way. While I ran the bar and did my gigs, she went on being Casey, the magnificent fearless kitten who challenged everything. She was a handful, argumentative, and definitely crazy, and every single moment I spent in her insane world made me fall harder in love with her.

Fuck, what my heart demanded, it wasn't just love, it was borderline obsession. I couldn't get enough of her. She was resilient in a wild way. Passionate in a reckless way. And she loved in a way that scared me because sometimes it became so intense, I worried we'd both detonate with the sexual energy generating between us. One thing was certain: she was mine and I was never letting her go.

The key with Casey was not to push her. She wanted to figure out her path on her own. So, I didn't steer her. I just held her hand and went on her life journey with her. One night, while I was working at the bar, she barged through the doors like a man—or woman—on a mission. She was covered in blood, and my life flashed before my eyes. I felt automatic pain in my chest. I thought she was hurt. My hands shook as I ran to her, checking her for wounds, screaming for anyone to call 9-1-1. If this world took her from me…

Thankfully, once I about lost my fucking mind, her laughter broke through my insanity. I cupped her face and kissed her hard and long. And when I pulled back, I asked her what in the goddamn hell happened. She went to explain how she was on her way here and saw a dog get hit by a car. She demanded the bus she'd been riding to stop and jumped off and tended to the dog. She knew right away the poor pup's leg was broken, possibly more injuries, but she went on and on, telling this detailed story, her hands in the air, so animated as she explained how she saved the dog's life. She'd flagged down a car, and in so many words, made the man let her in, holding the pup, and rode with the dog to the emergency vet. After a few hours, she'd learned he was going to be just fine. She started to cry halfway through her story, and I continued to hold her as she finally had her moment. She finally found her path. It took that dog that day to help her realize her journey was to help animals. A silly idea as a kid was just buried under a pile of doubt and scrutiny. She wanted to go to school and dedicate every single moment of her time helping animals.

My heart kicked back into overdrive at the thought of her time being elsewhere, instead of with me at the bar, in my bed, or keeping me happy and at peace. Her laughter, the sound no musical instrument can make, sifted through my ears like a natural high. She eased my worries with a kiss and told me she was going to go back to school.

And so, she did.

She had a few college credits under her belt, but after this week, she just finished her sophomore year at the local university. She knew vet school was a long road, but she didn't care. She pushed herself like I've never seen. Her dedication was so goddamn admirable, it made my chest puff just knowing she was all mine.

"Not only did you sleep the whole time, you snored like a boar in heat." Poppy stretches her head toward the backseat of their car. I laugh, knowing hell has no fury like a woman being called out on her snoring.

LAKE REDSTONE

She raises her feisty hand to take a whack at Poppy's shoulder when I intervene, grabbing her built-in weapon and cushioning it into my lap. One thing that hasn't changed is her love for violence. Her explanation is it's her way of being expressive. How can you argue with that? Did I mention she said that when she was naked as the day she was born and riding me like a cowgirl at bull riding competition? Another story for another day.

Mick takes a right turn down the steep gravel road, and everyone becomes silent as we share in the moment of the symbolism from the last time we all were here. When the trees open like wings, spreading across the way, it's hard not to catch your breath the moment they separate and the vast lake comes into view. The sun, just as I remembered, lays a silver cast on the water's surface, glimmering in tranquility.

Lake Redstone.

"Man, it's just as beautiful as I remember," Casey whispers, her voice filled with nostalgic. We pull up to the lake house, and go figure, we're the last ones here. Like deja vu, we see Jason and June swinging on the porch swing while Katie and Jerry unload coolers from their truck.

"How the hell did they beat us? We left almost an hour before them," Poppy gripes, checking the GPS.

"Well, if we hadn't spent thirty minutes at the gas station while Mick arm wrestled the attendant we would have."

"Hey! He complimented my muscles and wanted to test my strength and agility. You don't say no to that."

Casey shakes her head while I silently laugh. Mick kicked that dude's ass. No one messes with Mick "The Destroyer."

Okay, so it's a little nickname we came up with one night when we were drinking and playing cards. The girls had gone to go do what girls do and left us unsupervised. Jason had brought over a bottle of Malort, which is the devil's booze, and the dares started. Before we knew it, we were hyped up on gasoline and giving each other nicknames. It would have ended all good and dandy if the dares didn't become obnoxious and we hadn't ended up at the local tattoo shop tattooing each other's nicknames on ourselves. I definitely got the shit end of the dare on that one because *Mick "The Destroyer"* is a long tattoo. Unlike Mick, who only has *Jim's Bitch* written on his left ass cheek.

When Mick parks, we all climb out and make our way over to the rest of the crew. After a round of hugs and hellos, I excuse myself to have a chat with Jerry while Casey and the rest grab our things.

"S'up, my man," I say, slapping Jerry on the shoulder.

"Nadda. Everything is all good. You wanna see it?"

I whip my head around, making sure Casey isn't anywhere in sight. "No, I don't want the girls to catch wind. June's like a hawk. She'll sense something and start giving me that smile. The 'I know' smile."

Jerry laughs, knowing exactly what the hell I'm talking about. She's been eyeing us the last few months while Jerry and I get into our secretive conversations. "All right. Plans are in place. I'll hold on to it until later. When I hear you suggest the canoe trip, I'll sneak away and stick it inside the boat."

"Thanks, man. Don't know what I'd do without a friend like you." And that's the damn truth. Jerry, just like me, is huge into collecting antique vinyl records. There's money in it, not to mention priceless glory. Working in financial banking, he helped me move around some funds, invest in some small projects, and auction off some of my records. With the money coming in, the bar was flourishing, and the band was kicking fucking ass. Since Casey fell into my life, the writing hasn't stopped. So much so, Jerry hooked us up with a buddy who was a small-time recording agent. Our first album hits actual stores at the end of the summer.

But the most exciting part is the money I just spent, with Jerry and Katie's help, picking out a ring.

I'm going to propose this weekend.

At the place where it all started. Lake Redstone gave me life. Something I never knew existed. A love so deep, there's no true way to define it. I watch Casey and wonder how someone like me got so damn lucky. I don't deserve her. But I'm going to cherish her 'til I take my last fucking breath...if she says yes.

And if she doesn't? Then I hope she likes being tied up for the remainder of her life, 'cause I ain't ever letting her go.

Casey

"Same room assignments," Katie appears behind me as I wrestle my bag out of the jammed packed trunk. "Which means you two better keep it to a minimal this year. Between your moaning and Jerry's snoring, I'll be lucky to get a full five minutes of sleep during this trip."

My bag finally comes free, and I stumble backwards into Katie. "Jesus, did Mick really need to bring his portable stripper pole? A little much, don't ya think?" I grumble, regaining my stance and reaching for the bag I dropped.

"Oh, you know Mick, gotta beat out last year's competition. Saw the text chain between the guys. Pretty sure the loser's gonna have someone's name on their other ass cheek." I cringe at the mention. "Speaking of, is Poppy talking to Jim yet?"

By talking, does she mean two-word sentences and "you're lucky I don't kill you with my bare hands" stares? "They're getting there," I laugh and go in for a hug.

Lake Redstone was the birthplace of true romance. The kind where you glance at your soulmate, and even in silence, the words flow between you. The cuteness of finishing each other's sentences and all the sappy stuff like sharing meals, feelings, and movie dates.

No, I'm not talking about Jim and me.

It was love at first sight with Jim and Mick. Since the first handshake, they have been inseparable. A true bromance in the making. And let me tell you how annoying it's been. The inside jokes, the secret handshakes, the date nights, that *don't* include Poppy and I. What two men go to the movies to see a freakin' chick flick without their wife/girlfriend? They reminded us of two kids in their man-made fort drawing plans to rule the world together. Okay, maybe not the *world*. More so the world of pickleball as of the last six months.

After the debacle with the Malort and tattoos, Poppy grounded Mick. And by grounded, I mean, no drinking and no Jim. She lasted three whole days, bless her heart, until she couldn't take the moaning and groaning of how lovesick her husband was before she lifted the Jim-ban. But she stuck with the drinking. To say the least, she was not very happy to have my boyfriend's name on her husband's butt cheek.

So, the no drinking and doing dumb stuff rule in place, they found something else to keep them busy. Pickleball. Mick did his research, and through his agent, got in touch with the owners of the lake house. They, in return, got Mick and Jim a spot on a small time pickleball tournament. Six months later, they're still going at it. They currently rank at a 4.5/5.5 in the USAPA rating rubric and are well on their way to landing their own spot on the US Open tournament.

"Well, that's good," Katie says, grabbing for my bag while I fish for Jim's backpack. "'Cause Jim still looks a little scared of her." We both peer over at Jim, who's standing next to Mick, resembling a scared kitten while Poppy lectures them about something.

"I'd be too if I tattooed my boyfriend's name on my ass and had his wife go all cop gangsta on me."

And boy did she.

Nothing like having the best girls' night ever to come home to your husband incoherent and dancing around the house buck naked. Not that *that's* out of the ordinary but discovering his fancy new tattoo was.

After Poppy's reaction, Jim was out of his mind nervous to show me his.

"Just show me." I tap my foot on Poppy's kitchen tile, anticipating what the hell I'm in for. "It can't be worse than Mick's." I wait for him to agree. He doesn't. "Oh, you're kidding me, it's worse than Mick's?"

Jason spits out his drink laughing, earning a good smack from June. "Show me or I'm gonna take Poppy's gun and do more than wave it at you."

"Jesus, woman, fine." He throws his hands up in surrender. *"But keep the beating to a minimum. This wasn't my idea."*

"So, it was your idea?" Poppy snaps at Mick.

Jason doesn't quit. Tears of laughter stream down his face. June huffs, turning to her husband. "May I dare ask what's on your ass?"

"Babe, I'm not stupid like these two."

"Hey! You said it looked dope!"

Poppy smacks Mick. June smacks Jason. Katie visually murders her husband. "Don't look at me. This was just between those love birds." Jerry's hands go up in surrender.

We all glare back at Jim and Mick.

I take a menacing step toward him. "Show me or else—"

"Jesus, you scare me." He turns around, and with one quick swoop, shoves his shorts and briefs down, giving us all a nice moon view.

On his left cheek is Mick "The Destroyer."

I gasp. Poppy whacks Mick. June chokes on a laugh. Jerry smacks Jim on his freshly tattooed cheek.

"SON OF A..."

How can two grown men be so immature? I tried to stay mad at Jim. Silent treatment and all. But it was hard when he would stand on the other side of my locked bedroom door serenading me with "I'm sorry" songs. That voice. It did things to me.

"Oh come on, it *has* been six months."

"Yeah, and three hundred laser removal appointments. Not sure why she's still so angry." My comment drips with sarcasm.

"I'm gonna put my money on his hesitation to get it removed being the big factor. News flash, he *wanted* your boyfriend's name on his ass. I'd be a little ticked too." Katie wiggles her brows.

"What are we talking about?" June inquires, walking up and snuggling into me for a bestie hug.

"How Mick's still pouting because he couldn't keep Jim's name tattooed on his ass."

June shrugs. "Really? I thought it was because Mick suggested counseling for the three of them to move past the incident and not make Mick break up with him?"

That was a great phone call.

Poppy called, in her *"you're never gonna believe this shit"* voice, and explained how her husband, so worried she'd make him break up with Jim, suggested they attend couple's counseling. By couples, he meant him, her, *and* Jim! I had a solid five-minute laugh attack on the phone before I had to ask if she was pulling my chain. She wasn't. The funniest part was she almost considered it because she was so tired of Mick pouting. But I understood where she was coming from. It was impossible to deny the small amount of jealousy over their relationship. The dressing alike. Jam sessions, where Mick pretended to be in Jim's band. They'd cut each other's steak if no one would stop 'em. They were cute, yet so ridiculous. After Poppy got her long rant off her chest, we both got a good laugh out of it. Even more so, unlike Mick, Jim kept his tattoo. I didn't care. Was it awkward that I saw my best friend's husband's name every time Jim walked away from me naked? A wee bit.

But he took it a step further and did something even more unexpected. He tattooed "Beautiful Disaster" on his chest. Over his heart. It was in that moment my life felt real. My heart full. My entire world brighter.

The biggest lie I ever told was not about having a fake boyfriend.

It was that I didn't need a man to feel whole. Before Jim,

I was only living half a life. And now? I'm so complete, Jim filling each part of me with love, happiness, tenderness, and so much laughter.

He's my everything. He's patient with me, and kind. He trusts in me when I don't even trust in myself. And most importantly, he allows me to be me. There's no questioning the insanity inside my crazy brain.

I expected him to bail a million times. Find that Dear John letter, or a post-it saying it's not working out and I could keep his toothbrush. But he never did. And in times when my insecurities were at an all-time high, he'd ease my worries by doing something as silly as leaving more clothes at my place. Making me his "in case of emergency" contact at his dentist. When he got the tattoo, I cried like a baby. It was so permanent. What happened if I did something that really pushed him over the edge?

His response was always the same. "It wouldn't be true love if it wasn't a little crazy sometimes."

And gosh darn it, I was. I, Casey Kasem, was madly in love with this man. He stole my breath every time. He was full of passion, drive, talent—so much talent—in all areas, let me tell ya. We fought, but we loved harder. He took me for who I was and loved me all the way down to my core. He peeled back my layers one by one until he saw every imperfect part of me. And it only gave him more strength to love back.

I may have been living wild and free, but before Jim, it was just wild. The day he replied to my ad, he truly freed me from all the doubt, self-sabotage, and personal guilt I fought with to find myself. In the end, he found me first. And with his love and guidance, the past year, like a single musical note turning into a beautiful tune, I've orchestrated the perfect version of who I am.

"Why are you three staring at me?" Poppy breaks into my self-reflection, walking up to us.

"We wanted an update on your threesome." Katie chuckles, and ducks when I slap her. "What? I asked what you all were thinking."

Poppy swats at a mosquito. "Oh, we're all fine. I told Jim I wasn't mad anymore. That he could stop coming over and mowing my lawn. He's scaring off all the cute college kids home for break needing a few extra bucks." That earns a hefty chuckle from me.

"Anywho, I'm just worried once they get their surprise, they're going to run off and do something stupid, like get promise rings."

"Do they have any idea?" I ask, shocked myself Poppy made this happen.

"Not a clue. So, no videos when my husband cries, okay?"

We all share in a good laugh when the sound of a vehicle catches everyone's attention. My eyes shift up the steep drive as a white SUV pulls down the road. Poppy peeks at her watch. "Right on time." We all stand still, the guys joining us, while the car parks and two people get out.

"Holy shit, *Larry*?" Mick takes two hefty steps and throws his hand out, shaking Larry Rodger's hand.

"In the flesh, Mick. Great to see ya again. It's been too long." Mick's smile is gigantic, while Jim looks nervous as heck. Mick turns, calling for Jim to join him. "Jim, you still scared of me?"

Jim walks forward, shaking Larry's hand. "Nah, just nervous on how to act around a US Open all-time pickleball champ. I didn't mean to defeat you in that last game—"

Larry throws his head back, a gust of laughter so loud,

it echoes across the lake. "Son, you beat me fair and square. You should be proud. It's why we're here actually."

Mick and Jim's expression morph into confusion, just as Sherry turns the corner of the large vehicle. We met the owners of the lake house shortly after the guys' first tournament. The duo was making such a quick name for themselves, Larry and Sherry challenged them to a pickleball game. What no one expected was for Mick and Jim to win.

"Oh yeah? We didn't get the dates wrong, did we? I swore we confirmed the rental for this weekend."

Sherry comes up, leaning into Mick for a hug. "Hello, dear." They share a sweet, motherly embrace. Mick always said she reminded him of his own mother. "We're not here to stay. Larry and I are jet-setting off to the Cayman Islands here shortly, but we wanted to stop here first and give you both something."

Mick's eyes find Poppy's. "Don't look at me. Look at your boyfriend." His eyes widen even more as he focuses his attention on Jim.

"Us?"

"Unless you're cheating on him with someone else," Larry snickers and pulls an envelope from his back pocket. "This is for you both. Wanted to see your faces when you opened it."

They both share a look. Confused, but Mick steps forward, accepting the envelope. He rips open the seal and unfolds the document. Only a minute passes, but it feels like an eternity as we all watch his facial expression morph into disbelief.

"You're shittin' me," he says.

"What? Did we get disqualified 'cause you took your shirt off at the last match?"

Mick waves for Jim to come closer. "Dude..." His eyes raise to Larry's. "Dude..."

"Just spit it out, man." Mick's stopped functioning, so Jim snatches the paper out of his hands and reads through the letter.

"You have to be shittin' me!"

"Oh, Jesus, just spit it out. Enough shittin'," Katie gripes.

Mick and Jim stare at one another, in shock, until the excitement of the news starts to sink in. I got wind of this about a week ago, and it's been hell keeping it a secret. Poppy had the Rodgers' plan a detour before their trip to give the guys the news.

Since neither one can spit out the news, Larry does the honors. "That letter is an invitation to play at the US Open."

"You've got to be shittin' me!" Jason spits out.

I can't help the happiness forming in my tear-filled eyes watching the elation of Jim's face. If I were mistaken, he may also be just as emotional.

"It's very unheard of, two people making their way to the top of the ranking so fast. Especially ones who've only been playing the sport less than a year. But the board is impressed and would like to see your talent on their courts at the end of this summer."

"I don't...I don't even know what to say." Mick fights back his own emotions.

"Say you'll accept, so the missus and I can get on with our vacation."

Jim steps up since Mick is still broken. "Yes. Fuck yes." He sticks his hand out and vigorously shakes Larry's. "Thank you. This is—"

"Awesome! We're going to the US Open!" Mick's back in action. The two face one another and chest bump, hooting and howling.

I look over at Poppy, who's wiping a tear away, her smile just as full of appreciation. The guys hug and express their gratitude, until the Rodgers insist it's time they get going. Everyone says their goodbyes, and as we all watch the SUV trek back up the hill, until the sound of a beer cracking open breaks the silence.

"So! Now that *that's* over, let's get this show on the road. I've been thinking about drinking Casey's shitty spritzers all week long." Katie takes a swig and gives us her back as she makes her way down toward the dock.

One by one, everyone follows, Mick throwing Poppy over his shoulder and carrying his bride to the boat. When it's just Jim and I, he gives me his full attention, my body turning into Jell-O at the way he stares at me.

"Did you know about this?"

I shrug. "Maybe."

"Is this when I caught you under a bunch of blankets in the bathtub?"

Another shrug. "I didn't want you to hear me. Ruin the surprise."

He brings his hand around my neck and tugs me close, my breasts finding comfort in his solid chest. "I love you."

Three words I will never get used to hearing. As if I'm being gifted them for the very first time, the fullness in my heart overflows.

"Love you too."

His hand extends outward, and his fingers thread into my hair. "There's nothing in this world as beautiful as you."

"Even your vinyl collection?" I ask.

"Only a spec in comparison," he replies, placing a small peck to my lips.

"Even Mick?" This is where I lose him. But then he shocks me without even a second of denial.

"Mick who?"

At that, I laugh, smacking him on his shoulder. Just as fast, he plants his lips back on mine. He kisses me with every fiber of his being. And I accept it, pouring just as much love and devotion into this moment. When we finally pull away, we're both light on our feet.

There's a light breeze in the air, catching a lose strand of hair as it whisks across my face. Jim tucks it behind my ear. "Hope you're ready for another crazy weekend."

"Me? Oh, I was just hoping for some quiet time on the lake. Maybe jumping off a steep cliff, a dance off, running for my life from a psychopath. Who knows? Not sure if we'll have enough time."

His laughter is a flame to my soul, setting my entire body into a heated ball of fire. He startles me by scooping me up in his arms and starts our trek down the hill to the dock. "Looks like I have my work cut out for me. But I have a feeling this weekend will top last year. Just you wait."

I would agree, considering tonight, I plan on telling him I'm pregnant.

The end.

Lake Redstone

ABOUT THE
AUTHOR

J.D. Hollyfield is a creative designer by day and superhero by night. When she's not cooking, event planning, or spending time with her family, she's relaxing with her nose stuck in a book. With her love for romance, and her head full of book boyfriends, she was inspired to test her creative abilities and bring her own stories to life. Living in the Midwest, she's currently at work on blowing the minds of readers, with the additions of her new books and series, along with her charm, humor and HEA's.

J.D. Hollyfield dabbles in all genres, from romantic comedy, contemporary romance, historical romance, paranormal romance, fantasy and erotica! Want to know more! Follow her on all platforms!

Twitter
twitter.com/jdhollyfield

Author Page
authorjdhollyfield.com

Fan Page
www.facebook.com/authorjdhollyfield

Instagram
www.intsagram.com/authorjdhollyfield

Goodreads
www.goodreads.com/author/show/8127239.J_D_Hollyfield

Amazon
www.amazon.com/J.D.-Hollyfield/e/B00JF6U2NA

BookBub
www.bookbub.com/profile/j-d-hollyfield

ACKNOWLEDGEMENTS

First, and most importantly, it wouldn't be a proper acknowledgement if I didn't thank myself It's not easy having to drink all the wine in the world and sit in front of a computer writing your heart out, drinking your liver off and resembling a crazy person while you talk to fictional characters day and night. You truly are amazing and probably the prettiest person in all the land. Keep doing what you're doing.

Will the real Redstone Crew Please stand up?
Matt, Jen, JJ, Kristen, the Dixie Chick who knew Earl had to die, Jeff and the other Jeff.

This book would never have been written if you all weren't so damn crazy. Of course, fun, amazing and quite possibly the funniest people I know. Thank you for such amazing memories and such an insane weekend that it made its way on paper.

Mary and Gary. Thank you for inviting us into your home and letting us turn it into a frat party. Even though you were the instigators for half the mayhem that went down. May every year bring us new memories and even juicier storylines.

To my bestie, Gary. You are the best manager. I'll forever be convinced you were a pimp in your previous life. I'm *your* biggest fan.

Thanks to all my eyes and ears. Having a squad who has your back is the utmost important when creating a masterpiece. From betas, to proofers, to PA's to my dog, Jackson, who just gets me when I don't get myself, thank you. This success is not a solo mission. It comes with an entourage of awesome people who got my back. So, shout out to, Ashley Cestra, Jenny Hanson, Amber Higbie, Gina Behrends, Melissa Rizzo Schaub, Amy Wiater, my boo thang Kristi Webster and anyone who I may have forgotten! I appreciate you all!

Thank you to Monica Black at Word Nerd Editing, for helping bring this story to where it needed to be.

Thank you to All By Design for creating my amazing cover. A cover is the first representation of a story and she nailed it, as she always does

Thank you to my awesome reader group, Club JD. All your constant support for what I do warms my heart. I appreciate all the time you take in helping my stories come to life within this community.

Thank you to Emilie at InkSlinger for all your hard work in creating all my beautiful promotional material!

Thank you to Nicole at Indiesage for all her hard work on promotions!

Big thanks for Stacey at Champagne Formats for always making my stories look so amazing!

And most importantly every single reader and blogger! THANK YOU for all that you do. For supporting me, reading my stories, spreading the word. It's because of you that I get to continue in this business. And for that I am forever grateful.

Cheers. This big glass of wine is for you.

Made in the USA
Lexington, KY
24 October 2019